The String Glove Mystery

A
Detective Simon Brade
Mystery

By Harriette R. Campbell

Originally published in 1936

The String Glove Mystery

© 2015 Resurrected Press
www.ResurrectedPress.com

Published by Resurrected Press

This classic book was handcrafted by Resurrected Press. Resurrected Press is dedicated to bringing high quality classic books back to the readers who enjoy them. These are not scanned versions of the originals, but, rather, quality checked and edited books meant to be enjoyed!

Please visit ResurrectedPress.com to view our entire catalogue!

For updates on future releases, LIKE us on Facebook: http://www.Facebook.com/ResurrectedPress

ISBN 13: 978-1-943403-13-4

Printed in the United States of America

Resurrected Press books in A. E. Fielding's
The Chief Inspector Pointer Mystery Series

The Eames-Erskine Case (1924)
The Charteris Mystery (1925)
The Footsteps that Stopped (1926)
The Clifford Affair (1927)
The Cluny Problem (1928)
The Net Around Joan Ingilby (1928)
The Murder at the Nook (1929)
The Mysterious Partner (1929)
The Craig Poisoning Mystery (1930)
The Wedding Chest Mystery (1930)
The Upfold Farm Mystery (1931)
Death of John Tait (1932)
The Westwood Mystery (1932)
The Tall House Mystery (1933)
The Cautley Conundrum (1934)
The Paper-Chase (1934)
The Case of the Missing Diary (1935)
Tragedy at Beechcroft (1935)
The Case of the Two Pearl Necklaces (1935)
Mystery at the Rectory (1936)
Black Cats Are Lucky (1937)
Scarecrow (1937)
Pointer to a Crime (1944)

RESURRECTED PRESS BOOKS IN ELAINE
HAMILTON'S *INSPECTOR REYNOLDS OF
SCOTLAND YARD* SERIES

The Westminster Mystery (1930)

Peril at Midnight (1934)
Tragedy in the Dark (1935)
The Casino Mystery (1936)
Murder Before Tuesday (1937)

MYSTERIES FROM THE JAMES "BONNIE" DUNDEE
MYSTERY SERIES BY ANNE AUSTIN

The Black Pigeon
The Avenging Parrot
Murder Backstairs
Murder at Bridge
One Drop of Blood
Murdered, But Not Dead

RESURRECTED PRESS CLASSIC MYSTERY CATALOGUE

Journeys into Mystery
Travel and Mystery in a More Elegant Time

The Edwardian Detectives
Literary Sleuths of the Edwardian Era

Gems of Mystery
Lost Jewels from a More Elegant Age

Anne Austin
One Drop of Blood
The Black Pigeon
Murder at Bridge

E. C. Bentley
Trent's Last Case: The Woman in Black

Ernest Bramah
Max Carrados Resurrected:
The Detective Stories of Max Carrados

Agatha Christie
The Secret Adversary
The Mysterious Affair at Styles

Octavus Roy Cohen
Midnight

Freeman Wills Croft
The Ponson Case
The Pit Prop Syndicate

The Uttermost Farthing: A Savant's Vendetta

Arthur Griffiths
The Passenger From Calais
The Rome Express

Fergus Hume
The Mystery of a Hansom Cab
The Green Mummy
The Silent House
The Secret Passage

Edgar Jepson
The Loudwater Mystery

A. E. W. Mason
At the Villa Rose

A. A. Milne
The Red House Mystery

Baroness Emma Orczy
The Old Man in the Corner

Edgar Allan Poe
The Detective Stories of Edgar Allan Poe

Arthur J. Rees
The Hampstead Mystery
The Shrieking Pit
The Hand In The Dark
The Moon Rock
The Mystery of the Downs

Mary Roberts Rinehart
Sight Unseen and The Confession

Dorothy L. Sayers

Whose Body?

Sir William Magnay
The Hunt Ball Mystery

Mabel and Paul Thorne
The Sheridan Road Mystery

Louis Tracy
The Strange Case of Mortimer Fenley
The Albert Gate Mystery
The Bartlett Mystery
The Postmaster's Daughter
The House of Peril
The Sandling Case: What Would You Have Done?

Charles Edmonds Walk
The Paternoster Ruby

John R. Watson
The Mystery of the Downs
The Hampstead Mystery

Edgar Wallace
The Daffodil Mystery
The Crimson Circle

Carolyn Wells
Vicky Van
The Man Who Fell Through the Earth
In the Onyx Lobby
Raspberry Jam
The Clue
The Room with the Tassels
The Vanishing of Betty Varian
The Mystery Girl
The White Alley
The Curved Blades

Anybody but Anne
The Bride of a Moment
Faulkner's Folly
The Diamond Pin
The Gold Bag
The Mystery of the Sycamore
The Come Back

Raoul Whitfield
Death in a Bowl

And much more!
Visit ResurrectedPress.com
for our complete catalogue

FOREWORD

Though an American, Harriette R. Campbell set her series of novels featuring the reluctant detective Simon Brade and his friend the psychiatrist Dr. "Jerry" Jerrold in Britain.

Simon Brade is an amateur detective whose is much more interested in Chinese porcelain than crime, especially murder. His friend, Dr. Jerrold is only able to induce him to take up the case with the promise that his host has a collection including a particularly fine example of Ming china. Alas, the collection has been sold to finance renovations to the estates grounds.

The case in point couldn't be more British as it involves a death that occurs during a fox-hunt. One of the members of the hunt died from a fall from his horse, his body being found at the bottom of a chalk pit. At first it assumed the death was accidental, but rumors soon start to spread and the family calls in first Dr. Jerrold and then Brade in an effort to dispel these rumors.

The novel follows the common pattern of "country House" murders, with Brade and Jerrold coming to stay at Marpen Hall while they investigate. The usual cast of characters are discovered to be hiding an assortment of secrets relating to the murdered man, providing Brade with an ample set of suspects. As typical, there are also a number of clues pointing in various directions, not least of which is the pair of string gloves owned by the deceased that have gone missing.

Though *The String Glove Mystery* is a straightforward detective story, later novels in the series such as *Magic Makes Murder* and *Crime in Crystal* took a more occult turn.

Harriette Campbell isn't well known today, but *The String Glove Mystery* is a fine example of the British "Golden Age" mystery, even if it was written by an America. Resurrected Press is pleased to offer this new edition of this 1936 novel.

About the Author

Harriette Russell Campbell (1883-1950) was an American author who married a Scot and eventually settled in the U.K.. She wrote a series of novels featuring the detective Simon Brade. Later novels incorporated supernatural elements.

Mystery of Saint's Island 1927
The String Glove Mystery 1936
The Porcelain Fish Mystery 1937
The Moor Fires Mystery 1938
Three Names for Murder 1940
Magic Makes Murder 1943
Crime in Crystal 1946
Murder Set to Music 1941

Greg Fowlkes
Editor-In-Chief
Resurrected Press
www.ResurrectedPress.com
www.Facebook.com/ResurrectedPress

Tel. Conversation, 10.30 p.m., Thursday, Feb. 9th

"Mulberry 6000. Yes. Is that you, Perry? Dr. Jerrold speaking. I wired Mr. Brade that I would call him tonight. Is he in?"

"Yes, sir—that is to say, sir—he's in his bath, sir."

"Well, get him out! Tell him I'll hold the line."

"Yes, sir."

To the operator: "Yes, I do want three minutes more. It's an urgent call. Don't cut me off . . . Yes, I do want three minutes more!"

"Dr. Jerrold, sir?"

"Yes, Perry."

"Mr. Brade says he's only begun with the sponge and hasn't touched his wash-rag. Could you ring later, sir?"

"No, I must speak to him now. It's urgent. I told him it was urgent. Get him for me, Perry, that's a good fellow."

"I'll try, sir."

"Yes, I do want three minutes more! . . . Yes, I do. . . . Hello, is that you Brade?"

A plaintive voice: "No, Jerry; at least, I don't think so. It's been reading theosophy and I—I mean—it isn't quite sure. Probably the reincarnation of a faded flower, and awfully wet!"

"Brade, I want you to do me a favour."

"You'll break the wire. You sound so robust!"

"Will you?"

"Will I what?"

"Take a case?"

"Do I sound like it?"

"You sound more than ordinarily feeble, if that's what you mean. I'm asking you to do something for me. Will you do it?"

"I shall be deaf in a moment, Jerry."

"Can I come round and tell you about it now?"

"But it's bedtime, and I'm dripping."

"There's no time to lose."

"What kind of a case?"

"I don't know. It may be murder."

"I never take murder cases. You know that, Jerry. You advised me yourself not to."

"You took the Willett case and solved it."

"It wasn't the murder I solved. That wasn't interesting. It was the faked Holbein."

"Brade—I'm coming now. You've got to see me—Yes, I *do* want three minutes more!"

"What's the use, Jerry? I'll tell you what—write it down—the whole thing—and send it round. Then you'll feel better."

"It'll take me all night!"

"Well, if you don't want me to do it for you—"

"Brade, you're trying to put me off."

"Well, if you won't do as I ask you—"

"I will. And if it's four in the morning when I've finished, I'll send it round and you've got to read it then and there. I'll see that you do."

"Write everything, Jerry," earnestly; "you know, 'every idle word that proceedeth. . . .' It's the little things that count. And suppression in the subconscious is dangerous to the balance. Write everything."

"It'll take a week."

"Thank God!"

"But I'll do it tonight. You shall have it for breakfast. I'll come at ten o'clock."

"This is interesting."

"Yes, it is interesting," eagerly.

"I always said you'd fall in love some day, Jerry!"

Click!

Operator: "Your number has rung off."

Jerry: "Damn!"

Written for the use of Simon Brade
10.30 p.m., Feb. 9th—6.00 a.m., Feb. 10th, 1933

Monday, Feb. 6th

The five o'clock appointment is the last on my list for the day, so I generally give it to a case not likely to be particularly unusual or perplexing. On this day, however, I found a name booked for that hour which told me nothing—Mrs. Danvers Carne.

When I was left alone, a few minutes before five, I reached for the *Peerage*. "Carne"—Yes, "see Belfare, Marquis of." I followed the minute print till I came to what I wanted. "Danvers, Archibald, born Utica, N. Y., U. S. A., 1901, son of the late Archibald Smith Rivers Carne, and grandson of the late Lord Archibald Pratt Fitzwilliam Carne; heir presumptive to the marquisate; m. June 4th, 1927, Mimionc Elizabeth, only dr. of late Lieut.-Col. Colin Maclean MacDonald of Falfie, Argyll."

This, then, would be Mimione Elizabeth—a Highlander—probably twenty-five or so. "No issue"—choice or accident? I wondered; but the Peerage did not run to that sort of detail, so I shut it up and rang my bell as a signal that the patient might be admitted.

She came, promptly. Everyone knows that a doctor in my line learns a great deal from details that others would not notice. That is why I work in a big room and place my desk as far from the door as space allows. No two people cross that thirty feet of parquet in the same way, and before my patient is seated I usually know something about his or her temperament and habits, character and state of mind.

It was not, after all, a stranger who came in and stood for a moment looking across the room at me. A memory, so unprofessional that it had no business whatever in my working day, entered with her. The congested doorway of a ball-room, young voices. "My dear, what a crush!" "Oh,

Bobby, you darling!" "There he is!" "I'll never find my partner!" "Oh, I say, let's go on somewhere. This is too awful, you know!" And I, annoyed with myself for having been dragged to such an affair by a persuasive hostess, searching without enthusiasm for my partner, suddenly shouldered against a girl who was crushed between me and the wall. She seemed to be the only one who was not pushing and chattering or gazing anxiously right and left, but was waiting, amused and perfectly at her ease, for a chance to move.

"You couldn't help it," she laughed at my annoyance.

"I'm not hardened to these—er—scrambles," I continued to apologize. "Why not dance? It's the only way of getting out, and if you see your partner or I see mine, we can part."

She agreed by moving a fraction of an inch into my arms, and we danced, and forgot our partners until the music stopped.

I went away as soon as I decently could after that, but though I had forgotten every other detail of that night, seven years ago, I had remembered her. She seemed to me to differ from the others, so like her in their dark-haired, clear-eyed, fair-skinned youth. She was one of the few so well made that the short, tight dresses became them. But it was not this that impressed her on my memory. "That girl is made for happiness," I thought.

She came towards me now, surprised and pleased. "Why, I remember you," she said. "We danced the Charleston, and my aunt was shocked!"

"I went to three dances that season, and I always hoped I'd see you again, but I never did."

"No—my mother was ill and I went back to Scotland."

She took off her gloves as she sat down, and I saw her hands—generous, capable, friendly hands. But her face! I had been right about her face, but those seven years had not done their part. She was built to be happy, and she was not.

And now she gave the first sign of mental distress—

she leaned forward and looked at me eloquently. Could I be trusted to help her or would I send her away as bewildered and frightened as she had come? In a moment the scrutiny was over.

"I have not come to consult you about myself, Dr. Jerrold," she began. "I suppose it's unusual for one person to come for advice about someone else, but—"

"If you'll tell me what the trouble is, I'll try to help you, Mrs. Carne."

"Of course you may think I'm a case for treatment when you hear what I have to say!" She smiled, quickly.

"I hear a lot of odd stories, you know." I smiled too.

"Yes. I've never met a psychoanalyst before. When I heard about you, I thought that you might understand. I must tell someone!"

"Please tell me."

"It is about my husband—he is a very peculiar man." Then she laughed. "I suppose most husbands are—I'm telling this very badly—but Dan is unusual —in an unusual way, if that isn't absurd."

"Could you begin at the beginning—his schools, his parents?"

"Yes, you'll understand better if I do." She seemed relieved at the hint and began to speak, concentrating on what she was saying so that the words came steadily. "He was born and brought up in the States. His father was far removed from the title then, but the war and an accident changed the circumstances. At that time Dan's father was out of touch with his family. I don't think he was a bad man—just a person who never stuck to anything. He was killed in a motor accident years ago. Dan's mother was a beautiful woman and very gifted, I believe, and she had the greatest influence over Dan till she, too, died, when he was eighteen. They must have had the oddest life, for they had no money at all except a small allowance from Lord Belfare, and they lived in luxury. Mrs. Carne appears to have been a kind of mystic, and people who were interested in such things surrounded her. She and

Dan were petted and flattered, and Dan grew up with the idea that he had a right to things others have to work for. Since he has become heir to the title, his friends encourage him to think so. You know the world is still full of people willing to do anything for as charming a man as Dan, heir to a good title and half a dozen famous places.

"Very few know how near Dan has come to public disgrace. He had to resign from one of his clubs for paying his gambling debts with a bad cheque—you see I am telling you everything! The Carne family does not allow itself to be disgraced. Lord Belfare can't stand Dan, but he has paid his debts more than once and has him at Farle once a year to keep up appearances. The same applies to his cousin, Sir Ralph Carne-Hilton, who is the next heir. Dan knows the family tradition and feels safe in trading on it. . . . Well, he has had his head turned in an unusual way. You would say that he hasn't been spoilt by it, but his soul has been warped by his privileges, and he goes through life like an Olympian, perfectly aware of his divine birth, priding himself on being able to hob-nob with a beggar, never doubting that the beggar will be aware of it too. Do you understand?"

"I think you make it very plain."

"You see, it isn't altogether the fact that he will be a marquis some day—it's much more personal than that. He and his mother always got what they wanted without paying for it, and the result is that he takes what he wants without hesitation or scruple of any sort. He has only one vice—gambling—but he has no morals at all. He is fantastically generous, but someone else pays. I can't remember that he has ever gone without what he wanted, but he is always giving away money. The point is that sooner or later his friends find him out. He is always surrounded by adorers, but they are usually people who have not known him long, and gradually he is collecting enemies who hate him with extraordinary passion. These are of all classes and types—old servants, former friends, women, even animals. It is incredible, and I am frightened."

She paused abruptly as her voice faltered on the last word.

"Have you any reason for being especially frightened now?"

"Yes, oh, yes!" She looked at me again, searchingly. "I hate mysteries. I can't bear ghost-stories and fortune-tellers and table-turning! But so many strange things have happened lately that I can't ignore them. And you, perhaps, understand such things."

"I'm a student of the human mind, you know. I have to take many things into account—things other people can forget."

"Yes." She drew a deep breath and plunged into the rest of her story. "Dan is superstitious. No one, except myself and his servant Otway, knows how superstitious he is. He uses disinfectants as if they were a magician's mixtures." She made a little gesture of despair. "You are laughing, of course. I can't explain, but it is revolting— Dan's cleanliness. He spends pounds on antiseptic wash-rags which he never uses twice, and he never travels without a big suitcase filled with every sort of mouth-wash and such things. It is superstition— not sense.

"Well, we have been travelling abroad, and for the last month one thing after another has happened to shake Dan's nerve. He always wore a small gold coin, with hieroglyphics inscribed on it. I believe it was Egyptian; it was given to Dan by a Brahmin whom he had helped, and the man told him never to part with it, or disaster would follow. He kept it on the chain he used for his keys; it must have fallen off when we were travelling—the ring may have been worn—for it was gone when he took out his keys at the Customs in France, and we never found it. That was the beginning of almost daily trouble.

"I've told you about his mother. He makes a cult of devotion to her memory. He had one photograph of her which he said was the only one that conveyed her 'aura'— that is what he called it; it was a sort of shrine and followed him from his bedroom to his writing-table in the morning and back again at night. While we were in Paris the wind blew over a vase of flowers, the water ran into the ink, and the portrait was overturned and ruined. No one saw it happen. . . . Then we went to stay with some people. Dan had won a lot of money from our host at bridge, and they played for very high stakes. The only cards in the house were two shades of green. Dan is superstitious about green. He lost ruinously. . . . Other smaller things happened—perhaps because he was looking for them. And then, driving to Le Touquet, his medicine-case dropped off the back of the car. It must have been opened in some way by the fall. Some of the bottles were broken and others had been put back in the wrong places by whoever picked it up and returned it, so that the labels were all wrong. The pockets were labelled, you see. He took out what he thought was his eye-wash, but luckily I took it away from him and smelt it: it was purified methylated spirits.

"Then our new Delage was delivered to us, and it had been painted dark green instead of dark blue, by mistake. The colour was so dark that you could only see it in the sun and we had loaded it up before we realized the error. I wanted to go by train or let Otway drive. After everything else I couldn't bear to have Dan drive that car! But Dan took it as a sort of challenge. He told me I could stay behind if I liked. Well, I didn't. Of course we had an accident—Dan's driving was fantastic—a child was hurt." She stopped, caught her breath, and went on: "Dan couldn't understand why I wouldn't tell a lie to save him from arrest. Luckily or not, Otway will do anything for Dan, and another witness was found who said it wasn't Dan's fault, and he got off with a fine. The child did not die—I did everything I could. . . ."

She took a moment to recover. Then she leaned forward and spoke very slowly. "Tonight we are going to stay with the Carne-Hiltons in Bramshire, for a fortnight's hunting. In that house everyone hates him.

I've tried to persuade him not to go, but he will. He will hunt too, and, though he is a brilliant horseman, he is never safe on a horse: he excites them and they are afraid of him. I've seen them dripping with perspiration two minutes after Dan has mounted, just from pure nerves. He is in no state to take risks!" She stopped short.

"And he has been having trouble with Ralph Carne-Hilton about a horse he bought and sent down to Marpen. Ralph called him up last night. Dan wouldn't tell me what he said, but I caught enough to gather that Ralph considers the horse vicious and won't keep him in the stables. I'm so afraid Dan will try to ride him. It is just when he is in danger, or thinks he is, that he is most reckless."

"Is there anything else?" I asked.

She drew a deep breath. "Yes, there is!" I saw that she continued with great difficulty. "Dan has always trusted me, and because he has, I have been able to keep him from some consequences of his behaviour. But lately it is different. He seems to connect me with his bad luck. He keeps things from me, even avoids me. He is suspicious of me, Dr. Jerrold. I cannot go on, yet if I leave him I feel some terrible disaster may happen. I don't know what to do!"

For a moment or two I talked about nothing, until I saw that she was calmer.

"Am I hysterical?" she asked. "Or am I right to be alarmed?"

I considered her for a moment.

"I think you are right," I said. "I should stop your husband hunting at present if you can." I explained why. I told her of cases I had known—flying men who had lost their nerve, a jockey convinced that if he rode a particular mount he would be killed. "There's something that acts, in the face of danger, in the place of conscious thought, and that something is governed by the subconscious. A man who has faith in his safety stamped on the subconscious is safe, if the emergency leaves any margin for escape. A man who expects disaster will find it. Where nine chances are in his favour, it will be the tenth he subconsciously takes. I've cured men of this state of mind. Perhaps I could cure your husband."

She shook her head. "I couldn't suggest it. You are known as an authority on nervous and mental cases, and there was mental weakness in Dan's mother's family, I am sure. I think Lord Belf are knows about it. He warned me once. That is why we have no children. Once I spoke to Dan about his nerves and he flew into a passion— almost the only time he has ever been really rude to me. He is a very sweet-tempered person." She said this rather pathetically. "No, you've helped me by putting into reasonable words what I felt, but couldn't understand. I knew that Dan was in danger; now I know why. Will you help me again if I ask you to?"

"Mrs. Carne, I should like to know one more thing before I answer that."

"What is it?"

"You have drawn a picture of a man who wins strong friends and alienates them. Are there any exceptions, and are you one?"

She hesitated. "There are exceptions, yes. One of Dan's old uncles, one man friend, his servant Otway, who has stuck to him for years in spite of the fact that I'm sure Dan is in arrears with his wages, a woman or two. As for me—may I tell you a rather absurd dream I have every now and then? It explains how I feel about Dan." She looked at me for her answer and then went on. "In my grandmother's house in Ireland, there used to stand in the drawing-room an enormous Sevres vase. We young people thought it common and ugly, but she adored it and considered it very valuable. It was a modern piece, sixty years old or so, I suppose, very gold and blue, with paintings on each side. It stood on a pedestal, and was as heavy as a man. Well, I dream that I am sitting there and see that it is too near the edge of the pedestal for safety. As I get up to push it back, it starts to fall. I put out my arms and catch it, but haven't the strength to lift it into place or move it. I wonder, as I stand there, if it is really worth saving, but I call for help, and wait, while it gets heavier and heavier and my arms are nearly breaking with the weight. Just as I feel I can't hold it another minute, and the pedestal slips farther back, I wake up.— That is exactly how I feel about Dan."

"I understand."

"And now—" she put a hand to her throat, an expressive gesture, for she was certainly a person of great self-control, "I seem to have arrived at that stage of the dream where, so far, I have always wakened."

I repeated: "I understand."

"And you will help me?"

"I will."

She got up quickly, shook hands with me, and went out.

Usually I wind up my day's work and forget it, play a game of squash at the club and think no more of my patients until I go back to my desk, often late at night for a couple of hours and again at eight the next morning. But this case bothered me, and, as often happens, I was reminded of it by a conversation that took place at dinner the same night. I can't afford to waste time, and never go out to dine to be bored, but my hostess on this occasion was a lady to be trusted. Some of her guests I already knew, but one was a stranger, a woman of fifty, with a large, good-humoured face, who made more amusing remarks, without being vulgar or malicious, than anyone I ever met before. Her name was Lady Caroline Scott. I was startled to hear her say: "I know at least six people who would put him painlessly away with the best of consciences."

"Who is the unpopular man?" asked the lady sitting next me, who must have found me an absent-minded listener, for she had been attending to the conversation opposite.

"My nephew, Danvers Carne. But he isn't

unpopular—quite the reverse. Do you know him?"

"But, my dear, that agreeable creature? I sat next him at dinner somewhere or other."

"Yes, at dinner, but there's breakfast and lunch and quite a lot of time between."

"Somebody did say something—I forget what it was—was it racing?"

"Oh, he's a gambler, but it isn't that. He has a wife, and I adore her."

"Is she one of the murderers?"

"No. She's the sole reason why he is still alive, I should think."

From that the conversation turned on murder.

"I suppose you just are a murderer or you aren't. That's what saves people like Dan," said Lady Caroline.

"What about that, Jerry?" my hostess asked, slyly. She knows I hate to be shown off in my professional capacity. She also knows I hate to let her down.

"I should say it was more a matter of all of us being murderers, saved by our inhibitions, and it doesn't take much to break them down. Of course there's the criminal type, but that's another matter."

"I'd never have dared admit it, but I've murdered a certain sofa cushion of mine every month or so for thirty years," said Lady Caroline. "Of course it doesn't always answer to the same name. Now, suppose it wasn't a sofa cushion, I take it those inhibitions would get between us? What would break them down? It might be just as well to know!"

"I should have to know you a little better to say for sure. Drink might!"

"No use—I only go to sleep. To be sure, I snore. It might be enough to frighten a nervous victim into a heart attack."

"Music for some people, or a drug, fear, mob-fever, violent anger—depends on the type."

Lady Caroline shook her head. "I'm not musical. I always keep time with my foot and they say that's a sure sign. And as for drugs, I once used sewing-machine oil instead of castor oil, and since then I never keep anything in my medicine cupboard except tooth-paste and liquorice drops, and I'm not afraid of anything but mice and wouldn't kill one for a fortune, and I hate crowds. My inhibitions will have to stop by me. Thank God for sofa cushions!"

I would not repeat all this but it led to another little talk after dinner. Lady Caroline made a place for me on a seat beside her when the others paired off for bridge.

"I particularly wanted to meet you, Dr. Jerrold," Lady Caroline began, somewhat abruptly. "In fact, if you must know, I called up Kitty Grant and asked her to arrange it, so here we are, and, as you see, here we stay until the rubber is over. What did you think of Mimi?"

"Mimi, Lady Caroline?"

"Don't pretend to be a stupid, because I happen to know you are not. In fact, I sent Mimi to you today myself. I've heard about you. Do you like her?"

"If you mean Mrs. Danvers Carne, certainly I like her, but you know she consulted me professionally, and in such cases—"

"Come, come, my dear man, you're not as old as all that! Forty-two—forty-three?"

"Sometimes I wish I were older and sometimes younger."

"I can quite believe that," she remarked shrewdly. "Are the gay young things already putting you in your place as the older generation? It makes you as angry as it makes a deaf person to be told he didn't understand what you said. I know. Well, we'll leave Mimi— but what do you think of her husband, my nephew Dan?"

"I've been thinking quite a lot about him. What do you think, Lady Caroline?" She laughed good-naturedly.

"That's called turning the tables on me, isn't it?— though, come to think of it, I never did know what that meant. However, I'll answer. I don't know what to think of him. It would have been different if I'd known him as a child, but his mother kept him in the States. Belfare disapproved of her so thoroughly, though he never met her, that he took no notice of Dan, and of course then there seemed no prospect that he'd be the heir. She was either a psychic genius or had a religious mania—some people say one, some the other. Anyway, she made a good living at it, and taught Dan his creed. You can imagine just how well she fitted in with the Carnes, who have discovered the perfect pattern and cut their lives to it. I suppose that complete lack of responsibility about money does belong to saints as well as crooks, and Dan is always so open about it that you can't help thinking he is rather noble even when the nobility is extremely inconvenient to yourself—a test, I think!" She laughed ruefully. "Mimi hasn't an ounce of that kind of folly. She was brought up to think debt the most serious form of immorality."

"But she implies that her husband is—well—unreliable in other respects."

"So he is," answered Lady Caroline thoughtfully, "but when you take individual cases, there are explanations, once you admit his own contention that personality can be developed beyond law. Take that accident: he saw it as inevitable. From his point of view it did not matter if he drove seventy or ten miles an hour—it was bound to happen. From her point of view it was his fault. People who admire him—or, to put it more literally, follow him—say that they never lived at all until they knew him. Even women. I don't think he's particularly keen on them, but they often are on him. He says every call on him is a duty and he must respond. Well, *I* don't know. I'm no mystic. He seems to behave like a blackguard, yet he does what no ordinary man can—pulls people out of the depths."

She was watching my face shrewdly.

"What do you mean by that, Lady Caroline?" I asked.

"Well, this, for instance. A friend of mine has an only son. His father was killed in the war, and of course she spoilt Tim, and it was a pity, because he was made of slight stuff, I should think. His mother is a dear, but no heavyweight herself, and was surprised when the lovable boy went wild at Oxford, in all the usual ways. It was serious, for he was entirely irresponsible when he had been drinking, and got himself into all sorts of trouble, which he hadn't the character to deal with afterwards. Consequently, he drank harder than ever to forget it. (Easy to understand, I think. When my cook gives notice, I always ask everybody to dinner!) Lydia Revel was quite aged by worry by the time Dan got hold of Tim and reformed him as easily as you'd change a black tie for a white one. Now Tim follows Dan like a well-trained spaniel and has the spaniel's faith in his master. Lydia never stops talking about Dan. She says he's a reincarnation of Buddha, or someone. And she's not the only person to say so. He'd be a sensation in any religious movement, but he will not be identified with any sect. He says religion is universal. He says—he says a lot of things, you know!"

"Evidently!"

"Well, you can't dismiss Dan like that, young man. He's a saint or a devil. You can choose. But he's not an ordinary, good-for-nothing neurotic!" She had hit on my private thought.

"I'm sorry for his wife," I could not help saying.

"So am I. My sympathies are all with her. But then, I'd never have been an early Christian—I'd have been converted about the time of Constantine, when it became the respectable thing to be! I've an uneasy feeling that Mimi is in danger. I want you to help her if you can."

"I certainly will."

"Is it a promise?"

"Aren't we being rather intense about all this?"

"Everybody is intense when they get mixed up with Dan. I'd like you to promise."

I promised. I am a year or two younger than Lady Caroline guessed—but old enough to have known better, I admit.

Tuesday, February 7th

The case of Danvers Carne took hold of my imagination, and I should have liked an hour's interview with him. It must be a unique person who could defeat the judgment of so wise and experienced a woman as Lady Caroline Scott.

Mrs. Carne's account of him had given me a distinct view of his character. Charming, magnetic, unbalanced, evasive of responsibility, and adroit in eluding consequences. Such a combination, carried to extremes, explained all she had told me. Yet did it? Easy enough to understand that he should alienate most of his friends in time. His eccentricities in regard to money were enough to account for this. Not so easy to dismiss the few who were faithful. Who was the man friend his wife had spoken of? Was he a crank—or a crook? And the servant who had stuck to him for years? A servant might suffer considerably in such service, and Mrs. Carne had, in fact, said that he did. I felt a curiosity about the friend and the servant.

Mrs. Carne herself had won my confidence, but, considering her type, she would certainly not be likely to go far along the unfamiliar and difficult way of apostleship. She would be held back by ordinary scruples, and these might blind her to what was beyond. There were forms of genius which did atone for flaws in behaviour, serious enough to condemn the average man. Would we do without a Coleridge because he was addicted to drugs, or Shakspere because he deserted his wife?

On the evening after my interview with Mrs. Carne, I sat down at my desk and drew out the notes I had made. So far as I knew, it was a closed case. Mrs. Carne had come to ask if her uneasiness was justified and I had answered her. True, both she and Lady Caroline had asked for my help if it should be needed, but this event was unlikely—at least I told myself so. I could not feel that it was. Instinct, as I believe, is the sum of our experience, acting independently of conscious thought, and instinct told me that I should hear more of the matter. I was right. For while I sat there, looking at my notes, the telephone bell rang, and I took down the receiver.

Lady Caroline's voice spoke.

"Dr. Jerrold?"

"Yes. Lady Caroline Scott?"

"Yes. I have had a message from Mimi, my niece. Dan has been killed in a hunting accident. She asked me to tell you. I am going down there at once. If we need you, will you come?"

I said I would.

Wednesday, February 8th

The papers next morning had ample details of the tragedy. I cut out the notices that gave the fullest account and studied them.

Mr. Carne had left the hunt at the village of Marpen and was seen to enter a wood called the Wilderness, through which a bridle-path led towards Marpen Hall. The weather was inclement, and the field was reduced to a small number. The time was stated to be about three fifteen.

At five o'clock Mr. Timothy Revel, another member of the Marpen Hall party, riding back across the farm on the edge of the Wilderness, discovered Mr. Carne's body, in a chalk-pit, between the field and the wood.

Investigations had resulted in a complete reconstruction of the accident. Half-way down the bridle-path, the branch of a fallen tree extended in such a way that a rider would be obliged to stoop to the level of his horse's neck to avoid it. Through some chance only to be conjectured, Mr. Carne had been thrown at this point, and his horse had dragged him through the wood and swerved at the chalk-pit, the change of direction resulting in loosening the stirrup and releasing the body, which fell down the steep side of the pit to the bottom—a forty-foot drop.

There were no witnesses to the tragedy, as hounds had found in Chess Spinney near Marpen village and had run in a semicircle back to Cranmere Farm. The inquest was fixed for half past two on the following day, and the funeral would be conducted from Farle, the historic seat of the Marquis of Belfare, to whom the deceased had been nephew and heir.

I laid down the papers feeling distinctly relieved. Then it occurred to me that this was surprising. What had I dreaded to find?

My work distracted me from this problem, but soon

after lunch my servant brought me a note:

> *Dear Doctor Jerrold,*
> *Will you please come to the inquest? It is to be*
> *held in the village hall at 2.30 tomorrow.*
> *Mimi would like you to be present.*
> *Yours sincerely,*
> *Caroline Scott*

Well, I decided to go. The trouble and pangs of professional conscience I went through to arrange it must be the measure of the compulsion I felt to keep my promise to two women I scarcely knew. Perhaps at the bottom of it was my intense curiosity about the character of the dead man. I was against him, no doubt about that; and probably I wanted my judgment of his wife confirmed. I did not believe that she was spiritually stupid and could live side by side with an exalted soul for five years without knowing it. In short, I wished to prove to my own satisfaction that Danvers Carne was a fraud, self-deceived probably, and genuine to that extent; otherwise how explain his hold on the imagination of so many persons?

Thursday, February 9th

It was an occasion to use my new Rolls two-seater, and, since I had made up my mind to cut work for the afternoon, I enjoyed the drive into the rolling Bramshire country, with its strips of pine and beechwood and its pleasant villages, grouped in curves of winding roads. Modest but prosperous farmlands, and an occasional private park were silvered over by cold sunlight.

I turned off at the town of Agminton and drove past gates, two miles up a gentle rise, which I thought led to Marpen Hall, Sir Ralph Carne-Hilton's place. Farther on, a couple of turns brought me to the village hall, where cars of every type and degree of prosperity, drawn up beside the gate, testified to local interest in the tragedy.

I gave my name and was admitted and shown to a seat from which I had a good view of the witness-stand, improvised from forms and planks of wood for the occasion.

The official account of the inquest will be available, so it is only necessary to describe what struck me as important. There were the usual formalities. Evidence of identification was given by Sir Ralph Carne-Hilton and the lawyer, and the usual formal questions were answered. The third witness called was Timothy Revel.

I could not recall for a moment where I had heard the name before. Then I remembered. Lady Caroline had spoken of a young man who had reformed his life under the influence of Danvers Carne. I looked at him with close attention. He was a warmly coloured person with an impetuous manner. He would be good at tennis and polo, I thought, and bad at golf. He seemed to feel ill at ease before the jury and assumed a public-school expression to hide it.

Yes, his name was Timothy Revel, no profession at present, just down from Christ Church, in fact. Yes, he had been the first to discover the tragedy.

"Will you tell the jury exactly what happened?"

The young man paused. Then he spoke rapidly, as if he had rehearsed what he had to say. I can use a kind of shorthand, and I took down most of what he said, word by word.

"As you know, there was a meet of the South Lodesdale Hounds on Tuesday. Sir Ralph Carne-Hilton kindly mounted me. We had a disappointing day, owing to fog and rain, but shortly before four o'clock hounds found in what is called Chess Spinney and went away, turning to the right at Barwell Cross, straight past Beech Wood to Cranmere. Here the fox went to ground and, owing to the failing light, the Master called hounds off and the day was over. Besides the Master and hunt servants there were not more than half a dozen of the field left. I looked round for Sir Ralph Carne-Hilton, but I had waited to see if they meant to dig the fox out, and in the mean time he had gone. None of the others from Marpen Hall were in sight. One of the servants showed me the shortest way home and I set off towards the wood they call the Wilderness."

"One moment, Mr. Revel," the Coroner interrupted. "You are a stranger in this part of the world, I think. How do you come to know the names of the fields and coverts so well?"

Mr. Coroner looked very wise the man whom nothing escapes.

Revel answered: "I've looked them out on the Hunt map. Of course, I knew I should be asked questions."

Someone tittered. Young Revel stood in silence trying not to show how annoyed he was. His recital was evidently a trial to him, and the silly interruption made him furious. From then on he told as little as he could. I think the incident had its effect on other witnesses too; if the Coroner was watching to trip them up, they would be careful to say no more than was needed.

"Please continue, Mr. Revel."

"On my way I skirted the edge of the chalk-pit "

The Coroner was looking at a map. "Was this necessary? According to the map I hold and, I may say, my memory, you would have joined the Wilderness farther along if you had ridden in a direct line. In fact, you must have ridden in almost exactly the wrong direction."

"I rode up to the chalk-pit because I had been warned about it, and as I hoped to hunt again during my visit I thought I should like to see exactly how it lay. Besides, there was a rise of ground which concealed the Wilderness from the place where we were, and between that and the bad light, I took a slightly wrong direction."

"I see. Proceed."

"I looked down to see the depth of the hole, and thought I saw a pink hunting coat. I had to dismount to make sure that the body of a man was lying there. I tied up my horse and climbed down the side of the pit. Then of course I recognized the body and realized that Mr. Carne was dead. I thought someone might hear me if I shouted, and, in fact, Mr. Furness was riding across the far end of the field and came to my assistance. I remained with Mr. Carne's body, disturbing nothing, until Mr. Furness brought back two labourers who lived near by. He had also telephoned for a doctor. He suggested that they keep watch while I went to notify the household. I agreed. As I turned in at the gate of Marpen Hall, I passed Mrs. Danvers Carne's maid on her way to post a letter. I sent her back to warn her mistress that there had been an accident. The door was opened by Lady Carne-Hilton's maid, who must have seen or heard my horse at the door. She fetched Colman, the butler, and I asked him to inform Sir Ralph Carne-Hilton and to send for a groom to hold my horse. I went into the house and found Miss Trent, as I thought someone ought to go to Mrs. Danvers Carne, and Lady Carne-Hilton had only just come in and was dressing. When I had explained, I remounted and rode back to the scene of the accident. We waited some time for the doctor, but as he did not come, we lifted the body and conveyed it to the road, where a car met us. I think that is all I have to say."

"There was no sign of Mr. Carne's horse?"

"No. I believe she found her own way back to the stables."

"Thank you, Mr. Revel. I shall want to ask you a few questions later, perhaps."

Richard Furness was called next. He said he was a friend of the family and had been staying at the Hall for a fortnight's hunting. He had seen Mr. Carne leave the field some time after three o'clock. He had followed him to say that he had seen his second horseman looking for him and had told him to go on to Chess Spinney, which was the last covert on the way home. Mr. Carne said, however, that the weather was so bad he would go home. Mr. Furness then left him and rejoined hounds. As Mr. Revel had said, hounds found in Chess Spinney, and the small remaining field enjoyed a good fast run to Cranmcre. He was riding a youngster, who made a mistake at the last fence and gave him a toss. By the time he caught up, the hunt was over and the light was failing fast. He dismounted to examine the young horse, to make sure he had done himself no serious damage, and lit a cigarette. Then he remounted and rode slowly towards the Wilderness. He heard Mr. Revel shout, and answered. The rest of his evidence coincided with that of the previous witness. The village constable had arrived soon after Mr. Revel left him, and together they had made such observations as were possible, it being practically dark now. There were hoof-prints and marks left by the dragging of Mr. Carne's body, leading from the wood to the precipitous side of the chalk-pit. Investigations conducted the next morning showed plainly that Mr. Carne must have fallen as he rode along the bridle-path, the fall occurring where the branch of an uprooted tree overhung the ride in a dangerous way. He was then dragged, probably by the stirrup, and his mount no doubt swerved on seeing the chalk-pit, loosening the stirrup in

this way, so that the body rolled over the edge of the pit.
This was in fact what the hoof-prints seemed to show.

Mr. Furness's testimony ended here. I looked at him
as he came out of the box. He was such a type as you
meet all over the Empire, an alert, vigorous, by no means
brilliant person, but good company and with plenty of
experience, some of it obtained in the war.

The village constable and an Inspector from the
county town confirmed his reading of the accident, and
two witnesses from the hunting field testified to the
dangerous position of the overhanging bough. The field
had ridden down the ride earlier in the day. It was
necessary to stoop low to avoid it, and those riding fresh
mounts had made a detour rather than risk an accident.

The local doctor said that death had occurred within
three hours of his viewing the body soon after six o'clock.
There were several injuries, any one of which might have
caused death. The neck was broken and there was serious
damage to the skull. It was impossible to say whether
death had occurred before or after the fall into the chalk-
pit, which was forty feet deep. At the place where the
body had been thrown over, there would have been an
almost unbroken fall to the bottom. He was prepared to
sign the death certificate in terms of accident.

A scared young groom named Rogers testified that
Mr. Danvers Carne had insisted on having the mare's bit
changed at the last moment. She was usually ridden on a
snaffle, but Mr. Carne had insisted on replacing it with a
double bit with a sharp curb. There had been trouble
about the stirrups too. Mr. Carne rode very long, and the
safety stirrup didn't suit him. Mr. Barnet, the stud
groom, had been annoyed about the change of bit, as the
mare wasn't used to a curb.

I had begun to wonder why I had been asked to attend
the inquest. The case was clear, it seemed. When Barnet
was called I followed his evidence at first with half my
mind elsewhere, but his earnestness brought back my
attention. "Sarah can't stand that bit, sir," he was saying.

"She ain't used to that bit not that one. A Pelham, now, that wouldn't 'ave been so bad, but I wouldn't put anybody on Sarah with that curb, not unless it was Mrs. Danvers Carne. They 'aven't got the 'ands for it no, sir."

"Then you think that Mr. Carne, suddenly seeing the bough, may have used the curb rather roughly, that the mare reared and plunged, bringing her rider into contact with the bough?"

"Yes, sir, I do. Mr. Carne was absent-minded on a horse. And 'e wouldn't ride slow. Walk the first mile and the last that's what I teach children. But Mr. Carne, Mr. Danvers Carne, 'e didn't agree. Brought my 'orses in in a lather. You can take it from me, 'e was gallopin' along that ride, sees the bough, pulls in sharp like this. No, Sarah, she wouldn't stand for it. And them stirrups was too long, sir. They ride long in the States, I'm told. And Mr. Carne's spurs were long too, so if 'e once got 'is foot right through the stirrup it wouldn't come out, not without a big wrench. You can take it from me that's what 'appened."

"The mare is not vicious under ordinary circumstances?"

The little man flushed as if the Coroner had cast insinuations against a personal friend. "Vicious, sir!" he exclaimed, indignantly; "Sarah vicious? Why, I'd teach a child to ride on Sarah. Why, Sarah she's foolproof. It's this rough 'andlin' she won't stand. Why, I've known Sarah, when a gentleman 'as done a voluntary, I've known that mare " Suddenly he stopped, looked down to where the party from the Hall sat waiting, and finished lamely: "No, the mare ain't vicious, sir."

I wished he had gone on. Why had he stopped? Was he only afraid of being loquacious?

Soon after that, young Revel was recalled.

"You knew the deceased well?"

"Yes."

"For how long?"

"Over a year."

"You had hunted with him before?"

"Yes."

"He was an expert horseman?"

"Brilliant."

"Is this explanation about the bit reasonable?"

"I suppose so. He did use severe bits. He said he wouldn't ride a puller."

"Did this mare pull on the snaffle or don't you know?"

"I have ridden but not hunted her. She did not pull on that occasion."

"Mr. Revel, you were the first to discover the body. Did you see any reason to doubt that the tragedy was not the result of an accident?"

"No."

But that last word left me doubting, for it came after an interval when he seemed to me to hesitate and look sharply at someone among the group of mourners from the Hall.

As was expected, the jury returned a verdict of Accidental Death, and with a few words of sympathy for the family the inquest was concluded.

I was moving with the crowd towards the door when I was tapped on the shoulder and, turning, saw Richard Furness.

"Dr. Jerrold?"

"Yes."

"Mrs. Danvers Carne would like to see you. Will you come on to the Hall now?"

"If she wishes to see me." I felt a great reluctance to meddle further in this affair, but the evidence of Barnet and Revel left me with my curiosity further roused.

"Please come." Furness directed me and drew back, and I made my way slowly to the door. A young man beside me, talking to another, said, almost in my ear: "That mare, I don't understand it. Reared, maybe, but drag a man all that way why—that mare, she—"

Other voices drowned the rest, and though I listened for further significant comments, I heard nothing but expressions of horror at the disaster, pity for the family, and subdued inquiries about the date of the next meet, which could not take place until after the funeral.

As I came out of the village hall where the inquest had been held I stopped to look at the surroundings. Before me lay a small village green, with its war memorial, a cluster of pleasant cottages, a church with a graceful spire, a vicarage behind a newly-trimmed hedge of holly. The sun had dropped on the other side of a large wood, and this I took to be the Wilderness.

There was something gloomy about the firs and beeches that shut out the sunset, and in spite of the well-cared-for aspect of the village, I thought I should not like to live here.

Following directions, I drove through the village to the high road, turned to the right, then left, into a lane. Five hundred yards farther on, the gate to Marpen Hall divided a row of beeches, and a winding drive brought the house itself into view a reassuring Georgian structure, built of dim red bricks whose balanced proportions and square window-panes gave a sense of peace and security.

Peace and security! I repeated the words as I stopped the car and got out at a low flight of steps. Looking over my shoulder, I could see the spire of the church. Here no wood intervened to hide the western sky. It glowed softly, the bare branches of old trees black against it. A group of cattle and horses grazed in the field below, a few crocuses already showed colour between the flagstones on the terrace, and snowdrops were in bloom at the edge of the lawn. The scene was calm and ordered by a succession of steady, loving hands. Tragedy and violence seemed to have no place here.

The atmosphere of undisturbed orderliness and pleasant living followed me into the house. I was received by a white-haired butler, who had taken the mould of long and respectful service. He seemed to know all about me and led me across a square hall full of daffodils to the door of a room where he announced my name.

Mrs. Danvers Carne came forward to greet me, and I
thought the room suited her. She, too, was sufficiently
modern without any air of rejecting the past. The modern
dislike of heroics was in her composure, but an inherent
gentleness and feminine appeal were there too. There
were no emphatic touches of mourning about her black
dress. I recognized Furness, standing near the fire, a pipe
in his mouth, and Sir Ralph Carne-Hilton, who had given
evidence at the inquest. He was a slight man of fifty or so,
who limped as he came forward to meet me. There were
marks of suffering around his mouth, his eyes were
joyless and patient. Young Revel was sitting at the tea-
table with three women. The one behind the tea-urn I
took to be Lady Carne-Hilton. At first sight she appeared
to be an amazing creature, but I had not talked to her
very long before I saw that it was only the elaborate
dressing of her dark hair, her make-up, and her atrocious
ear-rings that were amazing, and that they were the sign
of an immoderate craving to attract attention. I
understood this better when I heard that she was the
sixth daughter of a country clergyman. She seemed to me
to be highly excited rather than depressed by the
situation.

The other two ladies were Miss Trent, an American
girl, who showed more signs of distress than anyone in
the room, but was triumphantly pretty in spite of it, and
Averil Legend. In common with all Londoners, I had seen
her many times before, although I had never met her. She
is to be seen at first nights, at the opera, at Ascot, at all
the right places at all the usual times, and her
photograph appears every week in some paper or other.
She is very fair, very English, and quite flawless. So far
as I know, she does nothing except maintain her
reputation for beauty. She has not even married, though
she must be thirty. No scandal has touched her
personally, but I seemed to remember that her mother
was equally lovely in Edwardian days, and not equally
virtuous, and that Miss Legend was reported to be of

exalted but unofficial parentage on her father's side. There was nothing unexpected about her until I looked at her hands. They were well-kept, cleverly manicured hands, but they were broad and ugly as a man's, and I liked her better for having them.

Lady Carne-Hilton gave me tea in a beautiful Chinese cup without a handle. When I admired it, she began to talk, and then I admired her memory, which must have been prodigious. It sounded exactly as if she were reading out of a text-book on the subject of Ming porcelain. There was no rejoinder but a murmur of agreement to such a display of knowledge. Furness spoke once or twice to Sir Ralph without getting much response. Young Revel went back to his chair beside Miss Trent. She gave him a grateful glance and a woebegone smile as he talked to her in a low voice. Miss Legend, who seemed to have finished her tea, sat still, with her ungainly hands in her lap, I think she saw me look at them, for she raised her eyes and let me see their colour, as nearly violet as eyes could be. They made me think again of the story that she was the daughter of some southern prince.

Mrs. Danvers Carne drank her tea thirstily and reached for a cigarette, which Furness lit for her, as if he had been watching her and was waiting to do her some service.

As soon as I had finished a second cup of tea and refused cake, Sir Ralph said: "Can we get on with this business now, Mimi?"

"Please," said Mrs. Danvers Carne.

Lady Carne-Hilton raised her eyebrows. "I'll show Dr. Jerrold my room while Colman takes away the tea," she announced, rising.

No one spoke, and I followed her through the hall into a room on the left.

"Ralph allowed me to do what I liked with this room," she explained as she switched on the lights. "What do you think of it?"

"It is very interesting," I answered.

"But do you like it?"

It was the strangest room I had ever seen. Although it must have been exactly the size of the dining-room, which I saw later, it seemed so much larger that it spoilt the balance of the house. Paintings and mirrors were placed to give an illusion of distance. Even the colours of the frescoes were dim and remote, like something remembered rather than seen. Everywhere I seemed to look down vistas where Doric columns, temples, statues, were vaguely defined against pale skies. Close and tangible, harshly white marble seats and tables stood on a marble floor, with skins of white fur thrown over them. Alabaster pillars intercepted the light. It was the colour of this light that shocked and startled me. Spirits waking in a royal tomb at the call of the master of evil might throw such light on their gorgeous surroundings. Its bluish-white brilliance suggested death.

I looked at Lady Carne-Hilton again. The patches of rouge on her cheek-bones were purple. My own figure was reflected in a mirror opposite. I looked like a spectre, dressed, with slightly obscene effect, in a black morning coat and grey trousers and their usual accessories.

She laughed a disagreeable sound in that room.

"Why?" I asked mildly.

"Aren't you clever enough to guess?"

"No, I don't think I am."

"You can't understand? This is one place where the commonplace does not flourish."

I am afraid she was very much disappointed in me, but she continued on rather a high note: "I cannot endure the commonplace. Have you ever thought how the average person accepts everything ready-made? Tastes, habits, morals? I have rejected everything I was ever taught, and begun again. Life is so clean, once one can do that."

"But isn't it just a little uncomfortable, Lady Carne-Hilton?"

I think I spoke for the sake of interrupting her, but

she answered me literally.

"Oh, no. Quite the reverse. These chairs are delightful made to a special design. This is my writing-table" she showed me a roomy marble slab on carved pedestals, occupying the central position along the outer wall "and here are my cubby-holes." She pressed a hidden spring, and a mirror on one side of the table swung out, disclosing a cupboard in the wall, fitted with different-sized nooks for letters and stationery.

Colman opened the door, and a stream of yellow light flowed in.

"Sir Ralph is waiting, my lady."

She shut the panel and led me back to the other room.

Everyone was smoking except Averil Legend when we came in. Mimi Carne stood between Sir Ralph and Furness. Marion Trent had drawn her chair nearer to them. She looked up at me with a little gasp, as if something she had waited for and dreaded was about to happen. Revel was standing behind her chair.

"Shall I stay?" asked Lady Carne-Hilton.

It seemed out of character that she should ask such a question at such a moment, for she was certainly a person to assert her importance and enjoy a situation so obviously dramatic.

"I think we all should be here, yes," her husband answered.

She sat down and drew a long cigarette-holder from her bag. Sir Ralph turned to me.

"The truth is, Dr. Jerrold, we want to consult someone, and Mimi—Mrs. Danvers Carne—has suggested you. You are an outsider and we all know your reputation also, a doctor and a lawyer are about the only two people who can be trusted to hold their tongues. For certain reasons we don't want a lawyer at the moment. You see, none of us is convinced that Dan met his death by accident."

"Then why—"

"Yes, I know—why not say so at the inquest? Because,

so far, this doubt is only a sort of instinct, and we don't trust ourselves to sift it. We are all too much involved. We only want you to listen to our reasons and give an opinion tell us if there is enough in it to make it our duty to go further."

"But, my dear sir—"

"Please, Dr. Jerrold!" Mimi Carne leaned forward from the chair in which she was seated.

I turned to Sir Ralph. "It seems very definitely not my business, but of course I will help if I can."

He looked round the room. "Well, you see us all," he said, shortly. "We knew Dan well. I disliked him. So did my wife, I think. Furness was supposed to be his best friend. Revel was devoted to him. Mimi was his wife, and Miss Trent—admired him."

The American girl gave a little cry. "I adored him!" she exclaimed.

"Averil Legend—"

Miss Legend looked at me. "I had every reason to hate him," she remarked quietly.

"And the point is, whether we hated or loved him, we all think there is something unexplained and mysterious about his death."

"Why?" I asked. "The facts seemed plain enough."

"You see," Mimi Carne spoke impetuously, "I almost predicted the accident in a conversation with Dr. Jerrold the day before Dan died. I've told you what I said to him."

Revel broke in. "We have some reasons—but they hang on our knowledge of Dan, and circumstances."

"Can you explain?"

Sir Ralph straightened out his leg as if it hurt him. Then he said: "There's the mare. You see, I'm lame and my hunters are trained to stand if I fall. Sarah is fifteen and I've hunted her for ten years. My boy and his friends ride her in the holidays. If we want to give a lady a safe mount, we choose Sarah. It is practically certain that she wouldn't drag a man five hundred yards. Unless—"

"Are you going to suggest that theory to Dr. Jerrold?"

demanded Revel angrily.

"As I understand it, we aren't suggesting theories at the moment. But Sarah certainly hated Dan, and when I said she wouldn't drag a man, I did have some doubts if she might not drag a man she wanted to kill."

Lady Carne-Hilton, restless because the conversation did not include her, made small gestures to attract attention. She smoked, knocking off the ashes every moment or two. She leaned forward, she leaned back, she looked at her rings and finger-nails. Now she spoke.

"Why shouldn't a horse commit murder?" she asked, in her high-pitched voice. "I believe she did it."

"It's absurd," protested Revel, violently. "I won't have the issue confused like this."

"Dr. Jerrold had better hear the rest," suggested Furness.

"Yes." Sir Ralph took the lead again. "Dan thought he might be killed, and from certain things he said to me, I believe he was afraid he might seem to die of an accident which wasn't an accident. It appears that he told his servant, Otway, and Revel, that attempts on his life had already been made. He seems to have had suspicions of the most unlikely people."

Mimi Carne interrupted him. "Dan suspected me of wanting to get rid of him," she said.

"Dan may not have been mad, but I don't think he was quite sane," Sir Ralph added.

"I absolutely deny that," cried Revel. "The family misunderstood and belittled him. Lord Belfare resented the fact that his mother was an American and neither rich nor distinguished by birth. Dan was a genius—a genius at living."

"There's something in that," said Furness, taking his pipe out of his mouth, "but there's something in what Sir Ralph says too. I've known Dan for years, and sometimes I would have agreed with one, sometimes the other."

"Why do you think there is a doubt about the accident theory, Mr. Furness?" I asked.

"I don't exactly think it. But I certainly feel a doubt. The mare for one thing— Dan's horsemanship for another. And then, to be quite frank, it's so devilish convenient. I wouldn't dare write Dan's death into a story, the way it seems to have happened it lets too many people out of intolerable situations."

"You see—" Revel turned to me, his1 hands outstretched.

Marion Trent covered her face with her hands, shuddering.

"Don't you believe that the devil sends his agents about the earth, and that wherever they go, lives are broken and disaster follows, Dr. Jerrold?" asked Lady Carne-Hilton, hysterically.

Revel turned on her. "The saints upset things too, wherever they went. Don't forget that!"

Marion Trent looked up. "Dan was too great for our little souls," she said fiercely.

"I'd like to see Dr. Jerrold alone," said Revel, drawing back with an effort.

"Yes, I think that's a good plan. You see, we are in some disagreement about my cousin's character," Carne-Hilton remarked dryly. "What do you say, Mimi?"

"Yes, oh, yes. And then he will tell us what we ought to do."

"Then, shall we all go out and leave Revel with Dr. Jerrold?" suggested Carne-Hilton.

"I think I should like to see you first, Sir Ralph."

I had selected Carne-Hilton because he seemed to me to be a man whose emotions were negligible. He had, I thought, a few deep-seated feelings, and one of them, Mimi Carne had told me, was for the honour of his family. Every word he had spoken so far had come carefully considered; nothing on impulse. I did not want colour just then, but design. Cold facts. If he lied to me he would do so deliberately, but I had no reason to expect this. He shared Mrs. Carne's opinion of his cousin, and Averil Legend took this view. Revel and Miss Trent were on the other side, Furness doubtful, and Lady Carne-Hilton yet to place, unless her remarks about the devil could be taken to mean that she shared her husband's views. It has to be remembered that some people regard Satan as a hero.

They all filed out and left us alone.

He gave me a wry smile. "It's a first-class bore for you, being mixed up in all this," he apologized, "but Mimi is in an awkward position. There's no doubt about it. And anything that will help her— After all, you may be able to persuade Revel and Marion Trent to drop it."

"They are the ones who demand an inquiry, then?"

"Well, not altogether. Now it's come up, we are all in the same boat. You see, if Dan's death was—well— assisted, suspicion would be likely to fall on me. I can't let the thing rest there. At the same time, if there's a chance of convincing everyone, we must find it, for Mimi's sake, and the family's."

"Why should suspicion fall on you?"

"Why not? Dan's death is all to my advantage."

"You mean because you are now Lord Belfare's heir?"

"Yes. And because I belong to the family. So far we have successfully escaped disgrace, and sooner or later Dan would have disgraced us. He wasn't very likely to have a son—Mimi refused to have children when she knew of the peculiar strain in his mother's family—a form of religious mania. But he could have done a lot of damage to the property and family name before my son inherited. He was an ingenious as well as an unprincipled person. Oh, there's plenty to tell against me. I had a first-class row with Dan the night before he was killed, and I've no doubt one or another of the servants could testify to it."

"Was the quarrel serious?"

"Yes. It began about a horse and ended about Mimi. It was serious enough."

"What did he say to make you think he was afraid of being murdered?"

"He told me he had made his will. If he had no heirs and lived to be fifty, all his property would go to my boy at his death. If he died earlier, everything not entailed would go elsewhere."

"And the effect of this?"

"We have three uncles. Two of them are very well off and childless, and made wills in Dan's favour. If Dan should leave all this money as well as all the rolling-stock and valuables, not heirlooms, away from the next heir, the estate would be badly crippled. It would be to my advantage to see that Dan lived to be fifty. He knew that my first interest is my son. But what he did not know, or thought I didn't know, was that lately the old men have changed their wills and put the property in trust for Dan during his lifetime and for his heirs afterwards. This means that my boy will benefit now."

"Why did your uncles alter their wills?"

"I gather that some information reached them. Dan was in financial difficulties, you know. It must have come pretty straight or they wouldn't have believed it. Dan had them under his thumb."

"They were fond of him?"

"They thought the world of him. He could be remarkably charming."

"But Lord Belfare—?"

"He had to deal with Dan. He knew him."

"Will you tell me why you disliked him so much?"

An expression of distaste, such as I've seen on the face of a man who hates oysters and sees them on his plate, was his instinctive response.

"Must I? The man's dead."

"Well, you see, at present I don't quite understand your attitude. You evidently feel that someone quite probably hated him enough to kill him. Others feel the same way. If I understood that better, I should be better equipped to judge whether or not you are right."

"Yes, I see. Well, Dan was a rotter."

"Drink?"

"Not more than a dozen good fellows I know."

"Drugs? Women?"

"I don't believe he took drugs unless—as an experiment. Women—I don't know."

"Did he gamble?"

"He did. Nothing would stop that. He had to have excitement, so the stakes had to be more than he cared to lose."

"Did he love his wife?"

"How can I say? He was always charming to her in public. He depended on her, I think. But quite lately he has distrusted her."

"She cared for him?"

"She seemed to be devoted to him."

"But she had a lot to put up with?"

"Naturally. She has a sense of responsibility and he had none, as you and I understand the word."

"But she was devoted to him?"

"Yes. I think she dreaded a smash if she let go. He did a lot of harm to a number of people as it was, but without her he would have done more."

"Do you suspect anyone in particular in connexion with his death?"

"No, I don't. I could name a dozen with sufficient motive. But, to judge by myself, there would have to be more than that. There were moments when I could have cheerfully murdered Dan, but only moments. The moment, the opportunity, and the assurance that I shouldn't be found out would have had to coincide."

I believed him.

"I see. And you think just this may have happened to someone on Tuesday?" I asked.

"Yes. But I still think it may have been the mare. Sarah is half human, and you can't hang a horse."

"But why did she hate him?"

He sighed impatiently. "Dan had a craving for power. He wanted to be master. He would go to extraordinary lengths to get his way. Now, Sarah has been thoroughly trained, and she is old. Put a child of two on her back and send him out with hounds and he'd be in at the death if he could stick on. But she has her little ways a sort of 'Mother knows best' attitude which infuriated Dan. You heard about that bit. I should think that Sarah must have fought him steadily all day, and that both their tempers must have risen with every mile they went together."

"And if not?"

He looked at me thoughtfully. "Well, if not, and if Dan did not die through an accident, someone in this house must have been responsible. Naturally I prefer to think it was the mare."

"But why? I mean, why someone in this house?"

"Because, when Dan left the hunt, the field was reduced to half a dozen people besides ourselves, and of those none had reason to ride home by the Wilderness. If anyone had done so, he would probably have been seen. Furness rode after Dan, said something to him, rode with him for five minutes or so, and rejoined the hunt. Mimi's mount cast a shoe and she started for home about four. I saw the fox to ground, and Barnet rode up with a hack he had brought to meet me; I changed horses and rode home. Revel and Furness followed, as you heard at the inquest. Marion Trent had come home earlier, so she is out of it. My wife and Averil Legend were motoring and heard hounds some time after four, got out and walked a little way, thinking they might see the kill. We were all in that wood at one time or another between three thirty and four thirty that day, except Miss Trent, and, more than that, any one of us could have left the hunt for a short time during the run and rejoined hounds, as it happened, before the end. Hounds ran in a semicircle. Anyone dropping out the other side of Barwell Cross could have slipped into the Wilderness and met the field again this side of Beech Wood Farm. This applies to the rest of the field, too, but I've thought them over and there isn't the faintest reason to suspect any of them."

"What about the servants?"

"Barnet took my second horse back and came out to meet me with the hack, as I said. He didn't leave the stables with the hack till after four, and that's a pretty good alibi, as it would take all his time to get to me at Cranmere, as he did. He took my hunter along to the lane and then home at a walk. Revel had already found Dan before Barnet could have got there. Otway was riding Dan's second horse, but missed him, as he doesn't know the country well, and most of the other servants had gone home, owing to the weather. He picked up the hunt after Dan left it. We were some distance from the Wilderness then, so one of the hunt servants directed him to the high road. Vivien passed him hacking towards Marpen and saw him open the gate into the lower park. The chauffeur confirms this. He never went into the Wilderness at all, apparently. That covers the servants, I think."

"But Mr. Carne left the hunt about twenty past three. How long should it have taken him to hack home?"

"Half an hour to fifty minutes, according to the way he rode."

"And how long to the tree?"

"Not more than fifteen minutes."

"And he must have been killed there."

"Why?"

"You mean he could have been taken back there and dragged from the place where the branch would make it look as if he had fallen? Yes, I see."

"It could have been done anywhere in the wood."

I thought this over. "I suppose I had better see Mr. Revel."

"I'll send him in."

Young Revel must have been waiting, for the door hardly closed before it opened again to admit him. This man would have trouble in keeping a secret, I thought. He moved as he spoke, tugged along by mental impulses like a kite in a strong wind. He sat down in the chair Sir Ralph had vacated. Where Sir Ralph had withdrawn nervously, a man whose will-power took the place of vitality, Revel rushed the interview, carried along by emotional excitement.

"You think Mr. Carne's death ought to be investigated further," I said. "Why?"

"Well, you've heard about the horse. Did Carne-Hilton tell you that Dan was a brilliant horseman? Did he tell you that Dan had enemies, and knew it?"

"Yes, but Mr. Danvers Carne seems to have been superstitious. Do you know if he had valid reason for his fears?"

"Dan wasn't afraid. He was never afraid of anything. As for being superstitious well, call it that! Only, with Dan, it was something more. He was sensitive to vibrations like a man who could catch wavelengths without a wireless apparatus. He knew when the unseen movements of the ether were with him and when they were not."

"But his reasons for thinking his life was threatened?"

"Oh, he had reason enough. There had been attempts on his life already. I've talked to Otway, his servant, and he confirms this. A year ago in this house they mounted him on a half-broken colt with a vicious temper. They gave him an ordinary snaffle, and the beast had a mule's mouth. He was all but killed then. Six months later Mimi Carne was ill in Gibraltar. Furness urged him to go out to her, although he knew that there was an epidemic of typhoid and that Dan would never be inoculated. Otway went too. He says he was nervous about his master and begged him to take him. Dan caught typhoid and nearly died. Furness went too, and Otway suspects him of changing the drinking-water in Dan's room."

"But I thought that Furness was Carne's friend."

"So Dan thought, till lately. But since then he found out that Furness was in love with Mimi."

I paused before asking him the next question. His statement startled me. If the facts supported it, these two must fall under suspicion.

"You suspect Mrs. Danvers Carne and Furness?"

"Mimi is a fine woman in her way. But she is under Furness's influence. She asked Sir Ralph Carne-Hilton to invite him to this party."

"You definitely suspect him, then?"

"I think either he or Carne-Hilton might have taken advantage of a chance to get Dan out of the way. Furness could have done it. He followed Dan into the Wilderness that day and no one saw Dan alive after that. I tell you, everything has been done to get this case over quickly and without due inquiry. Old Belfare disliked Dan. The Carne family is nothing if not stolid and British. Dan wasn't. He was unusual. He had visions of an international State. He was a pacifist. There isn't anyone in the family who regrets his death except the old uncles, and they are under Belfare's thumb. Mimi never understood him. Only a few people did. Otway adored him, but he's only a servant."

"To reopen the case there would have to be some evidence."

"How do you know there isn't? Has anyone bothered to find out? Look here!" He took a penknife out of his pocket and handed it to me. It was a cheap affair and looked new. "I found that in the chalk-pit, near Dan's body. It isn't rusty, so it can't have lain there long, and it certainly didn't belong to Dan. Who dropped it and when?"

I handed it back to him, but he said: "Keep it. Furness writes for the magazines—adventure stories, you know, murders and Wild West stuff. He uses pencils. He'd have to have some such thing handy."

"How do you know it didn't belong to Mr. Carne?"

"Of course it didn't. Dan never used a cheap thing. Wouldn't touch 'em."

"There seems to be a good deal of difference of opinion about Mr. Danvers Carne's character."

Revel leaned forward eagerly. "Carne-Hilton's been talking to you. He would! Haven't you found out that

most people stop short just where the important things
begin? To those people—and Carne-Hilton, old Belfare,
Furness, Mimi, are among them—Dan seemed
incomprehensible, unbalanced. His attitude about money
alone—it alienated them. He'd give money to anyone who
needed it and expect others to give it to him. He had a
horror of the commonplace. Most people accept
everything ready-made, even their morals. Dan began at
the beginning and made things for himself. He was free.
His religion was beauty. Dirty bank-notes seemed cheap
to him in exchange for anything lovely. He was
fantastically generous. If you, for instance, understood old
prints and loved them better than he did, he'd send you
all he had. He thought lovely things should be in the care
of those who valued them. If he found a poet writing
potboilers, he'd make him an allowance. Sometimes, of
course, he couldn't afford this sort of thing and Mimi
made a fuss. She thought he ought to pay his own bills
before he paid other people's."

During this speech I felt suddenly alert. Somewhere a
connexion had been made in my mind. Two wires had
joined and a message ran along them. I knew I should be
able to read it later, for the same thing often happens
when I am interviewing a patient. "This is what I want."
My reaction is as prompt as a woman's at a bargain-
counter.

"It's a point of view, you know!"

"Yes, but you can't expect a great man to be bound by
it. The little people ought to attend to such things. They
ought to think it a privilege. Can you see Mohammed
paying bills?"

"I don't suppose he had any."

"He didn't live in modern times."

"I seem to remember that you said something about
saints in this connexion before."

"Well, Dan was a saint in his way—he healed the
mind, he came to give life and to give it more abundantly.
Look what he did for me! It makes me writhe to think of

what I missed in life before I met him. My idea of excitement was to get tight and find a girl at the stage door. Dan taught me that every minute of life ought to be great, important, thrilling. He taught me to think of death as an incident—a link in a chain—not to be avoided or courted, but never to be feared. His courage! The first time I saw him, he saved a man from drowning. The man was tangled up in seaweed, and even the fishermen were afraid to go out to help. The seaweed had been washed into the cove by a storm, and the water was thick with it. He fought the stuff for half an hour, with fifty people watching. By the time I got there it looked as if they would both be drowned. Was that brave?"

"Very brave."

"That was only one of a thousand magnificent things he was too modest to talk of."

"I understand he was a gambler."

"Yes. He lived at such a pitch he had to have some relaxation, and he said the rhythm of chance was like music. It relaxed the tension. He studied Yoga. Do you know anything about it?"

"A little."

"Then perhaps you see—rhythm?"

"Oom!" I said solemnly.

"Are you laughing?" He was quick to take offence.

"I hear a good deal about such things."

"From neurotic women, I suppose. Dan was a man."

"You have given me a very definite idea of him, Mr. Revel."

"Then can you understand how I feel? That peerless man to be wiped out like that! A man the world needs—do you wonder I can't rest until I know how it happened, and if any cowardly brute had a hand in it, I'll see him punished or punish him myself."

"I do understand."

Before he got to the door it opened and Mimi Carne ran into the room. She wore a dark coat and held a hat in her hand. Her face was white.

"There's a man in the garden," she cried.

"Where? What d'you mean?" demanded Revel.

She turned to him and paused. "I went out. I walked down the path under the cedars. Just where the shadow is thickest someone stepped out on the path in front of me. It was a man—not very tall, in a soft hat and a big coat. I cried out—I was startled—and he drew back. I suppose I ought to have followed him, but I couldn't think. He seemed to vanish. I'm afraid I ran back to the house. Colman and Dick Furness are looking for him. I'm nearly sure I heard a car start up just as I got to the house."

Revel was gone.

Mimi sat down limply in front of me. After a moment she looked up. "Please ask me any questions you like, Dr. Jerrold," she said. "I suppose you've talked to Tim Revel?"

"Yes. Have you anything more to tell me?"

"Only that I'm surer and surer there's something more in Dan's death than appears. Sarah couldn't have dragged him, unless something far different from an ordinary fall had happened. Ralph can't grip with his right leg, and all his horses are carefully trained in case he should fall. Sarah is the wisest of them all."

"But is she as reliable with others as with her master?"

"Oh yes. Roy's schoolboy friends ride her. She's been proved again and again. Her cleverness is famous."

"Have you any other reason?"

"Instinct. And there are so many people here in this house who might have had motive for killing Dan."

"I understand about Sir Ralph Carne-Hilton and his wife. But the others?"

She looked at me and I knew that she had braced herself to tell me everything that was in her mind.

"Well, I had motive enough—far more than when I saw you the other day. Since we came here I've found out that Dan suspected Dick Furness of being my lover —that he wanted to divorce me and marry Marion Trent. She is rich. If Dick knew this—I hope he didn't. But perhaps he did."

"Miss Trent?"

"She was in love with Dan. But Ralph told her the truth about him. It appears that Dan had been investigating the facts about her fortune, and her lawyer had found it out. Ralph wrote to him and had an answer. I'm not sure if she was Dan's mistress. But she is a proud girl. If she believed that Dan had treated her like that— Then Tim Revel himself—he is in love with Marion. They were nearly engaged when Dan came along and took her away from him. He was so fascinated by Dan that he gave her up.—But you see, it was always the same. There came a moment when people found him out, and the more they had adored him, the more violently they turned against him. Suppose that moment had come to Tim Revel on Tuesday. As for Averil Legend—Dan ruined the only man she has ever really loved, I think—her brother. He is in the States."

"But, in the name of reason, why should Sir Ralph Carne-Hilton assemble such a party under his roof?"

"Well, Averil is a cousin of Vivien's. Revel went everywhere with Dan lately. Vivien asked Marion Trent. I asked Dick because he has always helped me with Dan and, as you know, I was frightened. But anyway, Dr. Jerrold, Dan attracted melodrama. Any seven people in one house a year from now might have hated and loved him just as intensely. If the devil went about in society, can't you see the house parties he would collect? Half worshipping him as a god, half loathing him in his true character?"

"A god or a devil—which was he? You loathed him at last?"

"I think I did."

"And that is the end of your dream?"

"Yes, I shall never have that dream again. The vase is smashed. I always knew horror would follow."

Furness and Sir Ralph came in.

"We've searched the garden. There's no one there," said Furness.

"You're certain you saw this man, Mimi?" asked Carne-Hilton.

"Certain."

"Do you want to talk to me?" Furness turned to me.

"I suppose so."

Mimi Carne rose, and she and Carne-Hilton went out together.

Furness sat down and filled his pipe. His face looked haggard. "Of course, Dr. Jerrold, I realize that if anyone's going to be suspected in this affair I'm the first. I saw and talked to Dan last of anyone. I rode after him, thinking he was going home because his mare had carried him all day, and I'd seen Otway with his second horse half an hour before and wanted to tell him so. But he said he was going home anyway, so I left him and rejoined the hunt. That was before we came to the branch that seems to have got him. But I'd have a job proving it."

"I still don't quite see how this affair could have been murder staged to look like accident."

"I do. Perhaps you know I write yarns. Well, I can think of a dozen ways of making it sound plausible in a story."

"Would you like an investigation?"

"Lord, no! Why should I?"

"Well, there seems to be doubt in a good many minds about the case, and you, as you say, are the person who would be under suspicion if anyone was."

"I could bear that, quite comfortably. There are lots of decent people who wouldn't cut me for it, even if they were sure I'd done it. Whereas if the thing is brought into public everyone will suffer—Mimi most of all, and she doesn't deserve it."

"That is why you didn't speak sooner?"

"Oh, I think we all tried to believe we thought an accident covered the facts, till Revel spoke up."

"You were a friend of Danvers Carne?"

"Yes. I owed him a lot. As for being his friend in the ordinary sense—that implies some things that weren't there. Dan was unaccountable. You enjoyed him, took what he gave, and gave what he took as long as you could stand it. Then you stopped. He had a way of seeing what people were good at. He started me on my writing. One night I'd been telling a yarn and he said: 'Write it down.' Not only that, he made me do it —worked over it with me. I hadn't a bit of faith in it. But it sold at once. I had a use for that money, but I lent it to Dan, and lending to Dan was giving. He was an inspiring sort of chap—had a gift for seeing and making other people see the amusing and exciting side of life. For a long time I was dependent on him for setting me going again when I got stale. Now I have a name of sorts, and a market, but I shan't write with the same confidence. He could always put me right. I never shook off the feeling that I owed my success to him. That's why I stuck to him—that and Mimi. I was sorry for her."

"So, when she called on you for help, you answered?"

"Yes, it got to be a habit. We were like a couple of doctors who take pride in propping up a rickety patient. Lately Dan got much worse—or else I got to the point where I failed him. I saw things I couldn't stick. I felt sure it couldn't go on much longer."

"What did you expect?"

"Some sort of public disgrace. Dan had to resign from two clubs. Or else his going too far and some man or woman getting his own back. You see, he was perfectly shameless. Look.at this girl, Marion Trent. Dan's affairs were at such a pass that even he had to pay some attention to them. Then she came along and fell for him— women did. So he made up his mind to take advantage of it. Mimi didn't matter—the girl didn't matter. He didn't even take the trouble to disguise his intentions. He wasn't ashamed of himself. To be fair, he didn't think he had reason to be. He thought money in his hands was used for the good of the world and he just took it."

"He seems to have felt that he had something so valuable that ordinary standards didn't apply to him at all!"

"That's just it. But there was something else. He didn't really credit other people with the scruples missing in him. He trusted people just as long as he felt sure that they shared his views about himself. When he began to think they didn't admire him enough, then he would believe anything of them, however base."

"Thanks, Mr. Furness," I said. "I think I've heard enough."

We went out together and found Sir Ralph in the hall. "Do you want to see anyone else?" he asked.

"I don't think so. I've made up my mind."

Averil Legend came down the stairs just then. She looked so lovely that I stopped talking to watch her.

"Is it my turn?" she asked.

"Dr. Jerrold has come to a decision."

She wore a black velvet dress. Her arms were covered with long sleeves which nearly hid her hands. When she spoke, her voice was charged with feeling, and her every word went home.

"Dr. Jerrold will be wrong if he advises you to go further in this matter," she said. "Why should Mimi suffer more than she has suffered already? Why should we be dragged through horrors for a man who has injured us all? Dan is dead. Why can't we all forget him?"

"Human beings don't forget, Miss Legend. And the harder they try, the worse they fail."

She cannot often have looked at a man as she looked at me. Every bit of her loveliness and the magnetism she seldom used was in that gaze.

"Don't do it!"

"I am doing nothing."

"Yes, indeed you are. I will persuade Mr. Revel to be silent. Everyone else is willing—except Marion Trent— and she can be forced to hold her tongue."

"I think, for the sake of everyone concerned, that this

doubt should be cleared up."

"But why?"

"So far as I can see, everyone feels responsible. Everyone doubts everyone else. I'm a mind-doctor. It seems to me dangerous and morbid."

A dog began to howl.

"It's Brune—Vivien's poodle," said Sir Ralph.

Mimi Carne ran down the stairs and came up to us quickly. "We can't find Otway," she said. "I've been looking over Dan's clothes. Did you know he was wearing chamois gloves when he was killed?"

Sir Ralph gave a short exclamation. "But they must have been soaked."

"Exactly. It was enough to account for an accident. But why? He always carried string gloves under his saddle flap. Where were they?"

"We'd better ask Colman." He rang.

Colman came at once and Sir Ralph put the question to him.

"Yes, sir," he said. "I put out string gloves for Mr. Danvers of course, but he was annoyed—he said he had to have chamois gloves for the meet. So I brought him a pair and laid the others beside his hat. Just then you came down, sir, and I attended to your things. Mr. Danvers mounted and rode off, but after you had gone I found the gloves lying on the table. He must have forgotten them. I sent the boy out to the stables, and he caught Mr. Otway just leaving with Mr. Danvers' second horse and gave him the gloves. Mr. Otway was put out, I understand, because his horse wasn't ready saddled for him and so he was delayed. He might have missed Mr. Danvers at the meet. In fact, sir, I believe that is what happened."

"Why, Colman?"

"Well, you see, sir, Mr. Otway was here this afternoon, attending to Mr. Danvers' things in the drying-room, so Mrs. Travers thought she ought to ask him to have a cup of tea, and he came into the hall. It seems Mr.

Barnet noticed the chamois gloves and mentioned it. I should explain that Mr. Barnet had dropped in for tea, as he sometimes does. Mr. Otway was much upset. He said he missed Mr. Danvers all day, being late at the meet, and when he did pick up the field, Mr. Danvers was not with the others. Mr. Otway said: 'I gave those gloves to—'; then he stopped short and got up. There's more in this than what's been told,' he said, and he was trembling, sir. I never saw him so upset. 'And I'm going to find out.' With that he left us, sir, and that was about five thirty. You can ask Mr. Barnet if these aren't the facts. We all heard him. Naturally, sir, we didn't try to stop him, not after what he'd implied, but being Mr. Otway, we didn't pay as much attention as we might."

"Thanks, Colman, that will do."

"We must find Otway. I've sent down to the cottage, but he isn't there."

"Probably gone to the pub," suggested Carne-Hilton.

Furness shook his head. "Hardly. Of all the people who are unhappy tonight, I suppose Otway is most heart-broken. I should think it far more likely that he has gone to find whoever it was he gave the gloves to. Someone whom he expected would see Dan during the run. I suppose he fell back with the other second horsemen and handed the gloves to some member of the field. But to whom? Well, he'll no doubt tell us himself when he comes back."

Revel was coming down behind Lady Carne-Hilton, and Marion Trent was with him. Lady Carne-Hilton was dressed in black, cut in some sensational way to show unexpected triangles of white flesh.

There were patches of rouge on her cheek-bones and the lobes of her ears. Her lips were vermilion and her finger-tips looked as if they had been dipped in blood. She awakened my professional interest. Such frustrated egoism as hers frequently leads to the chair in my consulting-room. She responded with a kind of frightened excitement to the strain under which everyone was labouring. You have only to watch and you will see that even the most civilized of us enjoy taking part in a tragedy. The sense of drama stimulates the nerves, and the fuss that poor people who lead monotonous lives make over the events of birth and death are an instance of this. Vivien Carne-Hilton had a dull mind, and her enjoyment of the situation was to be expected. Also she was one step nearer to becoming a peeress—a way of gaining just the sort of attention she craved.

"Well, we are all here. Perhaps you will tell us what you think, Dr. Jerrold?" said Sir Ralph.

"I have already said what I think. If I were in your place, Sir Ralph, I should have this matter investigated privately in the first instance. If you are all satisfied then that Mr. Carne met his death by accident, you can let matters rest as they are. An expert detective may be able to satisfy you that it was so. But at present it seems to me that you all suspect each other, and if nothing more is done, suspicion will grow. This seems unhealthy, if that isn't a frivolous way of putting it."

"I agree," said Mimi Carne quickly.

"But whom shall we get? Are there any private detectives who are gentlemen?"

Revel looked at Marion Trent. "I think we should be satisfied with a private investigation," he said, "if we found the right man."

"Did you ever hear of a man called Brade?" I asked.

"I have," said Marion, unexpectedly. "Papa employed him once. We were travelling in England and Papa began getting threatening letters. He cabled over to his man in New York and he sent him to Mr. Brade. Papa thought he was a marvel. I'd like to have him."

"Do you know him personally, Dr. Jerrold?"

"Yes, quite well. He's a very odd little man, and he hates murder cases. But he has one great merit. He's the last man on earth you'd take for a detective. And this isn't exactly a usual case, since what you want to know is whether it is a murder or not. I might persuade him."

"I remember, now," said Marion Trent. "He wouldn't take Papa's case at first. It was only after they got talking about Papa's collection of Egyptian hairpins that he accepted. He said Papa had a quaint mind and it wouldn't do for it to be shot at!"

"That's Brade!" I agreed with conviction.

"Then will you get him?" Carne asked.

"I'll try," I promised, just as Colman announced dinner.

Since I have been asked to write everything I can remember, I suppose I had better describe what went on at dinner. Lady Caroline joined us for the first time and she and I behaved like a pair of gramophones. Averil Legend might have been attending an ordinary dinner party, rather boring on the whole. Marion Trent excused herself after the soup had been served. She was very pale and said she felt ill. Revel ate gloomily, and Mimi Carne stuck it out, looking tired beyond all feeling. Lady Carne-Hilton introduced the subject of abnormal psychology and, but for Lady Caroline, I should have been at her mercy. If she had not been a stupid woman she would not have tried to talk to me on that particular subject. She had an extraordinary verbal memory and I could almost name the book she had read, out of which she repeated whole passages. Homosexuality seemed to interest her, whether because she thought it was a subject not usually discussed in public or not, I don't know. In fact, dinner, in spite of the excellence of the food and wine, was a very awkward meal, and Colman cut it short by suggesting audibly that the ladies might like coffee in the morning-room. Sir Ralph, who was suffering, I thought, got up with a gesture of relief.

Lady Caroline asked me to speak to her before I went. She led me upstairs, to a small sitting-room which showed that it was used by ladies. An embroidery frame with a piece of half-finished tapestry stood under a window, and knitting lay on the table. "It's Mimi's room," she explained. "We shall be quiet here."

She gave me a cigarette, took one herself, and we sat down.

"What are you going to do?" she asked directly.

I told her.

"Is it best—best for Mimi?" she demanded.

"I think so. Mrs. Carne will not recover from all this horror until the mystery is cleared up."

"Do you think it was murder?"

"I have no idea, Lady Caroline. These people all felt so strongly about your nephew in one way or another that their judgment can't be trusted. I have great confidence in Simon Brade."

"You realize that if there is an inquiry Mimi will be involved? Her friendship with Dick Furness will fall under suspicion. Her relations with Dan will have to be examined. And she must have passed the very spot where the accident took place soon afterwards. No one can tell what may follow. She has been through so much for so long—will she be able to bear it?"

"I think she will bear it better than secrecy and doubt."

"Perhaps you are right. But suppose all the signs were against her. Suppose it did turn out that Dan was murdered. Suppose she was arrested—imprisoned—put on trial."

"She is perfectly innocent."

"But innocent people have been hanged."

"Simon Brade will find out the truth."

"And you will stand by her?"

The door opened and Mimi herself came in. She stood in the doorway looking at us. Then she smiled and put out her hands. "Friends," she said.

Lady Caroline went to her and drew her in.

"Mimi, my dear, you want this inquiry to take place?"

"There is no other way, Aunt Caro."

She walked over to the embroidery frame and stood looking down at the work. Then she unfastened the canvas and rolled it up.

"I did those flowers while Dan was lying dead," she said. "I felt so peaceful—I was tired after hunting and my bath and I lay on the sofa working, waiting for my tea. I shall never touch it again." She thrust the roll into a drawer and shut it.

"Good-bye, Mrs. Carne, I must go."

"But you'll come back with Mr. Brade?" She put her hand in mine.

"Yes, if he will take the case, I will."

"You won't desert us?"

"I will do anything I can to help."

I went to find Sir Ralph, and as he was in neither the hall nor the morning-room I rang for Colman. I did not feel inclined to open the door of Lady Carne-Hilton's room or to wander about the house in search of my host. Before Colman answered my summons, while I stood before the fire, waiting, I saw Marion Trent's white face leaning over the banisters. She came down in a series of short runs and was at my side when Colman appeared. "I want to see you, Dr. Jerrold, please. Colman, the doctor will ring later." She scarcely waited until the servant was out of hearing before she began again, claiming my whole interest and attention with the confidence of a child who has never been repulsed. She seemed to me singularly unprotected, extravagant, a person who would give the whole of herself at once; easily injured therefore. And delightfully pretty!

"Did Sir Ralph tell you the truth?" she asked. "Did he tell you about Dan and me?"

"He told me a little. You made no secret of it, I think," I answered.

"I was proud of it. I am proud of it now. Did you know that I was sitting here, waiting for him, while he was being *murdered?*" She brought out the word as if it helped her to say it aloud. "Murdered," she repeated. "I had put on my pink dress—the one he liked."

"I am sorry, Miss Trent." I was.

"Did he tell you about this?" She drew out of her bag a

legal-looking envelope and held it towards me.

"No."

"I haven't opened it. And I won't. He—Sir Ralph— wrote to my lawyers about Dan. Papa died last year and I am rich. Sir Ralph dared to insinuate that Dan wanted my money—that he was prepared to leave his wife and marry me for mercenary reasons. He told me so. This is the answer to his letter. He asked them to write to me confirming his statement that Dan had made inquiries about my finances. Do you know why he did it, Dr. Jerrold? Of course you don't. But I do. Dan explained it all. Mimi refused to have children. So long as Dan was married to her he could have no heir. But he longed for children, and I would have been proud to have a son of his for mine. Sir Ralph knew it and meant to stop it if he could, so that his son should inherit. He said Dan was crazy, but it is Sir Ralph who is crazy. Crazy with family pride and ambition for his boy. Everyone knows it. He killed Dan because I told him last night that nothing anyone said would stop my marrying him when he was free."

She turned swiftly as Carne-Hilton limped towards us. "Did you hear what I said. I said you killed Dan. Here is the letter you thought would make me believe your lies against him. I haven't read it. There—" she knelt down and tossed it into the fire, watched it blacken and burn before she rose to her feet. "Now you know what I think. Oh, if only I had had a month, a week— even twenty-four hours as his wife! But I hadn't even that! Not even that!" She ran from us up the stairs, and we waited in silence until we could no longer hear her sobs and her running footsteps.

I looked at Carne-Hilton, but there was nothing new to see in his face or manner, unless it was deathly weariness.

"It did not occur to me before," he said slowly, "that there was that additional fact against me. If Dan and Mimi had been divorced and he remarried, there might have been an heir. You see, Dr. Jerrold, I did not believe it would happen. I thought she would believe the facts. They were so obvious to the rest of us."

"I am sorry for her."

"But not so sorry as you would have been if Dan had lived. We all benefit from Dan's death, but I'm not sure that Marion Trent doesn't benefit most. If I loved a woman, I would have killed Dan and suffered the penalty sooner than see her his wife. But I've never loved a woman so much as that. Other things have come first."

I knew what they were, but it seemed strange for this man to speak of them, even so vaguely. He was hypnotized by fatigue and the hysteria that pervaded the house tonight. He glanced at me a moment later as if he wondered what he had been saying, but was too tired to care.

"You still want me to get Simon Brade to investigate the accident, Sir Ralph?"

"Oh, yes," he replied without hesitation, but with the same dragging weariness that seemed to pervade all his speech and gestures.

"I will try to see him tonight."

"Thank you. The sooner the better, I suppose."

The burden of his immense fatigue began to affect me. Why had I allowed myself to be dragged into such an affair? A thousand times why? My work makes such enormous demands on my sympathy and vitality that for years I have kept my personal life barren of any but superficial interests.

The old house, so satisfying, friendly, sheltering, seemed to warn me. There was a second of startled awareness, when all the persons concerned were vividly present. Marion Trent, taking refuge from her grief in a passion of vindictiveness. Revel driven by a dangerous illusion. Furness floundering, bewildered. Lady Carne-Hilton enjoying a broth of turgid sensation. Averil Legend, aloof and mysterious. Carne-Hilton himself, armed by a battered fortitude which might or might not hold. And Mimi Carne.

Men and women come to me to be saved, and I save them if I can. This means that I make no reserves in my effort, but fasten on the purpose and do not let go. She, coming to me professionally, had roused this will to save. She was in danger, and I had taken her case. I could not abandon her.

"Then, good night, Sir Ralph!"

He shook hands with me.

"It is very good of you to help us."

The night was cloudy, with a wind muttering sullenly along the wooded lane. Just as I approached Agminton, the lights of a small inn interrupted the darkness. I pulled the car to a standstill, suddenly curious to hear local gossip about the inquest. I did not think I had been noticed that afternoon, not being of the party from the Hall, and hoped to pass as a traveller making for London.

The bar-parlour was hot, dim with smoke, friendly. I gave my order and sat down, picking up an old copy of the *Horse and Hound* and trying to appear absorbed in its contents. The girl who served me lingered a moment or two, so I looked up and asked how much farther it was to Agminton.

"Oh, only a matter of two miles," she answered briskly, "and London twenty-four miles on. You can't go wrong, if that's where you're going, sir."

"Yes, I'm for London. You get a lot of custom here for a week-day, don't you?"

"Not as a rule, sir. We're quiet enough. But, you see, the inquest has brought them along tonight."

I considered a moment. "Inquest? Oh, yes, there was a hunting accident the other day. I remember."

"Yes, sir. The Coroner said it was an accident."

She left me to wait on a group of men who had just come in. One of them was a small dark man who might have been a skilled artisan; another, dark too, but ruddier, suggested an outdoor life. I took him for a keeper. The other was a massive labourer with fair hair, blunt features, and a broad dialect, rather like a cockney's, but softer and slower. They were greeted by the company and sat down at the long deal table. I could hear the conversation quite well from my place in the corner. They were not discussing the inquest, which disappointed me, but some point-to-point race or other.

"And it was Mr. Danvers as rode Pink Livery," said one.

There was a momentary silence.

"Did he know?" someone else asked.

"That'd be saying." The first man winked. "But I wouldn't put it past 'im."

"And by—," the first speaker swore eloquently, "if it's not the same 'orse as Barnet's got in the stables at Marpen this minute, I'm a dud and I'll never lay a shillin' on again!"

The artisan spoke eagerly.

"You mean it was another horse that won under Pink Livery's name? And then he sold Pink Livery for top price? Mr. Danvers Carne?"

"I don't say it. It's my sister's brother-in-law, up at Oxford, told the story. 'E don't know if Mr. Danvers was fooled. But the 'orse was sold to an undergraduate gentleman, and 'e raised a row and went for the dealer and got chucked out. It all 'appened near two year ago. The Gentlemen Jockeys' Point-to-Point it was, and Mr. Danvers rode for someone else. It was all 'ushed up. But my sister's.brother-in-law is under-groom to the Master"of the North Bramshire, and 'e got the story straight."

One of the men glanced uneasily at me. The usefulness of what I had heard was doubtful, but I wanted to hear more, and already voices were being lowered, so I got up and moved over to the table.

"Was that the Open Handicap at Midley in April '29?" I asked boldly. "I put my money on Winter's Tale, and Pink Livery won by three lengths."

"Don't know that 'orse, sir. But that was the race all

right. I wasn't there. It was my sister's brother-in-law up Oxford way told me."

"Well, it's a queer story!"

"Likely as not there's nothing in it, sir. These things get about. Nobody thought much of Pink Livery. A Irish 'orse, I believe. And 'e's done nothing since."

"Well, it's very interesting, though I shouldn't have won in any case. Winter's Tale fell at the third fence. Good night to you all! Will you have one for luck before I travel on?"

I treated them all round, and they talked to me willingly enough about racing in general until I left, hoping I had not betrayed my ignorance, for it was only by accident that I remembered the name of the race meeting referred to, and if there is a horse named Winter's Tale, I have never heard of him.

Certainly the rumour had no bearing on the death of Danvers Carne, but it was interesting to know that one of these men, at least, thought him capable of a sporting sin so heinous.—'I wouldn't put it past him!'

Was he right?

If Danvers Carne had died by violence, it seemed to me that it was important to decide whether he was a saint or a villain. I had made up my own mind about that.

My dear Brade:
I have written down everything I can remember
while it is fresh in my mind.
I hope you will take this case. I shall come and
see you early this morning, as I said on the telephone.
Yours ever,
Jerry

Friday, February 10th

"Look here, Brade, do it for me."

Simon Brade put down the piece of jade he had been fingering and inspected me through his eye-glass. I think it was the first time he had seen me since I came through the door. Of all the people I have ever met he is, or can be, the most annoying, evasive as a shadow cast by a flickering light.

"But, Jerry, I don't want to."

"These people are in awful trouble. Don't you ever think of anyone but yourself?"

"Oh, yes, I have to, sometimes. But do I have to now?"

"You said I helped you once. Can't you help me when I ask you to?" Brade had had a serious breakdown, due to overwork on an ugly case, and I had treated him. Against my will, I used this appeal.

He suddenly gave me his whole attention—an embarrassing experience.

"So it's as bad as all that," he sighed. "I'd really better not take the case, you know."

"What do you mean?"

"I've read your notes, Jerry."

"Can't you speak out?"

"Oh yes, I can. You see, when I get interested I do sometimes hit on the truth, and are you sure the truth is what you want?"

"Of course it is."

He sighed.

"Once," he said, "a very old lady showed me a stem-cup. She said she had been told it was a perfect specimen of Ming porcelain—of the Hsuan Te period. She was very proud of it and seemed to think I might want to buy it from her, but she assured me that she would not dream of parting with it and had left it in her will to her favourite grandson. Finally, she asked me if I thought it genuine. It was a Japanese imitation, but did she want the truth?"

"What has that got to do with it?"

"Then you think Mrs. Danvers Carne is just as nice as she looks?"

"Really, Brade, you can't suspect that woman."

"But I can," he murmured mournfully. "I have a very suspicious nature. All collectors have. I'm sorry about it."

"You mean you think she did it? Well, you're wrong."

"I don't think anything. But suppose she did and I found it out."

"It's absurd. No woman could have done it."

"I don't think you're fair to the ladies. I've noticed it before."

"Of course, if you're going to be funny—"

"But I'm not, Jerry, I'm serious. Just because I don't know long words like you—"

"Will you or won't you take this case?" I demanded.

He put his hand to his head wearily. "Don't shout, Jerry. You'll break something!" He looked with concern at his collection of Ming porcelain, sheltered in a cabinet near by.

"Very well," I got up. "I thought you'd do it for me."

"Don't you see that I like you? And that's what makes it so confusing! Especially when you shout at me."

"I'll take the risk. Mrs. Danvers Carne is nothing to me except a sort of patient. I feel responsible and should like to help her."

"I wasn't talking about you, Jerry, I was talking about me."

"I wish you'd behave like a human being."

"Don't, please don't! You're going to talk about Behaviourism. I know you are. I don't like human beings—not the kind you read about in scientific books, all libidos and complexes."

I had an inspiration. "Lady Carne-Hilton employs an excellent chef."

He sat up and stared. Then he lapsed into his former state. "Bless you, how do you know? You like curry."

This was a sore subject between us and I cursed my

tactlessness.

"Doesn't it interest you that Averil Legend is in it? She is lovely, you know."

"I don't like Elizabeth Arden pamphlets, Jerry, not even the illustrations."

"Can't you drop your affectations for a moment, old man, and be the good fellow you really are? Can't you see I'm worried?"

Brade looked sad. I knew that there was something behind his reluctance to take up the case. He hated violence. To see a dog run over was more than he could bear. Yet his work lay among horrors. That was why he retreated between times to his jade and porcelain, his Chinese prints and pottery, into a world where everything was play, and people playmates. He could draw exquisite designs and might have made a career of it, but for some reason his passion for order and pattern had led him into the investigation of crime, and he had made himself so useful that he was frequently called in to help in any case more than usually subtle and intricate.

"Well, if you won't, you won't," I said. "I suppose I had better go to Holloway."

I did not do it on purpose, but my words had an instantaneous effect. He sprang up and grasped my arm. "Holloway! Oh yes, get him by all means. He'll find a murderer for you. Of course, it may not be the person who did it, but that won't matter. Holloway never fails! For picking holes in the most genuine alibi he's famous. Go and get him!"

"Who's shouting now?" I asked gently.

"I am. Everyone shouts Holloway's praises. What is the use of advertising rat-killer in pastels?"

"But I have promised to get someone." I hadn't, but I was not going to lose my advantage.

"I don't see why you came to me at all if you want Holloway. Might as well buy a knitting-needle when you are looking for a battering-ram."

"What about the C.I.D?"

"Bless us and save us, what next? Why the C.I.D. when there's probably a local football team?"

"I thought you admired the C.I.D.?"

"So I do. I can't live without the C.I.D. They do all my work for me, once I'm started. You don't seem to realize that if this was murder it was the work of a clever amateur. Find out who it was and then leave the C.I.D. to do the rest. But it's a one-man job in the first place."

"Well, whom do you suggest?"

He did not answer my question. Instead, he got up and wandered round the room, handling his treasures as he scolded me. "Really, my dear man, is it sense? You come to me with a string of characters, all nicely psychoanalysed, all apparently morbid and the victim of a fixed idea, and want me to investigate a murder that probably never happened. Really, you know—" He got no further, for a servant knocked on the door. "Oh, come in, come in," he called.

"A person to see you, sir. I told him you were engaged. He said he had come on the same business as Dr. Jerrold and had an important communication to make to you both. He gave his name as Otway."

"Danvers Carne's servant," I reminded Brade. "How did he know that you were concerned in this?"

"But I'm not."

"Mrs. Carne must have sent him. Show him up, Perry," I directed.

Brade sank into a chair and reached out his hand for tobacco and cigarette-papers. He rolled his own cigarettes, but rarely smoked them, as they usually came to pieces after a few whiffs. Engaged thus, his eye-glass falling off and interrupting him frequently, he waited for Otway, who had to climb three flights of stairs to reach Brade's aerie at the top of the house.

"You are being masterful, Jerry!" Brade reproached me plaintively while we waited.

Perry opened the door and made way for a trim, well-dressed little man, who suggested at once a military and sporting past. My first thought was that I should be glad to have him beside me in a tight corner, my next that I would unhesitatingly take his tip at a race meeting, and my third that in a house full of maid-servants I should see to it that he lodged elsewhere. I guessed that he was vain and unscrupulous, but I liked him, as I had found myself liking men imprisoned for sins against a society not arranged to suit them.

"You are Otway? I am Dr. Jerrold," I said, as Perry withdrew and closed the door.

Otway glanced over his shoulder.

"Oh yes, it's shut," Brade answered him, "and Perry's half-way downstairs by now. You can go ahead."

"Are you Mr. Brade?" Otway turned to him respectfully.

Brade did not deny it, though he seemed to wish he could. I nodded.

"Mrs. Carne asked me to come. She said that Dr. Jerrold was putting my master's case before you. She is very anxious to have you investigate it, sir, and she thinks you ought to hear what I have to say."

"You can sit down, you know. Somebody might as well be comfortable," Simon suggested sorrowfully.

"Thank you, sir, but it won't take me long to explain. I told Mrs. Carne last night that I know my master was murdered, though I'm not certain who did it yet. He fell, just as was described at the inquest, but he was not killed by the fall."

"Oh dear!" from Brade.

"Why do you say that?" I asked.

"Because, sir, his riding-boots were muddy."

"There might be several explanations of that."

"No, I think not. One of the stirrups was quite clean. If he had dismounted and then mounted again they would both have been muddy."

"Why didn't you say so at the inquest?"

"Because I did not observe it until Mr. Carne's clothes were taken to the drying-room for attention. I had already noticed the condition of the stirrups, which seemed odd."

"But the man had been dragged. Of course the boots were soiled."

"Yes, sir. But the soles were stuck with hard loam. The boots were new. He had been on his feet after his fall."

"You have kept the boots as they were?"

"Yes, sir."

"Have you anything else to tell us?"

"Yes, sir, Mrs. Carne tells me that you know the mistake made on Tuesday morning and that his string gloves were given me to take to him, that I was late in starting for the meet, and did not catch him; in fact, that I missed him all day for a variety of reasons, which I won't stop to explain now.

"I gave the gloves to Sir Ralph Carne-Hilton's chauffeur, who says he placed them with one or two other articles liable to be needed during the day. There was an extra side-saddle, as the second horse provided for Mrs. Danvers Carne required a different-sized saddle, and there was a cross-saddle for the groom, in case he had to take back a lady's mount. There was also some whisky and a syphon and a thermos flask of coffee. The small Morris often followed along when Sir Ralph sent out a large party and carried a groom, to ride home hunters if anyone wanted to leave the hunt. I thought Mr. Danvers might remember this and find the gloves. The chauffeur tells me that he left the car standing beside the road and walked with another chauffeur and the groom into the wood. When he returned the gloves were no longer in the car. The groom confirms this. There were several members of the field in the wood at the time, and he spoke to Mr. Furness and told him that the gloves were there, but he was not sure that Mr. Furness understood."

He paused and glanced quickly at each of us in turn before he went on.

"I was suspicious from the first about my master's

death. There was, if I may say so, a great sympathy between us. He had been very good to me. I knew that he was living under a foreboding of disaster. I knew he had enemies. I was not satisfied with the verdict. I could not understand what had happened to those gloves, and why no one came forward to explain the matter.

"Last night I left the servants in the hall and went out to study the scene of the accident. I took a powerful torch with me. But I was not the only person with that object, for when I reached the place I saw a circle of light, and suddenly I was standing in it myself. It had been turned on me and blinded me. When it was switched off, I could see no one, though of course I used my own torch. I thought it best to make a statement to someone at once. My evidence may be valuable and I should not be surprised if my master's enemy was mine too."

"You see!" murmured Brade. "It's perfectly simple— not my job at all."

Otway turned to me with a gesture that suggested protest and appeal. He seemed to wish me to say something for him which he did not feel at liberty to say for himself.

"But, Simon—" I began. Then, remembering that Otway was, after all, a servant, I hesitated to say what was in my mind. It was Otway himself who spoke out.

"The fact is, sir, that though I don't care what happens to Mr. Furness, it is a very awkward position for Mrs. Carne. If Mr. Furness murdered my master, there will be things dragged into it I'd rather weren't known. I have a great respect for Mrs. Carne. She got to lean on Mr. Furness a good deal at the last. I shouldn't like to be put in the witness-box and asked questions about it. I feel my master does not wish it."

I glanced at Brade. He was rolling cigarettes vigorously, his right arm working up and down like a pump-handle.

"It isn't my fault," said he angrily. "You both stand there looking at me as if I could decide on the most convenient person and wave my hands and produce a murderer, complete with evidence."

"I think that Mrs. Carne feels that if we put the facts before the police as they appear at present, they will arrest Mr. Furness at once, sir."

"And so they will, if they do their duty, my man."

"I should like Mrs. Carne to have every satisfaction."

"Then why did you take all that trouble?" Brade inserted his eye-glass. "The verdict could have been left as it was and no more questions would have been asked."

Otway showed dignity then. "I loved my master," he said simply. "I had reason to. I was down and out when he found me in the States and took me into his service. Worse than that, I was on the wrong side of the law. Mr. Carne trusted me. He trusts me still."

I looked at Otway with surprise. Did he believe what he implied—that his master lived on and guided events from another plane? There was nothing about Otway to suggest that he would be influenced by such an idea. I could imagine that he might be superstitious, with the gambler's superstition, but I should have thought he would regard a dead man, whether loved or hated, as a very dead man indeed. Danvers Carne must have been as persuasive as he was painted to have brought this attractive, horsy, solid little man to such a pitch of faith in the unseen.

"Oh, the consolations of religion!" Simon sighed.

"Mr. Carne had a remarkable personality, sir. You can't think of him as just—stopping—not if you've known him well."

"Yet he had enemies."

"Yes, sir. He was an enemy himself to many people. It's hard to explain. He hated greedy people. Well, it's like this, sir: nobody would like to be made to look always like they do in those queer mirrors at Madame Tussaud's— stretched out into monstrosities—everything wrong. He made some people look like that—and feel like it too— and they hated him for it. But others that had lost hope of themselves and never looked into mirrors at all for fear of what they'd see, he'd show them what they could be and help them to be it. He helped me like that and it's no wonder I try to think of him helping me still." He looked down at the hat he held in his hands as if, for the moment, he could not control his face.

"What good do you think I can do, Otway?" asked Simon, laying aside his cigarette-papers.

"I think it would be a comfort to Mrs. Carne to have you on the case, sir, and that you may be able to save her some trouble."

"You seem attached to your mistress."

"Well, sir, I don't know. I was taken up with Mr. Carne and he and she didn't always agree. It was a lot to expect of a lady—to understand him. She stuck to him almost to the last and, considering everything, she made sacrifices for him. They weren't suited, sir, hut I couldn't exactly blame her, seeing everything the way I did. To tell the truth, I didn't think much about Mrs. Carne, but I don't feel she deserves what's coming to her—maybe."

"So you want me to take the case, Otway?"

"I couldn't expect my wishes to weigh with you, sir. But since you ask me, it seems to me about the only thing I do want—my master's murderer found and found quick, and those as don't deserve suffering spared as much as possible."

The poor man could not know that he had from the first done everything and said everything likely to set Simon against the case. He had made it seem a simple and obvious business, and a very distressing one. His appeal was moving, but it was just that emotional element which made such an affair abhorrent to Simon. I gave up hope.

Suddenly Simon shot out of his chair. He dived almost bodily into a bookcase which filled the far end of the room and emerged with a weighty volume. He tore it open, fluttered the leaves, found his place, and bent over the page with an eagerness I had only seen him display on

one or two occasions when he had hit on the track of some
rare treasure for his collection.

"Come—ring the bell, somebody! Where is my hat?
Quick! Perry, my hat! Is your car there, Jerry, and does it
still go? Why, man, why didn't you say so before? It's
mere luck I happened to remember. This man inherited
the Hilton fortune and heirlooms from his mother. That's
why he tacked on Hilton to his name! He owns the
genuine Fuhkien porcelain bird of Kwan Yin. It's never
been shown. I've never seen it. He'll let me handle it. Sir
Ralph Carne-Hilton! How can I have been so dull as to
forget for one second that he's the luckiest man in
England and the only one who's got what I want. You
saved my life once, Jerry, but now you've given me
something really worth having, bless your heart!"

Five minutes later we were threading the traffic along
Lancaster Gate, and I was beginning to have misgivings.

"Look here, Brade," I ventured, "you'll be careful,
won't you? I know you, but these people don't, and you
don't always do yourself justice with strangers. Of course,
when you're called in by the police, it's different. They
know you're an expert. But I'm responsible, and I do want
you to make a good impression."

He raised his monocle, looked at me, dropped it, and
looked at me again. "I'm not applying for the butler's job,
or anything, you know."

"It's important that you should have their confidence."

"Well, just tell me how to behave, Jerry!"

"If you could be business-like—not go admiring the
furniture in the middle of an interview—that sort of
thing."

"Oh, that's all right. I shall probably hate the
furniture!"

"Oh, do be serious!"

"But I am. Furniture can depress me horribly,
darling."

"Don't call me 'darling' before everyone."

"But, Jerry—have they all got that sort of a mind? I thought it was only the lady with the ear-rings."

"Oh, blast—"

"Boyish," protested Simon, "too boyish for words!"

I was really anxious. I knew Brade and trusted him. So did the authorities, though his eccentricities annoyed them, no doubt. I had a pull with Sir Geoffrey Hill and felt sure Brade would be allowed a free hand, at any rate for the moment. But if he made a bad impression, the family might object and he would have to withdraw.

"Do you want to know anything else?" I asked.

"Not very much that you can tell me. But you might just recollect if you can whether there are shutters at the windows at Marpen Hall, as there are in these Georgian houses usually, and if the servants go round solemnly shutting and barring them at night just as they did when our great-great-grandfathers settled down to their port after a five o'clock dinner. These old customs intrigue me."

"Really, Simon!"

"If you won't tell me, I suppose I must find out for myself."

"Is it of any importance?"

"Quite a lot."

I seemed to remember that I had seen someone shutting up the windows of the hall bedrooms as I drove up to the door the night before. If only blinds and curtains had been drawn, chinks of light would have shone through. Of course there were shutters. I said so.

"That's my Jerry!" he said approvingly.

"What does it have to do with the case, anyway?"

"It's a point. It's a point. And, since you are so observant, have you any idea what Lady Carne-Hilton keeps in the cupboard she didn't open?"

I stared.

"But, Jerry, you told me the house was Georgian. Now, where did that writing-table stand?"

"In the middle of the long wall just opposite a

fireplace, built to look like a sort of altar."

"Exactly. That's what I gathered. And all the windows had been blocked out except one at the end?"

"Yes."

"And the cupboard she opened would be made by the space occupied by the old window?"

"I see. There used to be a window on the other side probably. But it needn't have been made into a cupboard too."

"You don't know architects. They have such tidy minds. And besides, you said there were cubby-holes for letters and stationery, but ladies like drawers and shelves for photographs and such things. The writing-table didn't have any drawers, now, did it?"

He was quite right, now I came to think of it.

"If there is a cupboard there, I don't know what's in it."

"And I suppose you didn't even ask the name of the architect?" He sighed. "Oh, Jerry, with the chance you had!"

"I don't see that it has anything to do with the case at all! You can't suspect Lady Carne-Hilton. You have only to look at her clothes. And to tell you the truth, I was much too much in a hurry to get away from her to ask unnecessary questions."

"She needn't have done it, but she might know who did it and tell us. Think what a lot of trouble it would save. And you've told me three very odd things about her already."

"I should have said everything about her was odd. Anyway, I should hope so."

"But these things wouldn't be so odd if she wasn't odd. You see what I mean?"

"No, I don't, and besides, she is much too stupid to keep a secret."

"But that's just it—she hasn't kept it. You said she looked frightened. 'Frightened and excited' was what you wrote, Jerry dear. And you explained all about why she was so excited, but you didn't explain why she was frightened."

"Good heavens, Brade, if you're going to take every careless word in that screed and hang these people on it—"

"*Did* she look frightened?"

"I suppose I must have thought so."

"Do you think so now?"

I tried to recall what I had written. I remembered that when Lady Carne-Hilton came down the stairs she did impress me as a woman stimulated by excitement and fear.

"Well, yes, I think she was afraid, but so must have been all the others. Consider the situation!"

"I have—quite a lot. But of all the people concerned, except Miss Legend, she seems to be the last who had reason for her fear, and the last to be disturbed imaginatively. She had no imagination, you see."

"She might be afraid her husband would be involved."

"So she might!"

"You mean she may have some reason to suspect him?"

"She may, and there are those shutters."

I decided to leave this and said: "Is there anything else you want to know?"

"There's this Mr. Furness. He intrigues me. A gentle soldier, brainy enough to spin a good yarn. He didn't detest our Dan as much as some of the others. He isn't what you'd call subtle or psychic or morbid. Now, why was he so sure this accident wasn't an accident at all? Because he knew it wasn't, or because he didn't want to be the only one to say it was? I didn't expect him to come out for murder, especially if he did it himself. It doesn't fit, now, does it? And I do like things to fit, you know." He finished on a complaining note.

"I like Furness," I remarked.

"It's quite likely that the murderer is a nice person in this case. That's the trouble. Besides, on the fact of it, if anybody did it, it was Furness. But why? He had a reason for keeping Carne alive, apparently. Or else he was inventing it, and it seems a futile sort of story to invent, not likely to be of much use with a jury. 'I wouldn't have killed him, because he helped me think up stories and encouraged me to write them down.' I ask you, Jerry, would that impress the average Britisher?"

"No, I don't think it would—particularly if it could be suggested that he was in love with Carne's wife."

"But it impresses me! It's painted under the glaze."

Simon's reference to the decoration of porcelain was expressive. I began to think of the characters in the drama in these terms. Which of them had given me the impression of colour applied 'under the glaze' and not smeared on top for effect?

"Go on talking about the people you like and the ones you can't bear, Jerry. It's so helpful."

"Don't be funny, Simon."

"But I'm not. I never am. I tried to tell a funny story at a dinner party once and the butler was the only person who laughed and he spilt the port down my back. You like this man, Furness, and you can't bear Lady Carne-Hilton. Now, who else do you like?"

"If I tell you you'll take it as evidence against the people I hope had nothing to do with it."

"Are you trying to obstruct the course of justice?"

"Oh, well—"

"Now, Jerry, we can turn round, you know. Or I can have a bilious attack. If there's somebody who mustn't be the murderer you'd better say so. This isn't a story-book. I thought it was only Mrs. Danvers Carne, but what about Miss Legend?"

"She's interesting, and she certainly didn't do it, but you could hang her, and our friendship wouldn't suffer."

"Miss Trent?"

"She's rather sweet, and very silly."

"Well, that's the lot, in the female line."

"Young Revel is a nice boy, but weak, I should think.

In a crisis? I don't know—I can't be sure how he would act. Carne-Hilton—no, I don't exactly like him. He suffers a lot of physical pain, and such people are often unpleasant. I trust him."

"The servants?"

"Colman is a type. I like the type. Barnet, true blue, I should say. I like him too. Footman and stable-boy, youngsters. I like youngsters."

"Otway?"

"You saw him for yourself."

"Do you like him?"

"I certainly feel sorry for him. Yes, I liked him, but I should not care to employ him."

"That Coroner was considering the family feelings and got the business over quickly. Amiable people, coroners. But he did manage to ask Mr. Revel a couple of pertinent questions."

"Revel seemed to think they were impertinent ones!"

"Were they, I wonder? Young Revel was a hunting man, and he spent three years at Oxford. The South Lodesdale Hunt isn't a far cry. Suppose one found out he had hunted that particular bit of country before and knew all about the chalk-pit?"

"Why should you think that?"

But Brade seemed to be tired of the conversation. He watched the country dreamily and made some characteristic observations on the new building in progress. As we turned the last corner before the town of Agminton is reached, he said: "And those rosy roofs before us mean that we are near the end of our journey, I suppose. The town figures in guide-books, I believe. Or have I mixed it up with Edgehill?"

"It is very picturesque."

"Elizabethan timber and a Queen Anne Town Hall, all complete. Tell me when the bungalows begin and I'll shut my eyes."

I confess I hoped the bungalows would hurt his feelings, but we had left these far behind when we turned into the gate of Marpen Hall. Colman opened the door for us and went so far as to say: "I am glad to see you back, sir."

He looked curiously at Brade. That little gentleman, with his thin fair hair, his general colourlessness, his air of straying vaguely in my wake, was not impressive.

Colman led us straight to the morning-room, full of early light, where we found Carne-Hilton alone. He got up out of his chair awkwardly, his lameness evident, and shook hands with us both. Brade dropped his eye-glass to the end of its string, popped it back again, and glanced at me like a child who does not quite know what is expected of him.

"Will you sit down?" asked Sir Ralph with somewhat stiff courtesy. "Something to drink?" His hand went towards the bell.

"I have only come to introduce Brade," I said. "I am going back to London."

Brade, sitting on the edge of his chair like an obedient small boy, gave a jerk of alarm. "You mustn't leave me," he said nervously. Then he explained naively to Sir Ralph: "I do so hate corpses, and Jerry is such a tower of strength."

"Don't be ridiculous, Brade," I muttered.

"But it's true. If he goes I shall go too."

Sir Ralph's expression must be left to the imagination. He turned to me.

"Brade always behaves like this. Don't pay any attention to him!" I tried to pass it off as a joke.

"He made me come, Sir Ralph. He did indeed. He's the only person who can manage me at times. But for him I'd be in an asylum today. He can't deny it."

I turned to our host. "Brade is one of the cleverest criminal investigators in England. You must take my word for that, Sir Ralph."

"I think, if you can spare the time, you had better stay, Dr. Jerrold." He hemmed and hawed a little. "Of course, it will be in a professional capacity. I know the value of your time."

"I'll stay, certainly, Sir Ralph, as Brade insists, if you will let me telephone to arrange with my assistant. As for my time, I should not care to be paid."

"That's my Jerry," murmured Brade. He drew out a tobacco-pouch and began to roll a cigarette, the light of peace on his face. Carne-Hilton took me to the telephone. When I came back Brade was still rolling cigarettes, his right elbow moving up and down methodically, with no other care in the world, and Sir Ralph was standing uncomfortably, waiting for me.

"Well," I said sharply, "do you want Sir Ralph to tell us what has happened or shall we go and look at the chalk-pit, or what, Brade?"

"You're being very professional, Jerry," he reproached me, his eye wandering—in search of the porcelain collection, I supposed.

He laid his sixth cigarette beside the others. "Will you try one, Sir Ralph? They are really quite good. It's my one talent." Carne-Hilton refused and Brade looked so hurt that he relented and took one of the amateur cigarettes.

"If you would like to see—" Sir Ralph hesitated; Brade sat up, on the alert—"the body—" Carne-Hilton finished grimly.

Brade sank back with a sigh of disappointment.

"Now, if it had been the bird!" he murmured softly.

If Brade had no curiosity to see the face of the murdered man, I had. There might be something in its features, in the shape of the head, to tell me what I wished to know.

"I think we should see the body, Brade."

"Very well, Jerry, very well! He's so conventional, Sir Ralph—always does the right thing. Jerry's the sort of person that exactly suits the editor of *Who's Who*. Club—the Bachelors; Recreations—squash and travelling. You know! They can't do anything with me. I told them I belonged to the Donkeys' Club, and it turned out to be for young ladies only, and I said my chief recreation was reading in my bath, but they seemed to think that unfit to print. So we had better see the body, I suppose."

Sir Ralph made no comment on these explanations, but led us through a sunlit corridor, up a pleasant stairway, and into a darkened room. He drew up the blind in silence. Brade stood, uncomfortably, making fussy gestures with his hands and looking at me.

"May I?" Sir Ralph nodded. I drew down the linen that covered the face on the bed.

Danvers Carne had been dead nearly three days, and during that time the face must have altered its contours, but even now it seemed to be guarding a secret. Dead faces often have that look, and I still find it mysterious and impressive. As I looked, my interest grew. The fine features all sloped downward, making a Pan-like triangle of the wounded head. There was a graceful freakishness in those lines. The closed eyes were set aslant too, in harmony. There was no distortion of the features.

"Did he look as peaceful as this when he was found?" I asked.

"When I saw him he did," answered Sir Ralph. He was not looking at his cousin's face. I replaced the linen and turned away.

"Is that all?"

"For the moment, Sir Ralph. But if you will allow it, I should like to take some measurements later on. I am interested and it might help us."

"Of course. Whatever you like."

When we had returned to the morning-room, Brade said suddenly:

"Why don't your servants like this man Otway, Sir Ralph?"

"How do you know they don't?"

"Just an impression. Something Jerry said. They didn't exactly want to ask him to tea, did they, though Barnet often dropped in?"

"I never said any such thing," I expostulated.

"But they don't, do they, Sir Ralph?"

Carne-Hilton looked annoyed. Then he braced himself to answer. "My servants are the old-fashioned kind. Barnet was my batman during the last three years of the war. Colman has been with us since boyhood. Otway is another type altogether. He is a clever and rather attractive little man, extremely devoted to his master, but he has not exactly the manners or bearing of a servant. That alone is enough to make the others antagonistic. And of course I suppose the older servants disliked Dan. I know Barnet did. He made a lot of trouble for them. That would be another reason for their not liking Otway, who saw that his master got the best of everything. In fact, things were so difficult in the house the last time he came that we arranged to give him rooms in the Lodge this time. It suited him better."

"Why egg-and-spoon?" inquired Brade suddenly.

Carne-Hilton stared, apparently thinking this was another question which he had not quite understood.

"He means the cornice," I explained wearily. "You know, I expect, that that particular pattern is called egg-and-spoon. I don't know why. Shall we go and see the chalk-pit? I have my car at the door. Perhaps you could send someone along as guide, Sir Ralph?"

"Barnet will go—unless you want me."

"Come on, Brade."

I knew he was longing to ask about the collection, but he got up reluctantly and walked to the window.

"Alterations in the garden?" he asked with animation.

"Yes, I'm straightening out those paths. Somebody early in the nineteenth century took the trouble to tear down the old walls and curl all the paths with a permanent wave. I want to restore it, but I have to do it gradually, because of the expense. In fact," added Sir Ralph with a short laugh, "I had to sell my collection of Ming porcelain to begin it at all!"

I thought Brade was likely to faint, but he did not. He looked for a full moment at the work in progress, then he looked at Carne-Hilton. "I see," he remarked.

Then we went out and found Barnet waiting for us at the car step. He touched his cap twice, once to Brade and once to me, and climbed onto the small seat at the back, leaning over the hood and explaining the landscape as we drove. Brade, unexpectedly, recovered his spirits.

"Now, Barnet," he said, "I'm the world's worst horseman. Absolutely champion at falling off, and I've got a very delicate neck—breaks much more easily than most people's. Can you lend me a horse to suit me? Something that warns you beforehand when he wants to trot and if we meet a steam roller, will walk past if I shut my eyes?"

"That'd be Sarah, sir," said Barnet earnestly. "She'll understand. Just a snaffle and a saddle with good broad flaps—Sir Ralph's saddle, because of 'is leg, you know, sir. You'll be safe as 'ouses, sir. And if you was inclined for a bit of a lep, why, just put 'er nose at it, sir, and the reins on 'er neck, and she'll take you over a five-barred gate as smooth as a cradle."

"God forbid!" exclaimed Brade devoutly.

"Course, you only 'ave o draw 'er up to it, gentle, and she'll most open it 'erself, once she understands you ain't in a 'urry, sir."

"Couldn't you explain to her beforehand that I'm never in a hurry?" suggested Brade.

"She'll understand. You can depend on Sarah, sir. Why, that mare, she . . ." He beguiled us for the rest of the drive with stories of the mare's intelligence.

"Sarah for me at half past two, Barnet," said Brade as we drew to a halt.

"You would want me to come with you, sir?"

"No, thank you, Barnet. I'm very private on a horse. I don't care to be observed!"

We had stopped on the main road at the end of the wood. I pulled the car onto the grassy edge and we left her, walking into the light shadow of larches and beeches still stripped by winter. It was an untidy plantation, dense in spots, but sparce elsewhere. The ground was firm, scattered with brown needles from the larches, and chalky underneath. Here and there a mossy ride showed ruts made by lumber-carts, and the marks of hoofs.

"It's his lordship's property—Lord 'illberry, you know, sir—and it's used a lot for 'acking, as there aren't many places where you can let a 'orse feel the turf 'ereabouts," explained Barnet. "Not unless you've got your own park. I often bring the 'orses 'ere on hoff days, for a change, and the riding stables use it too. Then there's the 'unt and the stag-'ounds." A groom, with a child on a pony, came by as we passed. Presently we reached a narrow wedge of timber, cutting into a big field, and emerged.

"This is Cranmere Farm, and there's the chalk-pit," Barnet informed us.

I looked with interest at the ragged edge of the pit, screened by gorse and coarse grass. At some time quarrying operations must have been started, for the side nearest us was artificially straightened by digging, while the far side descended in a cup-like slope. The surroundings were quiet and peaceful. "That's Cranmere Farm," explained the talkative Barnet, pointing to roofs just visible over a rise in the field on our right, "where Mr. Vane lives, 'im as breeds 'orses and trains them for sale. We've 'ad some good ones off 'im, too —nice-mannered and steady in the woodland and bold as you like at a bit of timber. And 'e gets a bit of blood from the shires too, and that's a 'elp when it comes to the vale. Takes a clever animal to carry you over our country, sir, fast at a flooded stream and careful over the staked-and-bound you get round 'ere, puttin' 'is foot in the right place, if you understand me, with rabbit-'oles thick as fly-spots on a dirty window."

A group of school-children were standing on the opposite side of the pit, looking curiously into it.

"They've just taken away the ropes," exclaimed Barnet. He waved an arm. "Off with ye, now! Get 'ome to your dinners. The gentlemen don't want ye botherin'. Swarmin' around the place they was, curious as robins, but the police kept them off."

The children reluctantly went on their way.

"That's where the body was found." Barnet pointed to a spot forty feet below. "And 'ere's Sarah's tracks—ye can see 'em yet, leadin' from the ride just 'ere, and ye can see where she turned sharp, but they couldn't pick 'em up so clear after that in the grass."

"Thanks, Barnet," said Simon. "Now perhaps you'd better go back and wait for us in the car. We want to do a bit of walking, and, as you say, these hoof-marks are still quite plain, so we can trace our way back to the ride where Mr. Carne fell. Dr. Jerrold is very particular about his car, and those children look inquisitive. If you'd go back and see they don't investigate too much—"

"It's a fact, they're bad as magpies for mischief," agreed Barnet, reluctant to leave us, but fully alive to the danger to my property. He stumped away, with the stiff gait of the professional horseman, and we went round to the opposite side where it was easy to scramble to the bottom of the pit.

"This is where the body lay, I suppose." Brade pointed to a spot where the ground was trampled down. "Well, any illumination, Jerry?"

"Only that Mr. Carne was certainly killed when he struck the bottom of this if he wasn't dead before." I looked up at the wall of chalk, tufted here and there with a few tenacious weeds. "I think, you know, he must have been killed in the wood if it is true that his face was so peaceful when he was found."

"And what do you make of Otway's remarks about his boots?"

"I should like to look at those boots."

"So you shall, dearest, so you shall! You know—I shall have to send for Ives."

"But—"

"Boots are not in my line."

"'Ave you found it?

The query came from behind us and above our heads. Looking round, we saw something squirming down the side of the pit. It straightened itself out into a small boy, about twelve years old, freckled, sandy-haired, and extremely alert.

"'Ave you found it?" he repeated truculently. "Because it's mine."

"Not yet," replied Simon, "but we've only just begun to look. By the way, what is it?"

The small boy subjected us to a careful inspection. Then he turned to me. "Are you a detective?" he asked dubiously.

Brade popped his glass into his eye and looked me over.

"Now, what made you think that? I suppose it's his jaw. Now I come to think of it, there is a spot of the Bulldog Drummond there."

"Well, one of you is," the small boy asserted, "and it can't be you."

Simon was delighted. "It takes the pure eyes of youth to see truth," he exclaimed with enthusiasm. "Now then, Jerry, darling, live up to your character!"

"What is it you're looking for?" I asked the lad.

"It's my penknife. I lost it 'ere comin' back from school last Tuesday. And them cops wouldn't let me in to look for it. Not after Mr. Carne fell in. They wouldn't even listen to what I said. They wasn't detectives!" he finished scornfully.

"What makes you think that?"

"Why, anybody knows a real detective pays attention to little things."

"But you're not so very little," Simon cut in. "May I ask your name?"

"It's Billiam."

"What?"

"Everybody's surprised at first. Dad, 'e wanted to call me Bill, and Ma, she wanted to call me William, so they 'ad a compermise. The Vicar, 'e says it's a sample to the parish."

"The parish!" exclaimed Brade. "A pattern for the

World to follow!"

"Well, I thought the Crowner's 'quest ought to know about my penknife, but nobody'd listen."

"We'll listen," Simon assured him.

"You ain't the detective, are yer?" Billiam regarded him.

"Not by nature, Billiam, only by accident. A very round peg in a very square hole. The world is full of them. Not a detective—just an unfortunate soul that's taken the wrong turning," he sighed.

"Does 'e mean 'e is?" demanded Billiam, turning to me.

"I don't know what he means. I very seldom do. But that's what other people call him."

"My word!" Billiam was absorbed in revising his view of the profession. "I'm going to be a detective when I grow up," he volunteered.

"Then mind you don't look like one! But, see here, Billiam, you're the man I want. You know your way about this place. Will you act as guide for a new shilling and the chance of studying the ways of the profession?"

"Will I?" Billiam's answer was punctuated by a finished and admirable illustration of the cart-wheel turn.

"Are you sure you don't mean to be an acrobat instead?" asked Simon.

"No, sir, that's what mother calls 'igh spirits. I get 'em off and on. I'm going to be a detective."

We climbed out of the pit after a brief survey, which convinced Billiam that his knife was not there.

"That's where I dropped it—where the corpse was found," he explained with relish.

"Now, if you'd come along to the ride in the wood where Mr. Carne fell from his horse," Simon suggested, "and mind, Billiam, that shilling will grow to two and sixpence if you keep all this to yourself."

"My word, you must be rich!" remarked Billiam. "What I say," he added, "is that that there penknife was there and it ain't there now. It's a clue."

"An exploded clue, I'm afraid, Billiam," I remarked. Then I glanced at Brade.

"Tell us all about the penknife, Billiam," he said.

"It was a present from my aunty. She's got a shop in Agminton and she's rich, so Mother said the penknife was too good to play with and I could 'ave it Sundays. What's the use of a knife in Sunday school, I ask you! So I took it to school because Tommie Baines has got one, and on our way home we was playing robbers, and the chalk-pit was our lair, and we was armed to the teeth, so I stuck my knife in my boot. Well, we 'eard the 'unt, so we thought we'd catch 'em if we ran, and when I got to the top of the pit my knife was gone, and I remembered I'd knelt down at the bottom of the pit to strangle Tommie Baines and it likely fell out then, but I couldn't stop to go back for it. We ran 'ard, but the fox went to ground and I was late for tea and the fog come down, so I went 'ome, but Mother, she missed the knife after all. She don't allow me to play in the chalk-pit, so I just said I dropped it, and I'd 'ave got a 'idin' from Dad if the gentleman 'adn't come in just then and told us about Mr. Carne, so Dad went out, and Mother was so excited she didn't notice 'ow much jam I put on my bread."

We were walking along the ride when suddenly the importance of Billiam's narrative struck me.

"You were playing robbers on your way back from school, I suppose?" I said as casually as I could.

"It's the only time anybody 'as for anything important," Billiam answered, a person with a grievance.

"And school lets out at four?"

"Yes, and it's only just beginning to be light enough to play anything much after that."

"Rotten system," Brade put in. "Now, the sensible thing would be to hold school from dark to midnight, when a lot of time is wasted in sleeping anyway. And so you're going to be a detective when you grow up, Billiam. Remember what I said about not looking like one."

"What do they look like," demanded Billiam, "I mean when they do?"

"Just like the gentlemen who wouldn't listen to you, I should say."

"Then I won't." He inspected Brade curiously.

"Would it be better to look like you, sir?"

"It would be a great deal better to look like you, Billiam."

"Oh!" The boy was obviously disappointed. Then he said more cheerfully: "But I could carry a gun in my hip pocket." He glanced at the place where Brade's hip might be expected to bulge.

"That is a matter of taste."

I went on thinking. If Billiam's story was true, and I could not see why it shouldn't be, he was in that chalk-pit when the hunt skirted Cranmere Farm, not earlier than four thirty. If Danvers Carne's body was not already there, where was it? According to the evidence at the inquest, he must have fallen at the overhanging branch soon after half past three at latest. We had already reached the spot. If dragged at once, he must have been thrown into the pit by three forty. It was inconceivable that Sarah should have stood still for nearly an hour and then run with him. I remembered Otway's story of the boots and his certainty that Carne was not killed by the fall.

"This is the place," said Billiam, "and that's the tree. You can see for yourself."

I put up my hand and could just reach the bough. I pushed it from me. It came back with a heavy sweep. The ground below showed the marks of many hoofs, but these were blurred by the rain that had fallen since Tuesday. Brade had wandered away and was looking thoughtfully at the ground, especially the harder and less marked spaces under the trees where some of the hunt had made a detour to avoid the low bough.

"I don't believe Mr. Carne died natural," said Billiam. "I think 'e was done in."

"Is that what other people are saying, Billiam?" I asked.

"It's what they're sayin' at the Red Crow."

"How do you know?"

"'Cause my Dad thinks what 'e 'ears over 'is glass is right, and 'e says it was murder, but everybody likes Sir Ralph, so they don't see no call to let it go farther."

"What has Sir Ralph got to do with it?"

"'E wouldn't like it talked about. It was that Mr. Furness. 'E's a nice gentleman too. 'E follered Mr. Danvers into the Wilderness and I think they 'ad a fight."

I suppose Brade was afraid I'd point out the discrepancy in time for he broke in quickly: "What about taking us on to the village, Billiam?"

"There ain't nothing to see there," protested the boy, "not 'cept the 'all where the Crowner's 'quest was. Was you there, sir?"

I told him I had had that privilege.

"I tried to get in. Sometimes a fellow is too little and sometimes 'e's too big!" With this pessimistic remark he led on.

He showed us the schoolhouse, with distaste, and the corner of the green where Danvers Carne had left the hunt. The blacksmith, working at his forge, and a man carting a load of beech logs to the chair-factory were the only people we saw. Brade suggested that we walk back to Billiam's home by the chalk-pit. "He'll be late for his dinner," said Brade, "and we can't have him scolded, especially as I want his help. Billiam, will you be my assistant? And if you will, there are two things I shall want you to be able to do—ride a pony, and hold your tongue."

Billiam was voluble in his assurances that he could do both. It appeared that the farmer at Cranmere had taught him to ride. Mr. Vane bred hunters and ponies and sold them to the local gentry, and Billiam had no prejudices whatever against falling off, so he made himself useful to the farmer on Saturdays and in the holidays. As for holding his tongue, it appeared he never did anything else. "Why, 'ow'd I ever 'ave any fun at all, sir, if I was always peachin'? And I'd never get anything to eat to speak of. Mother sends me to bed on bread and water when I do what she don't like."

"Billiam, have you heard anything about a horse called Pink Livery?" I asked.

"'Ave I? I'd say I 'ave! It's the same as is in the Marpen stable this minute and Mr. Baraet complainin' 'e ought to be put down. 'E ain't safe, that 'orse. No, sir. Mr. Vane, 'e says there's 'orses that'll throw you, and 'orses that'll kick you, and 'orses that'll bite you. But when you get one as'll do all three inside of 'arf an hour, it ain't a 'orse but a deviL That's wot Mr. Vane says. And that's wot 'appened when 'e tried out Pink Livery to oblige Mr. Barnet. 'E says 'e's blood brother to Cat o' the 'Ills, but when you've said that, you've said everything. Now, if Mr. Danvers 'ad been ridin' 'im last Tuesday, nobody'd 'ave wondered at wot 'appened. They'd 'ave wondered more if 'e'd got 'ome alive. That's wot Mr. Vane says. And 'e says Mr. Barnet told 'im Mr. Danvers wanted to ride Pink Livery, and Sir Ralph wouldn't 'ave it. A bit touched, Mr. Danvers was. That's wot I think."

Billiam had told his story eagerly, directing it to me, for it was impossible to tell whether Brade was listening or not.

"Mr. Carne brought Pink Livery to Marpen?"

"Yes, sir. Sent 'im by road. I saw 'im come. And 'e nearly killed Mr. Barnet when 'e tried to groom 'im that same night."

I thought of the Pan-like mask on the pillow. What was lacking there, besides the play of life on the features? Not courage, nor energy to keep step with the measure set—but something, I felt sure. Something we expect to find as a matter of course in the faces of our friends. Was it only that I was determined to condemn this man or was I right?

I timed the walk from the village to the chalk-pit. It

took us eighteen minutes. From there to Billiam's cottage took somewhat longer. His mother, Mrs. Lacey, received us at the door. She accepted Brade's explanation amiably and pressed us to come inside.

"I thought it was all settled like, about the poor gentleman?" she said eagerly.

"Yes, of course. But you see Sir Ralph thinks the village people are talking. And he asked me to see if I could explain in any way how his mare happened to drag the body when she was trained to stand. He has a theory that some animal may have alarmed the mare."

"That's what they're talking about at the Red Crow," Mrs. Lacey agreed. "I wouldn't disguise it, sir. There is talk. The village is a place for talk, it is—disgusting, I call it. D'you think it was an accident like the Coroner said, sir?"

"Well, Mrs. Lacey, I can rely on you not to repeat what I say?"

"Oh, yes, sir; indeed, I wouldn't say a word to trouble Sir Ralph. A kind master, sir, and hunfortunate."

Brade leaned forward impressively. "Well, I'll tell you, then, in confidence. We don't know."

She looked impressed.

"Well, I don't know as I ought to say, but people will talk! It's funny like, that mare dragging Mr. Carne. That chalk-pit, too—I always tell Billiam not to play there." She looked at her son with a mixture of severity and pride. "Don't know what fear is, 'e don't," she added.

"By the way," said Brade, "I understand he dropped a valuable penknife on the way back from school the other day. It may have been picked up somewhere. If I can I'll have it returned to him."

"If you could, sir, I'd be that grateful. It was the very day of the haccident, sir. You know, troubles never come singly. And Billiam was late and I'd missed the knife his aunty gave him, because I wanted to show it to a caller, you see, sir. And 'e'd been traipsin' after the 'unt, and come in with 'is clothes in a mess, and when 'is Dad come

in I was tellin' 'im about it, and then Mr. Furness opened
that very door you're standin' at, sir, and give me such a
turn, and of course Lacey went off at once to 'elp—not
that there was any 'elp for the poor gentleman. . . ."

"Billiam ought to be in by dark, certainly."

"That's what I say. And it was a dark day, and I'd 'ad
the lamp lit before 'e came. That's the rule—if the lamp's
lit and 'e's not in, 'e goes without 'is supper, and it's many
the time I've just about put my eyes out with tryin' to sew
in a bad light rather than light the lamp, for 'e does enjoy
'is supper, does Billiam. I don't know as I ought to say it,
sir, but it's all around the village that Otway thinks Mr.
Carne was murdered. Seems 'orrible."

"Then you won't mind if I borrow Billiam tomorrow,
as it's Saturday?"

"I'll ask 'is Dad to let 'im off 'is wood-choppin' for
once."

"Thank you, Mrs. Lacey."

Billiam followed us to the gate.

"What time will you want me, sir?"

"Not till afternoon."

"Can't I do anything in the morning? Dad'll make me
chop wood if I don't."

"Why, yes," said Brade, "you can look for a string
glove."

"Where?" demanded Billiam.

"Anywhere the hunt passed on Tuesday, except
between here and the village."

"That'll be easy."

"If you find it, bring it straight to me, mark the place
where you found it, and Billiam—silence!" He put a finger
to his lips. Billiam grinned with delight.

"Simon," I said, as we walked back to the road, "what
do you make of this?"

"Just one thing, Jerry. We can take Otway's word for
those boots."

"But—but—"

"Now, don't start quoting Rostand, dear man. You'll

distract my thoughts."

We walked back to the car in silence and found Barnet waiting patiently.

"Swarming all over it, them youngsters was!" he beamed. "Made short work of 'em. I doubt they may 'ave scratched your paint 'ere and there, sir."

They had.

We arrived at Marpen Hall very late for lunch.

2.15 p.m., Friday

When Colman opened the door for us he said: "Lady Carne-Hilton is asking to see you, Dr. Jerrold."

I turned to Brade, who was regarding me with a pitying eye. "I suppose you want to see everybody, Brade; you'd better come along."

"No, I am going to have my lunch. And then I'm going to exercise my liver, if Colman can find me some riding-boots and breeches."

I wanted my lunch too, and, definitely, I did not want a tete-a-tete with Lady Carne-Hilton, but I saw no help for it. Colman showed me into the Greek room.

I was startled when she wheeled round and faced me. At first I thought the effect of the light was playing tricks with my nerves. But when she spoke her high-pitched voice was like a violin string stretched too tight. I felt afraid it would snap.

"Tell me what is happening," she demanded, "I must know."

"Nothing much, Lady Carne-Hilton."

"But you have brought a detective with you. He is working on the case, isn't he?"

"Yes, I was asked to persuade Brade to take it up."

"Take him away, Dr. Jerrold. Leave us alone!"

"I have no power to do that."

"You don't care what happens to any of us. You don't care!"

"So far, I have tried to help you."

"Oh, I feel you are kind—I feel it. Leave this thing alone. The police will never find out anything. It will all be dropped unless this man Brade should discover— Marion Trent says he is very clever."

"I think he is."

"Take him away!"

"Lady Carne-Hilton, I think you are very much

overwrought. There is really no use in going on with this discussion."

"I'm afraid," she moaned. Then she turned towards me. "Do you realize that my husband was riding the afternoon Dan died, and that, being lame, he often makes use of his knowledge of the country to take short cuts from covert to covert? He could easily have disappeared from the field for a time and no one would have noticed it. He could have dropped out somewhere on the far side of Barwell Cross and rejoined the others when they turned towards home. I—I saw him riding home that day. I thought he must be in pain, his face was so white and drawn."

"Where did you see him?"

"Averil Legend and I had been following the hunt in the car in the afternoon. We stopped on the high road, beside the Wilderness, to listen, as we thought hounds must be near. I had my poodle, Brune, with me and she bolted after a rabbit, so I went after her. I couldn't find her, but when I came back to the car, Otway was just crossing the road, riding home. He said the hunt was coming our way. I didn't want to leave Brune, with hounds so close, but Averil wanted to go home, so I told Jennings to drive on and I would walk, as it was only a matter of ten minutes. Jennings opened the gate for Otway to take the short cut across the field and I went back to look for Brune, but I couldn't find her. It was then that Ralph passed me."

"And that was what time?"

"I'm not sure. I got home about five."

"But Danvers Carne must have met with his accident long before that."

"Yes, while hounds were running. Suppose my husband left them, as I said, and caught up with Dan in the Wilderness—"

"Are you trying to make me believe that your husband murdered his cousin?"

"How can you be so cruel! I am trying to persuade you

to drop this case."

"Yet you did not try to do that yesterday when you knew I meant to get Brade."

"I didn't think of this explanation then."

"So you were not frightened?"

"No."

"And after seeing your husband you only thought that he might be suffering from his wound? You had no suspicion of any other reason?"

"Certainly not. I walked straight home. Ralph took the short cut across the park and was in when I got here. I sent the chauffeur back for Brune and went to my room."

There was a mechanical note in her voice as if she had rehearsed the story.

"Dr. Jerrold, I beseech you—"

"That is ridiculous. I have nothing to do with it."

"Take this man Brade away!"

I got up and walked to the door. "If I were you, I should go and rest," I said as I went out.

I found Brade alone, finishing a dish which seemed to please him. Colman came in with coffee, brought me some lunch, and withdrew.

"Coffee comes last, luckily. One knows whether to risk it or not," Brade observed, sipping his with appreciation. "You were right about our host's chef, and I'm not so sure Lady Carne-Hilton is a stupid woman, if she engaged him."

I sat near enough to him to tell him in an undertone what Lady Carne-Hilton had said. "Write it all down, that's a good boy—put in everything—because I'm awfully busy." He sipped the coffee with an air of oriental leisure.

"Brade, I'm sure she was lying—some of the time anyway."

"Probably, Jerry dear. We'll find out." He got up and rang the bell.

"Could Dr. Jerrold speak to Lady Carne-Hilton's maid

a moment?" he asked.

"But what am I to say to her?" I ejaculated when Colman had gone.

"Just a little advice about her mistress's health— friendly and yet professional. The subtle mixture, you know! I'll attend to the rest."

"Here? Suppose the servants hear us."

"Let them!"

The maid came promptly. She was French and very smart. She stood looking at us expectantly, her prominent eyes bright and eager.

"Her ladyship has been speaking to me about her nerves," I said. "She is highly strung and requires quiet and rest. I will write out a prescription and I hope you will see she takes it, and try to persuade her to lie down and sleep. Does she sleep badly?"

"Oh yes, sir. She has hardly sleep at all since Tuesday. She ring for me in the night and say: 'Take the dog away.' That is strange, for Brune, she sleep on my lady's bed always. She love Brune best of everyone. That is why I think it so strange she come back without the dog on Tuesday. I say: 'Where is Brune, madame?' and she say: 'Jennings will find her.' She did not seem to care. And then she tell me to get her tea, and when I come back she is not there, so I leave it and wait and then she come in in a hurry and say: 'Mr. Revel is at the door. Go down and see what he wants.' So I go down and there is the awful news, and I go back and tell my lady. She is pale and she says: 'I must go and tell Mrs. Danvers. Come with me.' So we go. And Mrs. Danvers is sitting there, embroidering, as she often do. She look up, smiling, sad. You have seen her, sir—she look sad when she think, that lady. So my lady, she told her an accident had been, and just then Mrs. Danvers' own maid hurry in, very white; also Miss Trent. But Miss Trent, when she see us all, she say nothing, and then Mrs. Danvers' maid, she dropped the letter she was holding and ran and put her arms round her lady, and Miss Trent went out. So Mrs.

Danvers, she say gentle: 'Please will you all leave me?'—
so we went out and I picked up the letter not thinking—
like you do when something 'appens, and I put it down in
my room and forget it. And so the maids prepared a spare
room for the poor gentleman and Sir Ralph was in his
bath, but Mr. Colman told him, so he went out and we
waited. But it was terrible—that waiting! And we hear a
car, and it is the gentlemen bringing the body. Such a
'andsome man as Mr. Danvers Carne to be killed so! They
carried him up on a garden chair, spread out, and laid
him on the bed; and Mr. Otway, he come in and was like
a madman, for he would not believe his master was dead
till he see for 'imself. And then 'e made me tell 'im all I
knew, and 'e even made me show 'im the letter, which
was silly, but 'e was like that, not knowing what 'e said.
Mrs. Danvers Carne, she met 'im in the 'all, when she
come out of the room where was 'er 'usband, and she put
out 'er 'and to 'im, but 'e didn't see it, and walked past
her—blind—because that was not kind when the lady
was so in trouble. She looked after 'im, 'urt and sorry,
because I saw 'er, and she said: 'Poor Otway'—like that.
And that is all I know."

"Thank you, mademoiselle," I remarked, "but I only
wanted to see you about your mistress."

"There are no questions then, sir?"

"But you should have posted the letter, you know,"
Brade said gently; "it must have been important if Mrs.
Carne's maid was sent out with it specially."

"That is what I thought," said the Frenchwoman
eagerly, "but it was only to order more wool for Mrs.
Danvers' embroidery, and she 'as not touched 'er work
since that day, 'er maid says. But I did post it, sir. I am
very careful of such things. It was only because I was
upset. The wool, it come yesterday, so you see I post the
letter."

"Yes, yes, I see. Of course we understand everyone
was upset. And the poodle got back all right?"

"Yes. Mr. Jennings, 'e found 'er coming 'ome. But my

lady made me wash 'er mouth, and I did not like that, for Brune, she snaps when she is annoyed. My lady said she 'ad been 'unting and 'er mouth was smelling. She does not care for the poodle so much since then."

"Poor Brune!"

"Yes, I think it is not fair, for dogs are like that."

I don't know how much longer she would have gone on talking, but Brade seemed to have heard enough. He got up. "Now to exercise the liver!" he remarked.

"I will write that prescription," I said to the Frenchwoman, "and you will see that her ladyship takes it?"

She went away, still seething with talk, and I turned to Brade, who was smiling. "Write it all down, Jerry dear, while it's fresh. A written account is rather like a photograph. It shows up things one doesn't notice otherwise."

After finishing my belated lunch I walked out to the stables with Simon and found the young groom, Rogers, holding Sarah before the stone mounting-block. Barnet had taken Brade's confession of bad horsemanship seriously and hurried forward to assist in the mounting process, but Brade seemed in no hurry. He went from box to box, inspecting the inmates and asking amateurish questions, to which Barnet replied in a painstaking way. So ignorant did Simon appear to be of the simplest rudiments of horse lore that I began to be suspicious, but Barnet was not, and laboriously explained that by "fetlock" he did not refer to part of the horse's mane.

Meanwhile I introduced myself to Sarah. I like horses and was brought up with them, but as I do not care for circling Rotten Row and gave up hunting with nearly everything else some fifteen years ago, for the sake of my work, I seldom ride.

Sarah was a well-bred bay mare with a good shoulder and powerful quarters. I liked her intelligent head, with its unmistakable line of thoroughbred blood, and her steady eye, though there was a hint of temper there too, when Rogers annoyed her by pulling on her bit. She took my overtures of friendship with indifference, standing with trained patience, but saying plainly that she did not like it and would be glad to move on.

"What's his name?" drawled Brade.

"That's Pink Livery, sir," Barnet answered, with a considerable show of distaste, "and a wrong 'un if there ever was. I'll be glad to get 'im out of my stables. Upsets the others, 'e does, with 'is antics. Won't let the boy go near 'im, and 'e'd kill a man cheerful, 'e would, if I didn't 'ave my wits about me. Don't you go into 'is stable, sir. It's as much as your life is worth. Gentle as a lamb 'e looks this minute, and you can pat 'im and feed 'im one second, and the next 'e'd be at you with 'is 'eels and teeth same as a vicious mule."

"But the poor fellow looks quite harmless. Just open the door a second, Barnet. I won't touch him."

Barnet reluctantly unlatched the door, and Brade stepped inside. I went to look at the horse with some curiosity. He had tiny ears set far back and a humped forehead, but he was built for speed and stamina, and I could imagine that he might attract a speculator.

Brade was looking him over with attention.

"Only wants a bit of kindness," Brade murmured sentimentally.

"Step back, sir," cried Barnet.

It was too late. Timothy Revel, coming round the corner, kicked a water-bucket and knocked it over. The noise made Sarah jump. It sent Pink Livery stark mad. Brade had barely time to seize the halter which Pink Livery, alone, wore, with both hands. And then we witnessed an exhibition of ferocity such as I had never seen before. The horse lifted Brade off the ground and swung that little man from side to side, lashing out with his heels so that no one could get near him. He struck the wooden wall of the stable and cracked a board from end to end. His teeth were bare and his eyes red and rolling. He meant murder. Barnet and I tried to get at the beast's

head. Revel picked up Brade's crop, which he had left
outside, and beat the horse whenever he could get near it.
"Go away," gasped Brade, hauling at the bridle, before he
was dashed against the stable wall, and his breath
knocked out of his body. I was certain that every bone
must be broken by now. The noise was ghastly. Barnet
had got hold of a strap, and somehow he managed to lasso
one flying hoof. Pink Livery fell, and Brade rolled clear.
We pulled him out of that death-trap and slammed the
door.

Barnet wiped the sweat from his forehead.

"Are you 'urt, sir?"

Brade brushed some straw from his coat. "No, Barnet,
I'm not hurt. Is that what you call a vicious horse?" he
inquired as one asks for interesting information.

Revel stood frowning and looking at the brute, which
had risen, shivering, onto three legs.

"He'll have to be shot . Dan thought he could tame
him. Perhaps he might have done it. No one else can."

"Was he Mr. Carne's horse?" asked Brade.

"No, he was mine. A dealer landed him on me. I was
going to have him put down, but Dan asked me to let him
have a try. You see, he'd be a valuable animal if anyone
could manage him. His dam is Pink Lady and he was
sired by Livery Lad."

Barnet, like other sweet-tempered persons I have
known, was formidable in anger, and he was angry now.

"If I 'ad a henemy," he remarked, laying a hand on
Sarah's neck, "and wanted to see 'im dead and buried
quick, I'd give 'im that 'orse to 'andle. Is the stirrup right,
sir?"

Brade was mounted now and looked down on us from
Sarah's back nervously.

"She is shaking, Barnet," he said. "She won't run
away with me, will she?"

"Sarah? Not she, sir. If you'd pick up the hoff rein a
bit." Brade fumbled with the leathers.

Revel stood frowning beside me. "Are you riding too,

Dr. Jerrold?" he asked.

"No," Brade replied for me. "He's going to write everything down for me. Marvellous memory, Jerry's! Don't waste time, darling. Do it now."

We watched him ride slowly down the drive, bumping the unfortunate Sarah at every stride she took.

"'E'll be all right with Sarah," Barnet reassured me. "Trust that mare, sir, She hunderstands."

I think probably Sarah did, and I wondered if Brade had noticed that during Pink Livery's tantrum Sarah had stood, shivering with nerves, in her place beside the mounting-block. She had not moved one step.

5 p.m., Friday

While I was writing, I received a message that Lady
Caroline Scott and Mrs. Danvers Carne would be pleased
if I would have tea with them in Mrs. Danvers' sitting-
room. When I had finished, I went to join the two ladies
and found them waiting. There was a tea-table set with
bright silver, and enough food for a dozen people, a fire
burning gaily, books, knitting lying about, and a bundle
of papers that looked like old letters on the writing-table.
I think ladies look charming at a tea-table, and it is a pity
that the cocktail is banishing this pleasant hour of the
day. On this occasion Mrs. Carne's face, with its pallor
and strained attentiveness, made the scene sad for me.
My first impression of her came back. She was a person
built for happiness who had missed it—through no fault
of her own, I am convinced. Lady Caroline had recovered
her spacious calm. She poured out tea for us and went
straight to the point.

"We want to know what is going on," she said bluntly.
"You can't expect Mimi to sit here and do nothing and
hear nothing. She must be kept informed."

"Of course, but you must remember that Brade has
not been here long yet."

"What has he done?"

I did not feel free to tell them about Billiam's
evidence.

"Brade works in his own way, you know," I said, "and
I really have no idea what is in his mind." I added,
however, that we had been over the ground, and I tried to
make them laugh by telling them about Billiam and his
diplomatic name.

"I should like to meet Billiam," said Mimi Carne.

"Brade seems to have taken him on as assistant, so
perhaps you will," I suggested.

"I don't think we can keep this inquiry a secret for

very long," said Lady Caroline. "We have been talking to Otway and so has Tim Revel."

"Have they any further grounds for suspicion?"

Mimi spoke. "If those gloves could be traced— though I don't know what they had to do with it. It is conceivable that someone who wished harm to Dan took them and did not give them to him, knowing the difficulty of riding with wet leather gloves."

"Mrs. Carne, doesn't it seem extraordinary to you that Mr. Revel should have lent your husband that vicious horse, Pink Livery?"

She met my glance quickly, surprised, and did not speak for a moment.

"No, I don't think it is strange," she answered, deliberately. "Tim believed everything Dan said to him. He thought of Dan as a sort of magician, who could do what others couldn't."

"Please tell me everything you can remember about that horse."

She thought it over. "Dan won a good point-to-point race with him. I know that. I was away and knew nothing about it till I saw it in the paper. But there was some trouble about it afterwards." She frowned, trying to remember. "I went to Dan's room one evening, and as I started to knock I heard Otway's voice. He seemed to be protesting with Dan about something, and then I heard Dan say: 'Of course, I didn't know. After all, Pink Livery's as like him as one pea to another.' Otway spoke again, and Dan laughed. I felt nervous, for some reason. I knew Otway had Dan's interests at heart and that he must be very much upset about something, so I waited in my room and left the door open, to speak to Otway when he came out. But after all I didn't because—well—I saw from his face that he was angry. I've only seen him angry once or twice and I didn't want to discuss Dan with him then, so I never knew what the trouble was."

"Pink Livery did not belong to your husband?"

"No. We had no stables. Once in a while Dan would

buy a horse to sell. He often rode for his friends in point-
to-point and steeplechase races. Sometimes he was very
successful."

"You don't know who owned the horse at that time?"

"A gentleman dealer, I think. I don't remember his
name. Otway might know. Oh, I remember one more
thing. I don't know if it had anything to do with Pink
Livery. Dan said that night: 'I believe I'll have to get rid
of Otway one of these days. He's getting too big for his
boots.' Dan had said that before—and it was always when
Otway had been trying to keep him out of trouble. I knew
it would all blow over, but it frightened me."

"You trust Otway?"

"He was certainly faithful to Dan, if that is what you
mean. Dan was very irregular about his wages, but I
think he makes money racing, and Dan allowed him a
good deal of freedom. Sometimes we went away and left
him in England—I don't know what he did then. I think
he visits Mr. Vane's daughter, who lives at Cranmere
Farm, and he used to put up at the Red Crow
occasionally. He is attractive to women. He is always
perfectly polite to me—but I don't believe he likes me.
Adoring Dan as he did, perhaps that's natural. Dan made
a companion of him when I wasn't there—but when I
was, he had to keep his place. Sometimes I thought he
was jealous—but that sounds unlikely; I know." She
moved restlessly. "I can't think, or concentrate. I have
been down in the cellar trying to look over some of our
things stored there." She glanced at the table with its pile
of papers. "I've been reading over old letters—my father's
and mother's, and others that they kept, going back to my
great-grandfather's time. It takes my mind off the
present. I've been wondering if I could make a book of
them."

"A very good idea," I said. She picked up a letter with
a smile." 'Honoured and respected friend. . . ." she read.
"That was from my great-grandfather to his fiancee!"
Then she laid it aside with a sigh. "How peaceful to run

your race strictly between ropes you could see right to the end of the course!"

"But not everyone stayed within the ropes even then."

"Most of us would—if the ropes were so plainly to be seen. Remember, there was a fiery hell outside! You were shown pictures of it in books, just as one was taught history. And heaven was the goal. And those outside were outside and no mistake about it. Don't forget that!"

I looked at her in some surprise. Of whom was she thinking?

Just then a knock came at the door. It opened to admit Brade and Billiam.

"Colman said you were here, Jerry," said Brade, "and I thought you might feed my Billiam, with Mrs. Carne's kind permission. He's been working awfully hard, and fallen off three times. He likes falling off, but it makes him hungry!"

I introduced Brade to the ladies. They urged him to stay, but he refused. "Colman is going to send me some tea," he explained, "and I'm older than Billiam. Falling off makes me stiff. A hot bath with plenty of mustard is indicated. Mrs. Carne, you can do me a favour, if you will. May I look at your husband's clothes—everything he wore or carried at the time of the accident?"

"Of course," said Mimi. "His clothes are in the drying-room in the cellar. Otway has charge of them. But I put all the other things together in a drawer. Shall I show you now?"

"Please!" She went out with him, and a maid came in to draw the curtains. Thinking of Brade, I watched her. She unlatched and closed the heavy shutters, fastening them with a long iron bar that fitted into a socket. She was a tall girl and she could just manage it with a visible effort. Then she drew the curtains across, gave a professional glance round the room, and went out.

Lady Caroline addressed herself to entertaining Billiam, who was inspecting his surroundings with an observant air. He was dressed in a boy-scout tunic, a very martial belt, and riding-breeches. Splashes and daubs of mud were dispersed freely over face and clothing. He became aware of this, catching sight of himself in a mirror.

"Please, ma'am, if I could wash my face?" he said to Lady Caroline.

"Dr. Jerrold, will you show Billiam where to go?" she suggested tactfully. "The nearest bathroom is three doors down the passage."

I conducted Billiam to a bathroom fitted with all requirements. He stared at the pink tiled walls, the design of water-lilies stencilled on the ceiling, the silver taps and shining marble floor.

"Cripes!" said Billiam. He then looked vainly for that which was concealed by a chair painted pink and silver. "Cripes!" repeated Billiam solemnly, when I showed him its secrets. "Holy cripes!"

Throughout his toilet he missed nothing that a pair of sharp eyes could observe.

"Doesn't anybody ever come 'ere?" he asked.

"Oh, yes, I suppose three or four people use this bathroom."

"Well, them towels! They're washed, and 'tain't Tuesday."

"There are clean ones every day."

Billiam tried to grasp this. "I s'pose that there laundry van comes and takes 'em away and brings 'em back next day like this. Nobody don't 'ave to do the washin'."

"No, I expect the laundry does it."

"With machines," said Billiam.

"Most particular people like hand laundries."

"Why?"

I tried to explain.

"Yes," said Billiam thoughtfully, "she'd want 'er towels soft and white," and he pointed with his thumb in the direction of the room where he had left Mimi Carne. He looked at me with thoughtful eyes. "I always wondered what made ladies look like that," he confided. "Why, they don't ever have to scrub. They don't get dirty." He was solemn with profound thought. Then he said: "When I'm a man I'm going to 'ave a 'ouse with a bathroom like this for my mother."

He could hardly tear himself away from the pink bathroom till I reminded him of the waiting tea. Even then he stopped to ask me where the pipes went, fingering them experimentally and taxing my information about domestic plumbing and engineering, particularly why hot water could climb and if there was no danger of its boiling over and bursting the metal. I felt humble and exhausted by the time we returned to the ladies.

Billiam, plied with food, was not talkative, but Mimi Carne seemed to enjoy watching his appreciation of the scones and jam and cakes which disappeared rapidly under his attention. At last he could eat no more. Lady Caroline asked him what they had been doing all the afternoon.

"Riding, ma'am," said Billiam politely. "'That Mr. Brade, 'e can ride a 'orse, 'e can."

He seemed in awe of Mimi and fell silent whenever he looked at her, but Lady Caroline was apparently a less alarming person.

"I thought—" I began, and then checked myself.

"We 'ad a regular rodeo, we did," volunteered Billiam. " 'E said we 'ad to see 'oo'd fall off first. And I did. Mr. Vane, wot lets me break in 'is young ponies, says I fall off fine."

Lady Caroline looked at me, raising an eyebrow. It seemed a somewhat odd way for Brade to have spent the afternoon. . .

"Where did you fall off?" inquired Mimi.

"Mr. Brade said I wasn't to talk about it. 'E said some might think 'e wasn't paid for havin' rodeos." Billiam looked a little worried. " 'E's a grand detective though, certain 'e 'is, ma'am. Though you'd never know it to look at him."

Lady Caroline began to talk about horses, on which Billiam considered himself an authority. The merits of various individuals in Mr. Vane's stables came up for some enthusiastic comment.

"I shall certainly have to try out that chestnut," Mimi remarked.

Billiam looked at her, struggling with the shyness she inspired. "If you would, ma'am," he managed to say, "if you would—why, nothing'd stop you and that chestnut, ma'am! Not steeples!"

Just at this moment Colman opened the door, so suddenly that we all started up in alarm.

"Dr. Jerrold, sir, please come quick. Sir Ralph, sir— He never finished the sentence, for I followed him at an incredible pace down the stairs, through the hall, and into the Greek room. All the lights were on. The wide window at the end was open and the night came through, black and strange. Carne-Hilton was lying on a stone bench, blood trickling from his face. Furness was bending over him, and outside the window Revel's voice shouted something I did not understand.

"It's all right," said Sir Ralph, "I was stunned for a moment, that's all. Don't know what hit me—something hard." I looked up and saw that the cupboard which Lady Carne-Hilton had not shown me was open, and that drawers had been pulled out and ransacked.

Lights and voices from the garden told that the hunt for the intruder was on. While I bandaged Sir Ralph's forehead and nose with dressings Mimi brought me, he told us what had happened. He had been warned by Brade to see that the house was carefully closed at night, so he had gone into the Greek room to make sure that the shutters were fast.

"They were, sir, indeed they were half an hour ago," protested Colman.

"When I came, the window was open, and I felt sure that someone was in the room. I tried to switch on the lights, but nothing happened. I made a bound in the direction in which I thought I had heard a sound, and then I was hit by something that stunned me. That's positively all I know."

"But you must have rung the bell, sir; I heard it ring twice."

"Well, I don't remember doing it."

"I came at once, sir," said Colman, still trembling, "and shouted out. The lights was all turned off at the lamps themselves, so the switch didn't work. I could see the light of a torch on the lawn, but it was gone in a minute. Mr. Revel came running in and jumped out of the window."

Footprints were plain under the window as far as the path, but here the hard gravel told no tales.

"What is missing?" I asked.

"I have no idea," Sir Ralph answered. "In fact, I didn't know that there was a cupboard there at all. Colman, ask her ladyship to come here."

I knew Brade ought to be there, but there was no time to fetch him before Lady Carne-Hilton came into the room. She looked at the open cupboard, gave a terrified glance at me, and then crossed the room and stood with her back to the open drawers.

"What have you done?" she demanded shrilly.

Carne-Hilton explained. She turned and looked into one of the drawers, then into others.

"These are my private belongings," she said, "and there is nothing of value here—at least to anyone but me." She turned and saw that Averil Legend had just come into the room with Otway behind her. I thought for a second that Lady Carne-Hilton would spring at her, but she did not. Instead she covered her face with her hands and broke down completely. "Oh, why— why . . ." she cried.

Everyone seemed to think it quite natural that she should give way under the shock of finding her husband injured and her room forced, and I suppose it was, but I thought the glance she gave Averil Legend needed explaining.

"I'd better get Brade," I suggested, as no one seemed to have thought of it.

"Whoever it was has got away," said Otway. Billiam, standing by the table, coughed suddenly. Averil Legend had moved round the corner of the couch where Carne-Hilton still sat, and when I noticed her she was playing with a paper-weight, a bronze sphinx from the writing-table.

"Shall I close this, sir?" asked Otway.

"We shall have to send for the police," Carne-Hilton answered. "Better leave it as it is, Otway. Stay here and see that no one touches anything."

"Yes, sir."

"I shall stay too!" exclaimed his wife.

"Will someone ring the police station?" Carne-Hilton asked. "We'd better see Brade, Dr. Jerrold."

Billiam plucked at my sleeve.

"Tell Mr. Brade that lady—the pretty one—was looking at that cupboard like she wanted to know all about it," whispered Billiam, "and," he squirmed a little, "I ought to go back and say thank-you for my tea. My mother'll ask me if I did."

Mimi Carne came out then and I left him struggling with suitable expressions. When I arrived at Brade's door, the others had just opened it and were standing still, apparently lost in astonishment.

He was lying on the floor, playing, apparently, with a set of toy bricks.

6 p.m., Friday

I don't know what Carne-Hilton thought, but I was sure Brade had gone mad. Falling off horses with Billiam in the afternoon and playing with toys in the evening on the first day of his investigation of a case which I knew he thought involved a murder did not seem sane. He was so engrossed that he did not even notice our entrance. It was Carne-Hilton who recalled him by making an exclamation of amazement. Brade looked up without rising. Then, seeing us, he scrambled to his feet: "Darlings, you are so unexpected!" he said.

"Other things are unexpected, too," I remarked.

"You seem to have hurt your head, Sir Ralph," said Brade, looking at the bandages. "I'm sorry about that."

"A burglar broke into my wife's sitting-room and opened a cupboard which is supposed to have a secret fastening," Carne-Hilton explained briefly. "We thought you had better know."

"Ah, that cupboard! Sir Ralph, did you know it was there?"

"I did not," replied Carne-Hilton. "I dislike that room and never go into it if I can help it. I did not even look at the work while it was going on. My wife wanted one room to treat as she liked, and she got it."

"I see. So you don't know what was in that cupboard either." Brade looked thoughtful. "And you're sure your head is all right?"

"Oh, quite."

"Then that's a weight off our minds." Brade seemed to remember that he was supposed to be interested in this case. "Any finger-prints?" he asked with a knowledgeable air.

"We've sent for the police."

Brade was regarding us with an innocent stare. "Footprints?"

"Yes, plenty of footprints," I replied.

Carne-Hilton looked at us, half indignant, half bewildered. "Well, if you don't want to know any more—" he began.

"The policeman will tell me all about it when he comes," said Brade. "I'm sorry about that cupboard —but it may help to clear things up, you know."

"To me it seems another mystery."

I was left alone with Simon.

"Well," I remarked, "I suppose we're in for it now. This burglary, or attempted burglary, and attack on Carne-Hilton will bring the whole business into the limelight again. What the devil were you doing with those bricks, Simon?"

"Just a game, Jerry, just a game!"

I looked more closely at the toys. They were made of bone, and inscribed with writing too fine to decipher without a glass.

"It seems an odd time to play a game!"

"But what a game!" Simon inserted his monocle. I had always regarded this as an affectation, for I knew that he had an excellent pair of eyes, but it was useful. He could read the minute writing on the bricks with it. "Games are not understood in the West," he continued instructively. "Why, I don't suppose you even know the legend of Wong Chi, who was so much interested in a game of chequers that when he happened to ask the time he noticed that his beard had changed colour from black to white."

"I'm afraid I never heard of Wong Chi."

He sighed and shook his head. "Life is just one long process of correcting the effects of orthodox education, Jerry. I've told you so before."

He was extended full-length on the floor, examining his bricks. He would turn one over with his fingers and study the inscription on the other side, then do the same thing to another, and I watched him, interested, beginning to see how he used them, when a knock sounded, and at my signal Otway entered.

After the second of surprise at Brade's attitude and occupation, he said: "The police have arrived, sir. I thought I ought to tell you. I have measured the footprints in the bed under the window. They are unusually small for a man's, but the boots worn were certainly not a lady's. In fact, sir, I took the liberty of making an experiment, the shape and size were so uncommon."

"And the result, Otway?" Simon yawned.

"The result, sir, is that the boot I placed in the track exactly fitted it."

"Whose boot?" I exclaimed.

"The hunting boots of my late master, Mr. Danvers Carne."

"Active of him—very!" murmured Brade.

"But this means—the thief is in the house or on the place," I ejaculated.

"Yes, sir. The boots had been put back in the drying-room. They have been hastily wiped."

"Dear me!"

"Am I to inform the police of this?" asked Otway sharply.

"Oh, I should, certainly," Simon agreed indifferently.

"Do you see what it means, sir?"

"Well, not exactly."

"There's no man in this house or on the place who could so much as have got those boots on. Mr. Danvers had small feet, and very narrow."

"But there are several ladies?"

"Yes, sir. There are."

I thought quickly that here at least Mimi had an alibi.

Brade suddenly squatted on the floor, looking thoroughly Chinese, and gazed at Otway with flattering attention.

"How does this fit your reasoning, Otway?" he asked.

"It doesn't fit, sir, not yet. But it makes me surer than ever there's more in it than appears."

"You mean—there may be something in that cupboard

to incriminate a person—somebody else wants to shield? (There isn't enough variety in our dictionary, you know—somebody, someone—awkward!)"

"Well, sir, it looks like it."

"Now, Otway, this is urgent. You see those bricks? Well, the whole story's written there. Each cube has four sides. I've filled three. If I turn them this way, they fit, and Mr. Furness is pretty nearly caught. If I turn them the other, Mr. Revel looks guilty. Just turn them over and Sir Ralph focuses the attention. You see, I'm being open with you. The fourth side is blank, except for one mark. Just look at it." He handed Otway the toy and a magnifying glass.

"Yes, sir, I see."

"Well, I've looked at the hole in Mr. Carne's head. I didn't enjoy it, but I did. The doctors seem to have taken it for granted that he got it falling off his horse. You and I don't think he did. We think he was alive after that fall, but he certainly wasn't alive and walking after his skull was smashed. I've been over the ground. There's nothing I can find to make exactly the impression I found in his head. It might conceivably have happened during the fall if he had struck a protruding stone. But he didn't. The edge of the pit overhangs the side and he fell straight to the bottom, and there are no loose stones there. It's a smooth surface. It accounts for the damage to the back of the head, but not for that clear-cut hole above and behind the temple. Now, I want you to find those string gloves for me. Will you try?"

"But what have they got to do with— I see, sir." Otway paused. "You think they have, and that's why nobody's come forward to explain why the gloves are missing. It's an idea."

"Will you look?"

"Of course I will."

"Look everywhere!"

"I'll begin tomorrow as soon as it's light."

"Otway," I said quickly, "before you go, I should like to

ask you about Pink Livery. Your master rode another
horse under his name in 1931."

"Yes, sir. He didn't know. He was imposed upon. The
two horses were blood brothers and identical in
appearance."

"And Pink Livery was sold as winner of the race?"

"Yes, sir, to Mr. Revel. It was when it all came out
that he and Mr. Revel met first."

"You had words with your master over the matter?"

"Yes, sir. You see, I knew Pink Livery was vicious. My
master was extremely reckless."

"You tried to persuade your master not to ride the
horse?"

Otway looked at me squarely. "In this connexion, sir, I
do not wish to conceal anything. I thought my master's
life might be at stake, and it was only when I found out
that Cat o' the Hills had been secretly substituted for his
brother that I stopped my efforts to prevent him from
riding. I intended to go to one of the stewards and
protest."

"But you allowed the fraud to proceed?"

"If I had disclosed what I knew then, it might have
reflected on Mr. Carne's reputation."

"Why didn't you tell him?"

"I tried to, but he knew I meant to stop his ride if I
could, and he thought it was a trick. There was no time to
convince him then."

"You quarrelled about the matter afterwards?"

"Mr. Carne knew that I was devoted to him, and he
forgave me."

"I see. That's all, I think, Otway."

Otway had no sooner gone than we had another
visitor, heralded by a heavy tread outside. The doorway
was filled by a big man in uniform, which I recognized as
belonging to an Inspector from Scotland Yard. Exactly
what degree of inspector I did not know, and do not know
yet, but Brade and he looked at each other with
humorous recognition.

"This is Ives," said Brade. "We are inseparable. I told you I had to have Ives! Just Ives—not Scotland Yard in the mass. This is perfect!"

Ives glanced at me with the equivalent of a raised eyebrow. His features were too massive to yield to so subtle a gesture.

"Yes, dear man, this is Dr. Jerrold. I am helping him in this case. He is the real investigator. We have no secrets from Jerry."

"Then why did you send for me, Mr. Brade?"

"*I* send for you? My dear man! You are dreaming! You came down to see the Chief Constable about that hold-up on the Agminton-London road and happened to be there when they got a call from us."

"Well, all I know is I looked a fool. Marking time with Colonel Shields while he answered all my questions over half a dozen times, and waiting for my cue!"

"What did Shields say?" asked Brade inquisitively.

"If you want to know, I think he smelt a rat. Anyway, here I am, and it's irregular. The local Inspector is in charge of the case. But they know you're here, Mr. Brade, and you can't keep 'em off long. There's too much talk going about."

"Nonsense! There's been a perfectly good inquest and it's closed."

"The Colonel doesn't like it. There's no smoke without a fire."

"Now, Ives, dear man, don't start that! You know I hate it."

"Facts are facts, Mr. Brade."

"Help!" murmured Simon.

Ives grinned ponderously and then looked with curiosity and respect at the bricks.

"Sit down, Ives, sit down. Have a cigarette?" Brade offered him one, in so evident a state of decomposition that Ives looked at it and drew out his pipe, stuffed the tobacco into the bowl, and lit it.

"Hark to the story of the boots," Brade began, and told

him what Otway had told us.

"So there's a lady in the case!" Ives remarked.

Simon raised his eyebrows. "Well, I think so. But not because of those boots. In fact, boots bore me."

Ives was jotting down notes. He finished, and closed his book sharply.

"What are you here for anyway?" he inquired.

"It isn't me really," Brade apologized. "It's Jerry. It's such a nervy family, Ives. Haven't you noticed? Jerry is treating them and I came along. You don't know what an interest I take in Jerry's work. But he ought to study Eastern thought—really he ought, you know!"

"Who borrowed those boots, Mr. Brade?" demanded Ives. "Damned if I'm going to make a fool of myself over this. You know, you might tell me."

"What makes you think that?" Brade glanced at me proudly. "Now you'll see how a real detective works, Jerry!"

"But if you didn't know, you'd want to find out, and as it is, you don't care a damn. Plain as a pike-staff."

"I've asked you before not to employ stock phrases, Ives. It isn't worthy of you."

"Don't beat about the bush."

Brade winced.

"Tell me—there's a good chap. There's no man in the house who could have done it—that's obvious, I suppose."

"Is it?" Brade looked down at his own feet—as small as a woman's.

Ives stared. Then he laughed suddenly and heartily; and, rather late in the day, I saw light.

"You were always keen about that cupboard," I exclaimed.

"There's just one thing I can't forget," sighed Simon. "He sold his Kwan Yin bird for that woman!"

Ives looked at me inquiringly.

"You see, Sir Ralph inherited the Hilton collection of Ming porcelain, and, apparently, he sold it. His wife is no doubt an expense, and so is his garden."

"Suppose you make a clean breast of it," Ives suggested, briskly. "The Chief is worrying about this case. True, the jury brought in a verdict at the inquest, but the county is alive with rumours. This is going to stir up a nest of vipers or I'm an ass. Come along Brade, put me wise, as the Yankees say. What are you after? Did you borrow those boots and burgle the lady's cupboard or didn't you?"

"Can't you stop talking about boots? I ought never to have touched the things. But Jerry seemed to think I ought to look at them and they're quite comfortable, though on the big side, and I did want to look at that cupboard and I didn't want the ladies to know it. I don't like people to know that I've a suspicious nature. It's such an unattractive trait. And the ladies in this house are charming—ask Jerry!"

"Well, you've put me in a nice hole. What am I to report?"

"Tell the truth, dear Ives," Simon suggested, "but don't tell everybody. You see, I want you near me. I've been longing for you ever since I came. But I don't want you officially on the track of murder—not yet. Don't you see what a lovely place this is?"

"You're making a cat's-paw of me!"

"Stave off the Chief Constable for a few days and all will be well. You'll all be renowned for your brilliant feat of deduction. Think of it! The morning papers will have the murder sensation and the evening papers the solution, all worked out in a few hours by the local staff, assisted by Inspector Ives of the C.I.D. Consider!"

"Then there has been murder?"

"Yes, my sweet. Murder sure enough! Look here!"

"But, Brade, how was Carne-Hilton hurt? Surely you didn't attack him?" I interposed.

"That was his own fault. He was hasty. I'm always telling you not to be hasty, Jerry. He ran to the window, and the bar of the shutter I'd just unfastened fell on his nose. I assure you I saw he wasn't really hurt before I made my exit, and I rang and heard Colman coming, so then I jumped out of the window. If they had looked, they would have found that the garden door was unlocked too. It's awful, the fortifications of this house at night! I went to the hall and heard Sir Ralph Carne-Hilton talking to you, Jerry, so I knew he was in the best of hands!"

"Will you tell me what you were doing this afternoon when you were out?"

"It's no secret, darling. Billiam and I rode down that ride. I got off at the fallen tree and nosed around. And I'll tell you what I found. In fact, if you'll open that attache case and look in the cardboard box on top, you'll find it."

Ives and I together opened the box and saw the stump end of a cigarette. It had not been smoked in the ordinary way, but through a holder. A few letters of the maker's name remained visible.

"That is one of Danvers Carne's cigarettes and it fits the holder which he carried in his pocket. He would never touch a cigarette with his lips—one of his fads. Further, Carne's brandy flask was nearly empty when the body was found. Revel says he spoke to him a few minutes before he left the field that day. He saw Carne taking a drink and asked if he had any left, as his own flask was empty. Carne said: 'Take all you want. I'm going home and shan't want it again.' Revel poured a little of the brandy into his own flask and left the other more than half full. Somebody had a drink out of that flask between then and when the body was found. I wish we knew just how and when, don't you, dear lad?"

"After all, Carne may have taken another nip between leaving the hunt and getting his fall."

"Unless Revel is lying, he didn't—not fifteen minutes later—and half a flask of neat brandy! I don't think so. He is much more likely to have had it after his fall, at the same time as he smoked his cigarette, and what's more, he didn't drink it all!"

"But how do you know that cigarette wasn't smoked while he was still mounted?" asked Ives.

"Because it is nowhere near the marks of horses' hoofs. He was thrown, recovered, walked a few steps into the wood, presumably looking for his mount, which had wandered away, found he felt giddy, sat down on a stump and smoked his cigarette and took a nip at his flask, and then—what, Jerry, what then? That branch did not kill him and he was not dead at half past three."

"So Otway was right about those boots. Have you looked at his wrist-watch?" I suggested.

"That was either stopped by his fall or was altered to show three thirty-three. It tells us nothing, not even if that was the time of his fall. It may not have been right and it may have been tampered with."

"What else did you do?"

"Didn't Billiam tell you?"

"He said you both fell off."

"Nothing about potato-sacks?"

"No."

"Good for Billiam! It was quite exciting. Sarah doesn't care for the edge of that chalk-pit. In fact, she seems to be determined to avoid it at any cost. So we had to imagine the chalk-pit. We tried throwing potato-sacks, stuffed with odds and ends, down it. We decided it couldn't be done from a side-saddle or without the full use of all four limbs. But not until Billiam was very hungry with falling off and I was very stiff. And I never had that hot bath. I was looking at boots and jumping through windows instead!"

"I thought you couldn't ride, Brade."

He opened his eyes wide. "Didn't you know I was Irish?" he asked.

"I suppose you wanted to draw Barnet out about Sarah."

"Clever Jerry! And he didn't exaggerate. She has the mature wisdom of a schoolmistress combined with that of the madam of a professional establishment of another sort. But her nerves have been definitely upset, and she draws the line at that chalk-pit. Short of that, there's nothing she won't do for me."

Ives had been patient, listening carefully. Now he said: "Would you mind telling me what you are talking about?"

"We've no secrets from you, dear man!" Simon declared. "Jerry, just sum up the facts!" He settled down to listen.

"Everything?"

"In a nutshell, as Ives would say."

"Very well. Fact one—everyone in this house thinks that Danvers Carne was murdered."

"Why?" Ives demanded.

"For the most part, instinct, the only real reason given being the character of the mare."

"I've heard about that mare," Ives nodded. "Go on!"

"So far as I can make out, Mrs. Carne has no idea who did it. Otway suspects Furness. Lady Carne-Hilton suspects her husband. Revel and Miss Trent suspect Furness and possibly Sir Ralph. Miss Legend is keeping her suspicions to herself. The servants have been examined.

"To take them one by one—suspects first: Furness is obviously the most likely. On his own confession he was the last to see the victim alive. He followed him into the Wilderness and spoke to him, not more than five minutes and probably less, before the branch felled him at three thirty or thereabouts. He could have carried out the murder then. But he didn't. Because Carne was alive after the fall, and because his body was not in the pit at four thirty. Unless he can be proved to have returned and done the work later, he is innocent.

"Carne-Hilton didn't do it either, if what Brade says about the potato-sacks is true, because he has only one good leg and is not acrobatic enough to have dragged his victim to the chalk-pit and thrown him in. Besides, the time at his disposal was very short.

"Of the others, to take the men first: Revel perhaps might just have managed it, provided Danvers Carne was obliging enough to wait in the Wilderness for an hour after his fall, or if Revel knew the country well enough to leave the hunt, murder Carne, and dispose of his body later. On his own testimony, he didn't know the country. That has to be checked.

"The ladies now: Mrs. Carne had the time and opportunity to dispose of the body, but hardly to commit the murder, as this must have been done soon after his fall. She was in a side-saddle. I don't know whether she rides astride as well. If she does, it is conceivable that she might have mounted Sarah for this purpose.

"Lady Carne-Hilton was in the wood in motoring clothes and not under observation, for, say, fifteen minutes, but she walked home and was there before five, so did not dispose of the body. The same applies to Miss Legend.

"Miss Trent was at home and her alibi is perfect.

"The servants: Otway was seen riding home across the park about four thirty.

"Barnet was hacking to meet his master, but I don't know of any reason to suspect him.

"In short, Furness and Carne-Hilton, who had motive for the crime, seem to be acquitted by the facts, and it leaves us with Revel, who worshipped him, and three women, to choose from. Is that right, Brade?"

"But how do you know Carne's body was not in the chalk-pit at four thirty?"

I explained.

"You're basing your whole theory on a child's evidence?"

"We are," Simon replied. "That's the worst of Billiam's evidence. It's completely unshakable and confirmed in every respect by his mother and the school-mistress and Revel's finding the knife exactly where he dropped it. He was in the schoolhouse at four, at home at five. His knife, identified by his mother and himself, was picked up in the chalk-pit where the body was found. And there can't be a mistake about the day because of his mother's evidence and the fact that the knife would have told the tale if it had lain for twenty-four hours in the rain. But you've left out the important part, Jerry; I'm surprised at you!"

"What do you mean?"

"Was Carne a saint or a villain? If he was a saint we have to suspect the people who hated him, alibi or no alibi. If he was a villain, those who knew it aren't so likely to have killed him as someone who found it out suddenly after trusting him. There you have a reasonable motive that would explain it all. And there's another theory—a series of accidents led up to this murder, created an atmosphere of suspicion and fear. Was the murder premeditated over a long stretch of time? Was someone watching his or her chance?" Brade turned quickly and looked at me. "And you've neglected those shutters. Lady Carne-Hilton came in not long before Revel brought the news. Her maid was at the door to admit him, sent down by her mistress, before the usual servant could answer the bell. The windows of this house are closed at night, not only by ordinary blinds and curtains, but by heavy wooden shutters, and the rule is unbreakable that from November to March the house is shut at tea-time. Lady Carne-Hilton, in her bedroom, could not have seen Revel ride up to the door by accident. She had to perform quite a muscular feat to open a shutter and look out. Why did she do this? She sent her car home and walked back from the Wilderness without waiting to find her pet dog. Why? She has gone out of her way to cast suspicion on her husband. Why? She had a secret cupboard in her own sitting-room. Why? And you haven't asked me what I found in that cupboard, my dears!"

He took a typed manuscript from a drawer and threw it to me. Ives and I bent over it.

It appeared to be a collection of reminiscences. No name was attached, but from the bits of gossip I read here and there I did not think it would be difficult to place the writer. Most of it dealt with English and European adventures written at the time when the late King Edward was a lively Prince of Wales. I saw intimate references to the German Emperor, and the last pages took one up to and past the late King's coronation.

"Turn to page 247, darlings!" suggested Brade.

Here we found a racy chapter headed: "Life in the Near East." And Life indeed it appeared to be in a minor kingdom then in existence. There was a description of a certain party where the writer, a lady of beauty and charm, received a golden apple which opened to disclose a nest of emeralds. The donor was all but named, and again I saw light, for the author of this very interesting work was certainly the mother of Averil Legend, and the host of the party the Prince reported to be her father.

"An awkward document!" said Brade sweetly. "And better in our keeping. If a lady should wish to marry an ambassador to an Eastern State it might cause annoyance to somebody."

I remembered the glance Lady Carne-Hilton had given Miss Legend.

"Don't tell me Lady Carne-Hilton is a black-mailer," I said. "She hasn't the wits!"

Ives was delighted. "Truth is stranger than fiction," he observed.

Simon looked pained. "Ives doesn't do himself justice!" he murmured.

"But how does this bear on the case?" I asked.

"I don't know yet, Jerry!"

"And what am I to tell the Chief?" Ives demanded.

"Tell him I want you. Go on investigating this burglary for a day or two. And while you're about it, bear in mind that I want to know several things. Had Mr. Revel hunted before with the South Lodesdale? Did he know the country? Who was the stranger in the garden last Thursday night? And who was the American or Colonial gentleman who followed the hunt in a small Morris on Tuesday? Where are those string gloves? And check up those alibis: Otway's, Barnet's in particular, Ives. That's your job!"

"Hm! I see. Most irregular!"

"But consider the scoop!"

Ives considered it.

"You know how bad I am at routine work, Ives. Lend me a hand."

Ives rose. "One good turn deserves another!" he said cordially. "Personally, I think you're on a wild-goose chase, but I haven't forgotten past services."

"That's my one and only Ives!" Simon beamed on him. "And remember—you are looking for that burglar!"

When Ives had scribbled down several pages of notes and gone from the room, Simon took up his tobacco-pouch and papers, fluttering everything with his small and helpless fingers, which only seemed efficient in handling his treasures.

"Look here, Jerry, do you want me to go on?"

"What do you mean?"

"I came down here to find out if Carne was murdered. He was. I can say so and go home. But if I go on, I may find out who did it. Do you want me to?"

"Of course I do."

"Whoever it is?"

"Yes."

"Have you remembered that young Revel was a waster when Carne made friends with him and that he's a reformed character now?"

"Yes."

"I talked to a man I know at Christ Church, on the telephone. He says Carne had a marvellous influence on some young men, though he himself distrusted him."

"You think this points to his being genuine and reflects on his wife?"

"So far as it goes. There are people who are touchstones. If he was a saint, no woman could live with him for five years without becoming steadily better or worse than she was. Suppose it was Mrs. Carne who organized all this run of bad luck she described to you. Suppose she meant to kill him, and chance favoured her. Suppose she took and kept the string gloves on Tuesday, hoping for an accident. He would have felt her animosity as a threat to his safety, but might have loved her too deeply to connect the feeling with her. Suppose she and Furness are lovers, and he and she planned the whole thing and executed it. But for Otway and his boots and the end of a cigarette and Billiam, there would not have been a scrap of suspicion against them. You see that."

Simon had dropped all his affectations and stood still, watching me. He forced me to look into my own mind.

"I believe this murder was premeditated," he said quietly, "and if so, everything points to his wife—even her going to consult you. She tested your reactions. You would have been ready to say that, in Carne's state of mind, an accident was likely to happen."

Did I want him to go on with the case if it meant that Mimi Carne would be convicted of being a party to the murder of her husband?

"Is your theory that Furness may have killed Carne, and Mimi Carne may have known it and disposed of the body?"

"It is a possible—even a simple—explanation."

"Well, she didn't. If it were a case of a sudden shot —a blow in anger under intolerable provocation—I might hesitate. But she did not do what you suggest—I'll stake my profession on it. And I believe that her version of her husband's character is the right one. I believe he was rotten to the core."

"Do you believe it enough to give me a free hand? Even if I work along those lines?"

"Yes. You'll find out that you're wrong."

"Have you considered that she may be in love with Furness?"

"Yes."

"And that women are capable of doing a great deal for the men they love?"

"Yes. She could not have done that."

"Not even thinking that her husband had inflicted the final insult on her and was ready to throw her aside for a girl who was rich?"

"She knew her husband. Even that would not have come as a great shock. It only made her feel that she had finished with him." I thought of the Sevres vase.

"There's just this chance," Brade said. "The murder may have been premeditated, but the person who planned it may not have been the one who did it. I'd like to see that vase. Was it genuine or just a joke?" Simon had read my thoughts. We were both silent.

Then he suddenly returned to his usual manner.

"That was one of my bright thoughts, that burglary!" he murmured. "Ives would say 'it killed two birds with one stone.' I got the manuscript and an excuse for putting Ives on the job. I badly want those alibis checked up."

"But my dear Brade—" then I paused. After all, Otway was a dark horse. Was his devotion to his master real or mere self-interest? And Barnet's attachment to Sir Ralph might supply him with a motive for the crime.

"There's another danger," I said. "Innocent people have been convicted of crime. I believe in you, Brade. I hope you'll go on with this case."

"And you'll help, Jerry? I've been reading over your notes. Really, you know, I couldn't think of going on without them."

Brade drank a cup of tea from the tray which had been waiting. I watched him rolling cigarettes for a moment. "I'll certainly help if I can. But you must know that in one respect I'm hopelessly biased."

"I've noticed that, Jerry dear! There's one thing I haven't shown you." Brade pulled the attache case towards him. He took out a match-box, slid it open, and handed it to me. Inside lay a gold coin about the size of a sixpence, but surprisingly heavy, and inscribed with characters I did not recognize. "That was in the cupboard too," he explained.

"But this—what does it mean?" Of course I thought of the coin Danvers Carne had lost. "We must ask Mrs. Carne," I said.

"Not yet, Jerry. This is our secret. I want to brood over it."

"But—if it is the same one, it connects Carne with his cousin's wife."

"So, it seems, does that," Brade flicked the manuscript with his finger.

"You mean—Carne may have been playing the blackmailing game, using this woman as his tool?"

"Perhaps."

"But why the coin?"

"He might have given it—to his mistress."

"Horrible!"

"Yes. It doesn't seem exactly right somehow." Brade looked reproachfully at his bricks. "There's a twist somewhere."

"What are you going to do now?"

"Talk to Sir Ralph a little. Sarah is very funny about that chalk-pit."

"And what do you want me to do, Brade?"

"Talk to Colman. He's bursting with news, and he's not exactly open with me. Colman is biased too. In fact, all the nice people are, in one way or another. Talk to Colman and tell me all about it—if you like."

The meaning behind his last words was somewhat ominous.

7 p.m., Friday

I came away from my interview with Brade with a new feeling of dismay. He had led me to believe that everything so far pointed to the guilt of Richard Furness and Mimi Carne. The confidence I had felt in him, based on his previous successes, was shaken. Perhaps, after all, he had been more lucky and less brilliant than I had supposed. I knew him to have a penetrating mind, but if he erred in his hypothesis at the beginning, might not his ingenuity become a positive danger? Might he not build up a plausible case against two innocent persons?

The idea of premeditation was new to me, and I considered it as I sat before the satisfactory coal fire in my bedroom. Was it not a fantastic view to take of the incidents Mimi Carne had described to me? That she had come to me deliberately to test her scheme by my reactions to it I did not believe. Yet suppose she had not impressed me as sincere? What should I have thought of Brade's theory then?

If Carne had given the gold charm to Vivien Carne-Hilton, telling his wife that he had lost it, might not an unscrupulous person have thought out some such plan, knowing his superstitious weakness, knowing that the more afraid he was, the greater risks he would run? Hoping that an opportunity would arise in time to make use of this form of panic?

But Mimi was not the only person close enough to him to carry out such a plan. There was Otway.

What about him? He was clever, I felt sure, and had been in trouble with the law, as he himself admitted. If Carne was a villain it was more than likely that Otway was his tool. No doubt everyone believed him to be devoted to his master. And what motive had he, to compare with either Mimi's or Sir Ralph's? Nevertheless, I thought I should like to find out more about that alibi.

Ives was to investigate it, but I did not feel inclined to
wait for Ives, so I put on a coat and went out to the
stables.

The horses were being bedded down for the night, and
Barnet and Rogers were both there. I followed Rogers into
Sarah's stall.

"Look here, Rogers," I began, "I want to ask you a
question or two."

"Yes, sir."

"Can you check up the hours when all the horses,
except Sarah, were in this stable last Tuesday?"

"Yes, sir, pretty close."

"Well then, who was first to come in?"

"Pinnace, sir, the horse Miss Trent was riding. I got
him settled comfortable and give him his gruel half an
hour or more before Mrs. Danvers come in. She brought
Taffity straight to the stables, but I'd gone round to the
house to wait, so she put her in herself and told Colman
to tell me about the shoe she lost."

"That was about a quarter to five?"

"Maybe a bit later. Sir Ralph, he rode in while I was
groomin' Taffity and I helped him off and left the cob—
just unsaddled him—he not needing attention like the
hunters."

"What happened then?"

"Sir Ralph asked me who had come in and I told him
and he had a look at the horses to see they was
comfortable, and told me to give Black Watch the once
over. Mr. Otway wasn't one for over-groomin', and Mr.
Barnet says t'ain't Otway's place to groom our horses,
though if he wasn't so much the gentleman he'd lend a
hand when the work's heavy like it was that day."

"When did Otway bring in his horse?"

"Almost the same time as Mrs. Carne, or a bit before.
In a hurry for his tea, like he always is, so Mrs. Lovell at
the Lodge says, and argued it was late when it was on the
table five sharp, same as usual."

"And the others?"

"Sarah got in at her stable door and was munchin' hay when Mr. Furness rode home, leadin' Trews. Mr. Revel was in the car that went to fetch Mr. Carne's body. That's all I know. I hopes nobody thinks it was my fault—them stirrups—that bit. But orders is orders, ain't they, sir? And Mr. Barnet wasn't here to ask."

I reassured him and went back to the house.

So from four to five Otway had ridden home, seen by three people, stabled his horse, and made a punctual tea at five o'clock.

I remembered that Brade wished me to talk to Colman, and thought the best way would be to ring for a glass of sherry which I wanted. The downstairs rooms were empty. I supposed everyone would be dressing for dinner. One lamp was burning in the hall. The fire spluttered over a damp log, and shadows fell heavily where the light stopped.

As I moved towards the hearth to look for the bell, a stifled scream came from beyond the closed door of the Greek room.

"Help! You'll kill me!"

I threw the door open. There, in that extraordinary green-white light two women swayed backwards and forwards. Averil Legend, the placid, the lovely, was shaking Vivien Carne-Hilton, her powerful mannish hands fastened on the other's shoulders, and her arms moving with confident strength.

"Scream," she was saying, "scream! You rotter! You utterly poisonous little snake! If I hang for it tomorrow, I'll do what I like now."

I don't know how long she would have gone on shaking the unfortunate lady if she had not seen me, but as I stepped forward she let go, and Vivien Carne-Hilton fell on a couch, gasping and sobbing wildly. Miss Legend smoothed her hair with those odd hands of hers and smiled at me.

"She deserves it, you know," she said, calmly. "Better go up and tidy, Vivien, or somebody else will come along and we'll have to explain, which wouldn't suit either of us, would it?"

Vivien Carne-Hilton looked at her, honest rage taking the place of everything else in her face.

"You always were a brute, Averil, and strong as a lunatic." Then she seemed to remember me, and her vanity asserted itself. She certainly did not look her best under the influence of genuine emotion. Her oily skin showed through her make up, and her mouth was slack and coarse.

Miss Legend looked at her and deliberately picked up a bag from the floor, opened it, took out a gold vanity case, and powdered her own nose.

Lady Carne-Hilton, defenceless, stumbled out of the room.

"Can you spare five minutes, Dr. Jerrold?" Miss Legend asked, taking my answer for granted. "But not here!" She laughed. I suppose the expression on my face was funny.

I followed her into the morning-room, and we went to the fireplace where a fire of beechwood was burning brightly.

"That's better! You look like a human being again. And so do I, I hope. That ghastly room of Vivien's!"

Again she laughed. "It was Dan's idea, of course."

"Really?"

She was silent. Suddenly, I was amazed to find that, without speaking or moving, she had made me feel aware of her whole loveliness and charm. There was pleasure in standing there so near her, the firelight playing over her skirt and the walls of the room closing us in. I knew that she had willed me to feel this, for some reason of her own.

"Will you believe me, Dr. Jerrold? Vivien's and my quarrel had nothing to do with the mystery of Dan's death."

"Why should it?"

"When you are thinking so much of one thing, it is natural to connect everything with it. Also, as you have seen, I have a temper, I am very strong for a woman, I was in the Wilderness for a few moments last Tuesday, and I did hate Dan."

"I don't think it would occur to anyone to suspect you."

"No? I wonder why. I have a proposal to make to you, Dr. Jerrold."

"Yes?"

"It is this: You are interested in solving this mystery, I know, or you would not be here. I may be able to help, I can't say now how or why. But Mimi Carne is one of the few people in the world I like, and respect, and I would go to a good deal of trouble for her. That is saying a lot, for I'm a lazy creature. I know she had nothing to do with Dan's death. I'm pretty sure you want to prove that, too. If I help you, will you do something for me?"

"I should like to."

"That is non-committal." She laughed again. "You are a remarkable man, you know. Very easy to approach, but very hard to move, however near one may get."

"Indeed I'm not." I denied it with regretful sincerity.

"I think you are. Well, this is what I want: Tell me, if you can, who rifled that cupboard of Vivien's, and what did they find? Please!" She came nearer to me and let me look into her eyes.

"How should I know?"

"I think you do. Please, please!"

"You must want to know very badly indeed," I said. The fact is, I was annoyed. No man likes to think a lovely woman is using her arts to charm him for any reason except one. She must have been very confident of her power, considering my age and experience.

She drew back and spoke impulsively. "But I do like you, Dr. Jerrold!"

"And I like you, Miss Legend. I find you very interesting, especially—" I paused—"your hands."

"Look at them if you like."

It was a rash thing to do, but when she stretched them out to me I took them, and I did look at them. For a second I felt their magnetism, and thought of nothing else. Then I knew how deep was my wish to save Mimi, for they became suddenly the hands of the woman who had been in the Wilderness during that critical hour, who did hate Danvers Carne, and I glanced at her face, smiling.

"*Must* you marry your Ambassador?" I asked.

"I told you you were hard to move," she answered steadily, without taking her hands away.

"Didn't you mean me to say that?"

"Perhaps. But if so, I meant you to mean it," she retorted. "Look at my hands. You are interested in them. You study hands, of course. Tell me what they tell you, Dr. Jerrold."

"That you will do well to marry your Ambassador. They are hands to take and hold power, I think. It is what you want?"

"Yes. What else is there? Love? Well, when you are a woman like me you come to despise anything so easily won—and lost."

"And so easily missed altogether."

I was still holding her hands when the door opened and Mimi Carne came in. She stood looking at us in silence. All the warmth went out of her face, but she smiled at Averil and came forward.

Averil said nothing, a point in her favour. I dropped her hands and looked at the clock. "Time to dress, I suppose."

"Meals are never on time these days," Mimi remarked, lighting a cigarette. "I don't know what the chef thinks. No one has ever dared to be late for dinner in this house since he came. Vivien is much too afraid he'll leave, and there are plenty of hostesses ready to bribe him to. Dan found him for her. He said, since we had to stay here sometimes, we might as well have some form of pleasure!"

She talked quietly and evenly, not thinking of what she said.

"I can dress in ten minutes when it is worth my

while." Miss Legend moved towards the door. "That is the advantage of spending five hours a week in a beauty parlour and two at the hairdresser's." She walked out of the room, unhurried and composed.

But I did not. I was seized with a foolish wish to explain. There being nothing to explain, and no reason whatever to explain it, I was in a difficulty. Mimi did not help me. She went on talking in that steady voice, but I do not remember what she said. It gave me a chance to recover from one panic and plunge into another. For, looking at her, I realized her position in all its horror and felt afraid. It could not be many days before the case must be made public, and, unless Brade solved it before that happened, the police would find the two factors they would look for—motive and opportunity—in the evidence against Richard Furness. If he should be arrested and the testimony of Otway and Revel held under examination, the idea of Mimi's complicity was an inevitable result. She might be arrested, she must certainly suffer—she might be convicted. She might be hanged!

She turned to me and saw my face. Her reserve broke | as she looked at me.

"What is it, Dr. Jerrold? Oh, what is it?"

"I am trying to think what I can do for you. That's all."

"Are you? You want to protect me?"

"With all my heart."

"Then—I'm not afraid."

But I was, and showed it.

"Mrs. Carne, will you give me a free hand? I'm not a detective. Brade is. I brought him into this case, and now—"

"He suspects me! Listen! I had nothing whatever to do with it. I have no idea who did. The truth is there, somewhere. I believe it can be found. Don't be afraid. I am utterly innocent. Nothing can make me guilty when that is true." Her courage stiffened mine.

"I think Brade is on the wrong track, and he may find it out, but I don't intend to wait for that. Mrs. Carne, can you think of any way by which Otway could have brought his horse in at four forty-five and yet have been in the Wilderness between four thirty and four forty?"

"It is impossible. Surely you don't suspect Otway! It is unthinkable!"

"I suspect everyone except you."

"Don't waste time on Otway. His life was bound up with Dan's."

"That doesn't convince me. But—apparently—he did not have time—and that does. I must work on other lines."

"It is all unthinkable!" She moved, as if she tried to evade some intolerable pressure. "Who is there? Dick? No, no! Ralph? I can't believe it."

"Revel?"

"He worshipped Dan. You have seen that for yourself."

"He had known your husband for over a year. You yourself told me that sooner or later his friends found him out, and then, with the exception of Furness, who seems to have still felt a need of him, and you, who felt his need of you, and Otway, who, I suspect, shared his unscrupulousness and benefited by it, they turned against him. What if Revel did that? He is impetuous. He could act hastily, violently, I am sure. Why did he give your husband that vicious horse to tame?"

"Pink Livery? Why do you harp on that?"

"I'm going to find out about that horse."

Lady Carne-Hilton came into the room, and her husband followed. I asked to be excused from dining, on account of work to be done, and went to my room to write up my notes. But I had resolved to use my discretion about what I told Brade, and from now on I worked independently. The young footman brought me dinner, but Colman himself appeared with coffee and brandy, so I had an opportunity to talk to him. I found Colman so ready to talk to me that my inquiries required no preliminaries at all. He had the typical servant's mind, afraid of responsibility not in his province.

"The fact is, sir, I'm not quite clear about the rights and the wrongs of it, and I've got something on my mind. I'd rather talk to you than one of these detectives, sir, and maybe you'll advise me, seeing as you are a friend of Mrs. Danvers Came." He looked at me, making of the last remark a question, and I answered emphatically that this was so.

"Why not speak to Sir Ralph?" I asked.

"I tried, sir, but he shut me up. He said: 'If you have anything to say, Mr. Brade is the person to say it to.

"Just so."

"But suppose I'm not asked? There's things that come to my mind, and they may fit in with other things or they may be just imagination. We're all a bit nervy like, sir, and it's easy to see something strange in things we'd never think about in ordinary times. You see what I mean? And to tell the truth, Dr. Jerrold, sir, I care considerably more for Sir Ralph's peace of mind, and Mrs. Danvers Carne's, than I cared about Mr. Danvers."

"You are afraid that what you have to say reflects on one of them?"

"It might and it might not."

I thought of Brade and of all he had said to me.

Suppose what Colman had to say should throw suspicion on Mimi Carne. Did I want to hear it? Was my faith in her proof against evidence that she knew more of the truth than she admitted? Suppose she did love Furness and knew him to be guilty? I had to choose then and there. Women, even women like her, were capable of strange contradictions under the control of passion. So were men, for that matter. Did I mean to defend her from suffering, whatever happened? Could I believe in her in spite of any ugly fact that might come to light? I did and I could. If necessary, I would fight Brade himself for her sake. If Colman had anything to tell me that reflected on her, I would hear it, but I would not pass it on.

Colman was watching me. "I should like to tell you what is on my mind," he said. "It would relieve my feelings, sir, anxious as I am to do right, and not cause difficulty for my master, or for Mrs. Danvers, who is a nice lady, sir, and one we all respect."

I motioned to him to sit down, but he preferred to stand.

"This is all I know, sir," he began. "On Wednesday the house was very much upset, as was only natural. That being the case, the odd-man, whose duty it is to look after the furnace, let the fire down and Lady Carne-Hilton complained that the house was cold. I went down myself to see that the man had not over-stoked the furnace and put the fire out altogether, as sometimes happens if it gets too low. Well, sir, I was very much annoyed to see that someone had just dumped in a pile of rubbish, done up in a newspaper. No one is allowed to interfere with the furnace. All rubbish is deposited in a metal basket supplied for the purpose, and placed on the fire at the discretion of the servant in charge. The paper round the parcel flamed up as I opened the door, and I smelt some material scorching. I took the poker to see what it was. I was very much annoyed, you see, sir. The fire, though low, was extremely hot and the stuff burnt quickly, but the poker caught up what appeared to me to be the remains of a string glove considerably soiled or blackened by the fire, I couldn't say which."

I sprang out of my chair. "But this is important," I exclaimed.

"Yes, sir, but I wasn't positive, sir. Perhaps you will hear what followed before you deal with the information."

Chilled by his manner, I sank back in my chair.

"I thought I heard someone moving on the stair, and feeling sure that the parcel had only just been deposited, I followed the sound. You know there is a staircase, used chiefly by ladies' maids, which runs from the cellar to the top of the house. It is enclosed with doors opening at the landings onto passages, and anyone going up and down is concealed from persons in the halls. I ran up these stairs. Her ladyship's French maid is not liked in the house and considers herself above orders that apply to other servants, so I thought it quite possible that she might be responsible. Whoever was ahead of me seemed to go out into the hall that leads to the principal bedrooms, for the stairs leading to the top floor were empty. When I reached this hall, all the bedroom doors were closed except the one occupied by Mrs. Danvers Carne, and that was just closing."

"Did you make any further investigations?" I asked.

"Yes, sir. I went up and knocked at Mademoiselle's door. Receiving no answer, I looked in. She was not there. Going down again, I met Mrs. Danvers' maid coming up. She said her mistress had rung. I asked her where Mademoiselle was, and she told me she was out with the dog. I was well aware what that meant, sir. She is extremely friendly with Jennings, the chauffeur."

"You think that you followed so closely on this person's heels that he or she could not have entered one of the rooms and shut the door before you reached the hall?"

"That was my impression, sir."

"What did you do then?"

"I concluded that Mrs. Danvers had wished to destroy something and I went about my business."

"And you have not mentioned this to anyone?"

"No, sir."

I realized in what a predicament I found myself. If a new inquest should be demanded, Colman could hardly refuse to repeat, under examination, what he had told me, probably with the added information that he *had* told me. I remembered with a sinking of the heart the letters which Mimi Carne had pointed out, and her remark that she kept her odds and ends in the basement at Marpen Hall. She had certainly visited that cellar since Tuesday and would have had an opportunity to burn what she liked, and the letters might have made an excuse if she had encountered anyone on the stairs.

"Will you take me to the cellar?" I asked, more to gain

time for thought than for any other reason.

Colman led me down the stairs he had described. The cellar was more a basement than a cellar proper, and ran under the whole of the older part of the house. At one end were larders, wine-cellars, a boot-hole, and the drying-room, with a separate stair to the kitchen wing. At the other, servants' rooms, designed when servants did live half below ground, and sometimes used for menservants now. The store-room, where spare trunks and articles of furniture were kept, was at the bottom of the staircase leading to the central part of the house, and near the furnace-room.

"As I see it, almost anyone might have approached the furnace-room and gone out at one door when you came in at the other. It is a perfect place for hide-and-seek."

"Yes, sir," answered Colman doubtfully.

"Of course, if you are questioned—that is, if there should be further official inquiry into Mr. Carne's death— you will have to tell all you know, but for the present perhaps it is not necessary," I said.

"I thought you would feel that way about it, sir. It is a relief to my mind to have told you."

I had no doubt whatever that it was, but it certainly was no relief to my mind to have this burden shifted onto it.

10 p.m., Friday

At ten o'clock, while I was writing, Colman brought me a message that Sir Ralph would be glad if I would join him in his study. This was a small room on the eastern side of the house. A library of gardening and sporting books occupied one side of the walls, and hunting prints of some value hung between the fireplace and windows. Over the fireplace was a map of the county, and another map was spread on the writing-table when I entered. Carne-Hilton and Brade were bending over it, and a man I had not seen before sat beside them, a note-book and pencil poised on his knee.

Brade was struggling with one of his hand-made cigarettes, which had to be removed and re-rolled at every other puff. He looked up as I entered.

"Sir Ralph is going to tell us about the hunt on Tuesday," he explained. "I want you to listen and write it down, Jerry dear. This gentleman will take down what he says in shorthand, but you do put things so scientifically. It is improving to the mind!"

I swore at him politely and settled down in one of the easy chairs. Very soon there was a pleasant fog of tobacco smoke in the small room. Carne-Hilton seemed at his ease with Brade as he lit his pipe and began his story.

"Brade has asked me to tell him everything I can remember about the day, especially what I can recall about the members of our own party. Naturally, I had my eye on them all, as they were riding my horses, and Furness and Revel were mounted on two young geldings I had bought lately from Vane, so I wanted to see how they went. My horses and my garden are about the only interest in life the war left me, outside my son, and I take a good deal of pride in my stables. Also I have to pick my personal mounts with care, on account of my crippled leg. I fancied the colt Furness was riding and went out of my way to watch his performance. We met at Langdale Crossroads." He stopped to show us the place on the map. "The ladies motored to the meet with me, Barnet riding my mare and leading the other two mounts. Miss Trent rides astride, but Mimi Carne uses a side-saddle. Revel and Furness hacked to the meet with Barnet, taking a short cut across the park. Dan also hacked, but, as you heard at the inquest, he was delayed by the alterations to his bridle and stirrup leathers and arrived just as we were moving off. I noticed that Otway was not there with Dan's second horse, and was annoyed that he should be late. The country is a difficult one, and though Otway had followed hounds before, I was afraid he might miss Dan unless he rode with the other second horsemen. The small car which had brought the ladies went on to Groves Ford. I always keep one car out when a party from the Hall is hunting, for convenience of ladies and any who wish to go home before the end of the day. Barnet took the other car home and met me with my covert hack—a very old-fashioned proceeding, but one that saves me a good deal of tedious riding."

There followed a minute description of the first draw, and the hack to Groves Ford.

"As you see, the country is heavily wooded, and the weather was so unfavourable that it was a trying morning for the young horses. Furness had some trouble with his, and kept away from the crowd for this reason. I spoke to him once or twice. I also noticed that Dan picked us up while we were drawing the first covert and rode beside Marion Trent most of the time. This annoyed me; for certain reasons, which I think you both know, I was very anxious that Furness should not suspect anything. Dan's suspicions of Mimi and Furness seemed to me quite outrageous and I knew Furness to be quick-tempered, and wanted to spare Mimi anything like a scene. They had both stuck to Dan through so many impossible situations that I was prepared to use any pressure to stop Dan's manoeuvres. I knew he was unscrupulous, but it seemed past all sense that he should deliberately plan to force Mimi into the divorce court for the sake of marrying an heiress." He continued to follow the movements of the hunt. There was a flurry of a few minutes from Groves Ford. He described the line and the performance of his horses.

"Dan and Marion Trent were missing and I saw them later coming out of the wood below Noke Hill," he said.

"Who else in your party would have noticed that?" asked Brade, with more eagerness than I had seen him display.

"Why, all of us who were there, I suppose—Furness, Revel, Mimi."

"Furness was riding with the field then?"

"Yes. I think we were all there."

"How far were you from the cars and second horsemen?"

"Oh, they were below on the road. They could not see us."

"So only you four knew that Miss Trent and Carne were missing?"

"Yes."

After that they hacked to Noke Hill, where they spent some time over a hopeful drain, without result. "Then I made one of my detours, which save me a lot of tiresome pounding over the roads, as I knew they would draw Chess Spinney. I lost sight of the main field, but some of the second horsemen caught up with me, and among them was Otway. When I saw him he was apparently directing a stranger, following the hunt in a Morris two-seater. We get far too many cars from London and the neighbourhood taking a day's outing in this way. I noticed this man because something about the cut of his clothes suggested that he was an American or a Colonial.

"We waited for the field at Cookson's Pond and eventually heard hounds in the woods just above. I rode up to join them. By this time the tenderer members of the field had already dropped out, as the weather was forbidding—a misty rain on the hill-tops and a rainy mist below, thick as a fog in some places. All of our party were there except Dan and Marion Trent. Otway had stopped with the other second horsemen below at the pond."

He described the circling of the wood and the subsequent move towards Chess Spinney. "On the way we drew a small covert and started a likely dog fox. We ran fairly fast across Lee Farm and I was pleased to see the style in which Threws—the young gelding Furness rode—topped a bit of stiff timber. I kept behind to watch his performance over two or three cut-and-laid hedges— one of them supported by a ditch on two sides. The ditch was full of rather dirty-looking water and put the young horse off, and Furness, afraid of getting left, I suppose, rode down to the gate that gave on the road while the field cut away to the right. I followed Furness, for my leg was aching and I knew that the country ahead was cut up with ploughed fields. We ran into the second horsemen, following along the lane below, and I cantered along the grassy edge. We could not see the field over the rise, but I knew pretty well the line the fox would take. I saw Otway ride up to Furness. They drew behind and must have been talking for some time. I looked over my shoulder and saw that Furness seemed angry, and that Otway was talking to him earnestly. At the corner we heard hounds again and turned towards Marpen village. When I rejoined hounds, Dan was coming down through a gate, but Miss Trent was not with him. Furness rode up. The second horsemen had gone down another road that skirts the Wilderness. I saw Furness ride up to Dan, but Revel was talking to him, and I saw Revel help himself from Dan's flask. As we turned for Chess Spinney, Dan wheeled round and made for the Wilderness. Furness must have seen this at the same time, for he went after him. I had a moment or two of doubt whether to follow them or not, for I had a distinct impression that Furness was upset by something, and I connected it with his conversation with Otway, but of course I may have been wrong.

"We drew Chess Spinney. By this time nearly everyone had gone home and I should have done so myself if we had not been more or less heading for Marpen. There is a good bit of country on the other side of the Wilderness, and we found in the spinney, and the fox headed for Barwell, as you have heard. We had a bit of parkland to cross, with some timber."

Brade interrupted. "Please tell us everything you can about the obstacles—fences, water, timber and all," he asked; "and just what happened to each of the riders, so far as you can remember, and just when Furness rejoined you."

Carne-Hilton went over the hunt in minute detail. He seemed to remember everything. He saw Mimi Carne's horse peck at a fence. Furness had caught up with them perhaps ten minutes before, and he had seen Trews clear a stile in the best of form, also a small stream. It was just after this that Mimi drew up and turned for the Wilderness. Furness had been riding rather carelessly, he thought, considering the inexperience of his mount. He saw Furness say something to Mimi as she cut out of the field. At that moment Otway had ridden up. This was about four o'clock, judging from the time the hunt finished and the distance travelled. He himself caught up with Otway and told him his master had gone home. He also directed him to follow along, as they were near a lane which would take him to the road to Marpen.

"You will see from the map that Mimi left the hunt just before we crossed this lane." He put his pencil on the spot. "She might have followed this to the high road, but to ride across country and through the Wilderness was a trifle quicker, and no doubt thinking it softer going for her mount, lacking a shoe, she took that way. But by the time I spoke to Otway we had galloped nearly a mile in the opposite direction and put several big fences behind us, so his best way was by the road. I was enjoying the run, which was by far the best of the day, and we were all keen to get our fox before he went to ground at Cranmere, where the chalky soil is almost impossible to stop effectively. I watched Furness over four fences and saw Trews make a mistake at the last one and left him behind. It was just there"; he pointed out the place. "That must have been at four twenty or a little later. Revel and I carried on, but when I saw that the fox had got to ground I dismounted at once, and as Barnet was there with my hack, I got on and rode home. You'll see we had been riding back in that direction for about a quarter of an hour. It was a twenty-minute hack for me, but a good deal longer for a tired horse by road. As a matter of fact, Barnet lingered to watch them try to get out the fox and didn't get back till about five twenty, so he said. Revel came on later, as he told you. Barnet was down in the hollow with the huntsman and I suppose he didn't notice him, so he took his directions from the farm-hand and happened to pass the chalk-pit, which I had avoided by half the length of a fifty-acre field. Furness must have come up a few minutes later and ridden almost in my tracks. I was suffering from my leg by that time, and once the run was over, I got home as fast as I could. Rogers, the stable-boy, came to the door for my horse, and Colman was fussing over my bath. I was in it by the time Revel came with the news."

Brade had had his nose glued to the map most of the time.

"Damn!" he said earnestly.

"What's wrong?" inquired Sir Ralph, with the lift of an eyebrow.

"These times! It's impossible to check them. You say, for instance, that it was twenty minutes from Cranmere Farm, where the fox went to ground, to Marpen Hall at a fast trot. What about a fast gallop? The same thing applies to all the timing, you see. Mrs. Carne was in at the right time supposing she rode slowly. But if she hurried, she could have had fifteen minutes to spare. Likewise Barnet—likewise everybody! Also," he added,

"Mr. Revel seems to have ridden pretty nearly in the opposite direction he wanted to take to have visited that chalk-pit."

"It looks like it. But it's a much easier mistake to make than you'd think, in the mist. If he could see the Wilderness at all, it must have looked like a blur on the sky-line. And he says he rode up to the chalk-pit on purpose."

Brade nodded thoughtfully. He now went over every word of what Carne-Hilton had said, very much as if he was learning it for a part in a play. By the time he had finished I think I could have ridden the line the field took that day without going astray at a single point. He made one or two mistakes, which Carne- Hilton corrected, and drew from him further details. Even the exact spot where he ate a ham sandwich and took a pull from his flask were noted. Then he turned to me. "Jerry dear, I want you to run Sir Ralph up to London in the one and only Rolls," he said. "He tells me that Lord Belfare is in town and is anxious for news. It is an opportunity."

"Tonight?" I asked, not loath to avail myself of the chance of avoiding questions about my conversation with Colman.

"As soon as you possibly can go. And I want a little chat with Sir Ralph first while Colman is packing his toothbrush. You will both help me enormously by going at once."

Carne-Hilton looked at him curiously, but made no objection.

"And," Brade went on, "when you come back, I've a little plan, so don't be away too long or you'll spoil it!"

Half an hour later we were on our way to town, where we arrived about twelve thirty, to find that Belfare House was vacant and his lordship with friends in Surrey. "Better phone Brade," suggested Sir Ralph.

I did so, and heard Brade's voice urging me to travel to Surrey at once. "He knows what I want," said Brade. "Don't delay!"

"I suppose we had better go," said Sir Ralph when I told him.

"Is the information of such enormous importance as all that?" I asked. He smiled.

"He says he wants to know how Belfare heard about Dan's debts, but personally I think he wants us out of the way for twenty-four hours," he replied, "and I don't mind obliging him!"

While we slipped out of London, Carne-Hilton became almost talkative. "Brade has not told me why he believes that Dan was murdered," he said. "I suppose you know his reasons. Do you agree with them?"

"I know some of them, and I certainly think the matter cannot be dropped where it is."

"I suppose everything points to Furness. It is only necessary to prove that he knew Dan's plans for getting rid of Mimi to give him motive enough. And he was the only person who had the opportunity."

I did not reply to that, but, with a sickness at my heart, I realized that in view of what he had himself told us about the hunt Mimi Came might equally have had the opportunity. Carne-Hilton was still taking it for granted that his cousin had been killed and dragged long before four.

"Lucky I'm let out by the time," he said thoughtfully. "I suppose Dan must have been killed round about three thirty. And half a dozen people saw me with the hunt then. Otherwise, according to Brade's reasoning, I might have done it. I was the first person to leave when the fox went to ground, ten minutes at least before anyone else. Supposing Dan to have sat still for an hour after falling at that tree, and supposing I had happened to know it, I've no alibi, and heaven knows there's sufficient motive."

"But your leg, Sir Ralph. Could you have done it?"

"Well—I don't know. The doctors have always said I might recover the use of those muscles suddenly in a crisis."

This was quite reasonable. I myself had on record

cases of the kind. How had Brade missed this possibility? Or had he? We drove on in silence while I checked up what he had told me of the run. I did not see how it left a loop-hole for the suspicion that he had been absent from the field after Carne left it.

We had warned the Surrey household of our visit and found Lord Belfare waiting for us. He is a familiar figure to everyone and manages to suggest his reactionary attitude towards life by his dress, manner, and the very type of healthiness and vitality which has withstood his years. He greeted me warmly, with an air of knowing exactly who I was, whether he did or not. We settled down by the fire, and Carne-Hilton answered his quick questions. I offered to leave them alone, but they refused.

"No, no—you know all about it, and more than Ralph probably. This Mr. Brade—I've heard of him before—he seems the right man for the case. Is there any chance of its being kept from the public?"

"I don't know," I replied truthfully. "There is a certain amount of talk already in the village."

"Yes, the people always get hold of these things. Trust Dan to make trouble and scandal for the family, dead or alive., Now, about that letter. It came to me typed, without signature, and said: 'Go to the secretary of the Ace of Spades Club and ask for information about the resignation of your nephew, Danvers Carne. If you offer to pay his debts he may tell you the truth.' I destroyed the letter, but I carried out the advice it contained. And I found out enough from various people to convince my brother Donald that he could not trust Dan with capital, if he had the interests of the family at heart. The date on which I received the letter was June 30th of last year, and the postmark was Ealing. That's all I know."

I wrote down what he had said and gave it to him to confirm.

"If Furness should be charged, I suppose it means that Mimi's name will be dragged in." He turned to me. "I hope not."

"Unavoidable, I should say. The Crown wouldn't miss such a chance of finding motive. I should like you to tell her that I shall do all in my power to show that I support her. I have every possible confidence in her. I shouldn't blame her for falling in love with another man, but if that man had been Furness she would never have used him as she did to befriend Dan. Depend upon it, if there is any evidence of a liaison between them, it will be fraudulent."

"That is what I think," said Carne-Hilton. "But Mimi could not have foreseen such a situation, and appearances may be against her. Furness used to be in and out of their flat at all times and he often travelled with them."

"Yes, and there are no saving conventions nowadays. You no longer know what to think when a man is seen coming out of a lady's bedroom, but juries are old-fashioned in that respect, I believe."

Lord Belfare seemed to think we had talked enough about the matter. "What about the garden, Ralph?" he asked.

"Oh, it's going on slowly."

"You had better take my advice about that terrace."

"Can't afford it, my dear man."

"Nonsense! I know what your income is to the last penny. Can't think what you do with it all. And the sale of your collection went well."

Sir Ralph said nothing, but I thought of his wife, her clothes, the Greek room—what else? Unimaginative people are always expensive, because everything that amuses them has to be manufactured by someone else.

I left Lord Belfare with his nephew and went to my room to write up my notes.

When I reached Brade's comment on Revel's mistake in riding towards the chalk-pit, I stopped to think. It seemed to me that there were a good many points about that young man's behaviour which needed clearing up. Suddenly I resolved to set about it, and just then I heard Carne-Hilton come upstairs, talking to his uncle. I stopped them as they passed my door.

"Would you very much object to going back to Marpen now?" I asked.

"But it's nearly three," protested Lord Belfare.

"I want to go on to Oxford. I've had a brain-wave. It may or may not be of use—I can't tell."

Lord Belfare looked at me shrewdly.

"You are worried about this case?"

"Yes. And there isn't too much time to spare. As the facts stand, Furness may be arrested just as soon as Sir Ralph is obliged to consult the police. You must remember that Mrs. Carne came to me for help, and I intend to help her if I can. So far, Brade has succeeded only in bringing out facts that tell against her."

"Of course I'll go now if you like," Sir Ralph agreed.

My car had been garaged for the night, but Lord Belfare roused his own servant, who managed to get the key of the garage, and in half an hour we were travelling along nearly deserted roads, avoiding London and making the best time towards the Bramshire hills.

"What's the brave idea?" Carne-Hilton asked once.

"I don't think I'll tell you. It's too vague. But it's been growing, and I mean to find out if there's anything in it."

He did not ask me any more questions and I dropped him at his own front door just as the east was greying and the chill of the departing night blew drearily across the land. Carne-Hilton shivered. He looked exhausted in the light he switched on inside the door. "Come in and have some coffee," he suggested. "No use killing yourself."

"I'd rather not wait. I'll get breakfast somewhere."

He said no more, and I drove away.

I had a young nephew at Christ Church—a quick-witted young man, and interested in my work, with a great idea of my abilities. I had never done anything to enlighten him on this point, finding his admiration agreeable. I thought it would be useful now, and so it was.

By the time I drew up under the grey walls of the old

town, the day was already beginning for those who serve others more fortunate. It took me a few minutes to rouse the tousle-haired youth, and further seconds to convince him that I was not a figure out of a bad dream, but at last he let me in and, fully awake, made some tea and listened to my demands.

"Revel—yes, I've heard about him. Some feller got hold of him. Was it the Oxford Group or New Thought, or what? Weird—I know that. There's a man who used to run around with him a bit. I can find out for you, Jerry. But what's the game?"

I tried to arouse his interest without telling him more than I must.

"I've heard that story about Pink Livery. And now I come to think of it, there was a real proper dust-up over the business. A servant got into trouble. Oh, we'll find out, Jerry. What a chance to cut work for a day! Hurray!"

It may not have been his idea of work, but we were not idle that morning, and when we settled down to lunch at the Mitre I felt repaid for my expedition. My nephew's eyes were bright and inquisitive, and as he had certainly been helpful I rewarded him.

"Look here, my boy, if you want to do me a service, follow this up," I began. "Get all the evidence cut and dried for me. I may want to use it and I may not, but if I do, it will be a matter of life and death."

"Who to, Jerry?"

For some reason the question confused me. Mimi Carne with her innocence and her intolerable position was so constantly in my mind that it was difficult to speak of her to this curious young man.

"To a patient of mine."

"Female?" he inquired innocently.

"As a matter of fact—yes."

"Oh!" There was a short and, for me, embarrassing silence.

As we came out half an hour later, I felt my shoulder jostled and turned to face a man who glared at me with a pair of reddened eyes. His clothes were old and shabby, his manner insolent, and his face flushed with drink.

"You're here prying into my affairs," he remarked truculently, "and you're not the first in the last week either. I've had just about enough of it, I'll tell you."

I looked at Ted.

"Have a drink?" he said sociably. "Come along, I've got the stuff."

"Oh, I'll come fast enough! And not for a drink either, if you're a friend of that—swine that calls himself a gentleman."

"Now, now, all in good time, my man!" Ted hustled him along and presently had him seated, soothed by a large tumbler of whisky and soda, in the privacy of the room where I had already breakfasted.

"Now, tell us!"

"You've been prying into my affairs, you have, and I'm not going to stand for it. What's finished is finished and that's all there is to it. Not heard of the matter for a year, I haven't, and now inside a week three nosy people poking and prying. It's more'n a man can stand."

"Tell us the whole story—and there'll be something for you," Ted suggested pleasantly. "You see, we don't even know who you are."

"I'm a gentleman born. It's horses brought me where I am today. That and people like yourselves that take advantage of a man's misfortunes."

He showed signs of blubbering. Ted cut him short. Little by little we wormed out of him the facts. It was he who had sold Pink Livery to Revel. He swore the most elaborate oaths to convince us that he believed the horse to be identical with the one who carried off the open race at the Amateur Jockeys' Point-to-Point meeting in the spring of '31. The horse didn't belong to him. He sold him on commission. At that time he owned a business which, I gathered, was already marked for liquidation, hiring out hacks and hunters and dealing in horse-flesh. He didn't know the name of the owner for whom he acted, but was willing to handle the deal.

When "young Revel," as he called him, found out that he had been swindled, he sought out this man and attacked him.

"Tight as a sailor he was, and nearly killed me. I've got the mark yet." He threw back his hair and showed a huge scar. "Fell against an iron fence, I did, and lucky for young Revel I didn't peg out. He got off all right. He's rich, and I'm not. Nothing but injustice in life for me since I was born—that's the truth."

"And I believe you are drawing a comfortable allowance, as a result of the affair," Ted remarked gently, "and you wouldn't like to lose it."

He began to whine then. We tried to find out if he knew any more, but he did not, or he would have given it away, so we let him go, with a pound note.

"It's a fishy business, but pretty clear," said Ted thoughtfully. "The man who owned Pink Livery bribed Cat o' the Hills' groom. The two horses are blood brothers and alike in build and colour. Cat o' the Hills won the race under Pink Livery's name and your friend rode him, knowing or not knowing the fraud. If he did know, he probably pocketed some of the cash when Pink Livery was sold as winner of the race. I suppose that's what you wanted to know."

"Some of it. What I'd like to know is—did Revel believe Carne knew he was riding the wrong horse? Or has he found out lately that he did know?"

"And done him in eighteen months afterwards? Oh, come!"

"Not for that, Ted. But suppose, in the meantime, he had fallen under Carne's influence. Suppose he thought him a saint. Suppose he gave up the girl he loved to Carne—and then found this out? Wouldn't his faith in his hero collapse at one stroke? Wouldn't he see a hundred things he hadn't seen before? And suppose he faced Carne with it and Carne exposed himself, and he thought of the girl who believed in him still and meant to marry him.

3.15 p.m., Saturday, February 11th

The plan was this:

Carne-Hilton, Revel, Marion Trent, Mimi, Furness, and Otway were to ride as nearly as possible over the ground traversed on the day of the accident and I was to check off the times as well as I could from a table which Carne-Hilton handed me. From Groves Ford to Cookson's the action was to be sketched out roughly. That is, checks in the hunt and the wait in Cookson's wood were to be counted off without repeating the time wasted. But from three twenty, when Danvers Carne left the field, to the end was to be as nearly accurate, minute by minute, as possible, reading our watches with an hour's difference.

Barnet was to represent Carne. Rogers in the stables and Colman in the house were to check the times of arrival, and the whole action was to be moved forward an hour to allow for the difference in light between a day darkened by heavy mist and that of a clear, though clouded, evening. Lady Carne-Hilton and Miss Legend would repeat their movements, and everyone was to note the least divergence from pattern in the timing or behaviour of any one of the actors in this sinister drama.

The difficulty was to find a leader, since no one wished the affair to be made a matter of public gossip. The permission of the farmers had been obtained, but they were all well known to Sir Ralph and he trusted them to keep silence for a time at least. Eventually, he had asked the second whipper-in, who was a friend of Barnet's and had been on duty on the day of the accident, to lead the field over the line.

It was as grim and nervous a party as can be imagined. Brade alone seemed unconcerned and I was amused to watch Barnet's face as he noticed how comfortably he sat the dark chestnut gelding. The horses were infected with the uneasiness of their riders. We cantered across the park, having some difficulty not to break into a scamper, and crossed the Agminton high road, rode through a gate, up a hill, and down again to Groves Ford.

"Where is Revel?" asked Brade. "I thought he was with us."

I had not taken the boy's threat to ride Pink Livery seriously, but now I remembered it.

"There he is. My God—he's got that horse!" Sir Ralph exclaimed.

Pink Livery came along quietly enough, but his wicked head and slanted ears did not add to our comfort. Sir Ralph betrayed his annoyance by a tightening of his lips. Mimi exclaimed: "Oh, why has he done such a thing today? I am frightened!" I moved to her side.

"You must be careful," I said. "This is a mad scheme of Brade's anyway. Everyone's nervous. So are the horses. Don't jump more than you can help. And leave timber alone."

The young whipper-in, named Frank, was waiting beside a narrow bridge. Women came out to look at us from cottage doors, and children ran to the gates. We gathered in a circle, while Carne-Hilton went over his notes of the ride, directing Frank to travel over the line hounds had taken. "You, Miss Trent, ride with Barnet as nearly as possible as you did with Dan that day. Furness, you went by the lower field. I saw you jump three fences. From Noke Hill to Cookson's I can't direct you, as I took a short cut. Otway and I ought to meet below if he finds his way all right. I leave Otway at the pond and rejoin you in Cookson's wood. Miss Trent rides home, where she will help Rogers with the timing there. We don't know exactly what Dan did after Miss Trent left him, but Barnet can take up the trail at the gate on the lane which I've showed him. I follow Furness from Cookson's and we meet again at Chess Spinney, barring Furness. I can check things again when we get to Cookson's. We must be at Chess Spinney at four forty whatever happens. You've all got watches? I make it three forty-five now. Can we do it all right, Frank?"

"Yes, sir, if we cut out all the checks and the time it took to draw the wood."

"Then come on!"

I looked at Marion Trent. Her bright and intelligent eyes were fixed on Carne-Hilton's face, and she at least would play her part with passionate precision, I thought.

The horses were uneasy, taking it for some kind of a point-to-point race. I followed Mimi Carne, but I was able to keep my eye on Revel and admire the performance of that outrageous beast of his, which, for the moment, went like a saint in horse-flesh. It was a fast ride over firm turf and I hoped Pink Livery would be in a good temper for the rest of the day after such a beginning, but when Frank stopped us and led the way through gates and up a lane to Noke Hill, he was sawing at his bit and rolling his eyes. I distrusted him heartily.

Mimi's mare was nervous and refused a fence once or twice. I saw Brade watching her as she put the thoroughbred at it the second and third time. My horse, a confidential beast and the quietest of the lot, gave her a lead, and she was on the right side at last, but her face showed that it had cost her a struggle.

"I never thought I could find a ride so horrible," Mimi said as we cantered on.

I had memorized the ride from Noke Hill to Cookson's, according to the combined accounts of Mimi, Revel, and Furness. Barnet, in Danvers Carne's place, and Miss Trent were not in sight. Carne-Hilton was repeating his detour, and Otway, representing the second horsemen, was on the road below. But the others rode the same line, jumped the same fences, and kept roughly the same time. Once Mimi and I found ourselves alone, cut off from Revel and Furness by a strip of common covered with gorse. She pulled up. "I'm wrong," she said. "I should have taken the low ground. We must get back."

To do so without loss of time we found ourselves

forced to descend a steep, chalky hillside, pitted with rabbit-burrows. When we were half-way down, we saw Furness and Revel galloping ahead, in the field below. It was impossible to hurry the horses, who slipped and scrambled precariously as they made the descent. My mount took it calmly, but Mimi's pretty thoroughbred did not care for this work and tossed her head impatiently as Mimi held her back. She would have made a short business of it, one way or another, by galloping down to reach the others, if left to herself, with the likelihood of falling before she had taken a dozen strides.

"Keep in my tracks," I directed, and Mimi obediently slid along behind me. Once the mare bounced past me and slipped. I saw Mimi's face. She had lost her nerve, but not her courage, and regained her place in a moment. That descent seemed endless, but we did reach the firm turf safely, with Furness, Revel, and Frank far ahead and out of sight.

"Can you remember the way?" I called as we galloped on.

"I think so. That farm was on our right—the wood up there on the left. There's a stream somewhere. Yes. I crossed close to that gate, I think."

I had difficulty in keeping up with her, for my mount was not so fast as hers, and the thoroughbred no longer refused her fences. She flew at them, and Mimi gave her her head, afraid, I think, that if she tried to control her she would do the wrong thing in her nervousness. I have seen women win point-to-point races in the same spirit, and heard veteran horsemen declare that it sent their hearts to their boots to watch them. Mine was in my boots most of the way to Cookson's wood. The fences were not big, but they were stiff, and Mimi did not stop to choose her place.

We were the last to arrive at Cookson's wood, and the others were waiting impatiently.

"I went wrong at that common," Mimi apologized. "Sorry!"

Revel displayed a bruised eye, but no one made any comment on it. Pink Livery was giving him trouble now, in earnest. Once he kicked out viciously when Carne-Hilton moved up a step too close.

Furness came towards Mimi. "We're to do the next run now. Keep the farm on your left this time and watch for a haystack with some sheep-hurdles about a mile on. That's where we turn back towards the village."

Brade was looking plaintive. "I do hope everybody will remember everything this time. Mr. Furness and Sir Ralph are the only two who seem quite sure where they went and what they did!"

Revel spoke up furiously. "I remember perfectly. But this brute won't look at timber and it's no use to try to make him. He's nearly killed me once already."

"You needn't have brought him along, you know, Mr. Revel. Nobody asked him."

Pink Livery bared his teeth and bit the bark off a tree-trunk.

"Bless his amiable little soul!" murmured Brade.

Revel, infuriated, gave a wicked twitch at his bridle. Pink Livery responded by a plunge against my horse that nearly unseated both Revel and myself.

"If I were you, I should avoid those rails at the bottom. Go round by the haystack. There's a gate," Furness advised Revel.

But Revel's temper was up. Frank led us straight towards the rails. Mimi, Carne-Hilton, Revel, and Furness had jumped them before and they all followed Frank now.

"For God's sake, keep away from that brute!" I shouted at Mimi as we galloped side by side. It flashed across my mind that if Revel intended to spoil the experiment, he was going the right way about it. An accident would put an end to the proceedings, and he seemed to be riding for a fall. Pink Livery, thoroughly out of hand, flew the rails. There was a crash. Horse and rider were down in a confused mass, and Mimi's thoroughbred swerved, took the rails aslant, brushed into a thorn tree, which took Mimi in the shoulder and swept her off, as the mare galloped on.

I spared no thought for Revel, but reined in my mount and went to Mimi. She got up quickly, and Frank caught the thoroughbred's bridle and led him back. Revel was up, too; he had kept the reins and he and the horse seemed to be unhurt. "Put his knees into it, the bloody brute," he swore furiously. "Come here, you devil!" He set his teeth and scrambled to his seat.

"We're losing time, you know," Brade complained, his bridle over his arm, and his hands full of tobacco and cigarette-paper. He was trying to roll himself a cigarette, which he would have no chance to smoke, and failing more dismally than usual.

The clouds were sailing in rolling folds over our heads, a south-west wind was rattling the stiff branches of trees that dotted the hedges, the turf under my feet was springy and pleasant. It was a soft evening such as the huntsman loves. I could remember such scenes and such days in my boyhood, when a fall was an incident that added a tinge of excitement to the wild joy of a scamper across the field. But there were no hounds giving tongue ahead, to cheer us on. The joy of a ride with good comrades beside us and the urge of the chase were absent. Even my own mount knew the difference and moved restlessly, bewildered and scared. Mimi's thoroughbred was shaking under her smooth skin, and Mimi was shaking too, as she remounted from my hand.

Frank looked at his watch. "We'd better miss out the rest of this run if we're to meet Mr. Barnet at the village on time," he suggested.

"So we had," Brade agreed. "I expect we'll miss out quite a lot before we've done. Well, well, it will be interesting to see what we do miss out, won't it, Jerry dear?"

Personally, I think we'd better go home and stop this foolery," I answered with some heat. "It's a farce."

"No, no, I shouldn't say that."

"If it doesn't end in tragedy."

"Dear Jerry, don't be melodramatic! It's worse than being boyish!"

We followed Frank down the field to a lane and turned towards Marpen village.

"This is the way I came," Furness explained, "and of course it puts us all out. I fell in with the second horsemen and rode along beside Otway. Carne-Hilton rode through the village and I went on with the second horsemen along the lane. That was how Otway missed Dan, who must have crossed the lane behind us and got onto the road through that gate. Is that right, Sir Ralph?"

"Yes, that's how it was. The second horsemen rode on to the end of the lane and waited there, and the field turned back towards Chess Spinney. That was when Revel spoke to Dan. You came along behind. That's clear enough. Most of the grooms must have gone home then, seeing that their masters had gone, but Otway must have ridden up the lane and joined us just when Mimi turned for home. There's Otway!"

We were sorted out again. Revel, Furness, Mimi, and I followed the lane with Frank to the crossroads below Cookson's. Furness joined Otway behind us. We turned back towards the village and saw Carne-Hilton coming on with Barnet. Revel moved up to Barnet to repeat the episode of the brandy-flask, but Sarah backed away from Pink Livery, her ears pointing at her tail.

"She's cross as two sticks, she is, sir," Barnet confided in me. "Never seen 'er in such a temper. This play-actin' don't suit 'er, that's wot it is. Tain't sensible, and she knows it. And she can't abide that 'orse. No more can I!"

"I wish we could all go home, Barnet, and stop this business. It's dangerous."

"And so do I, sir," he agreed earnestly. "Why, Dr. Jerrold, sir, they're my very words. Why, sir, it'll surprise me if I don't 'ave a stable full of lame 'orses before we're through."

I smiled for the first and last time that day.

The light was changing, but full darkness was more than an hour away. I looked at my watch. It was four twenty.

"Ride on, Barnet," ordered Carne-Hilton. "You know what you have to do."

I looked at Brade and remembered suddenly that Barnet did not know. So far, Carne-Hilton had directed his movements and he believed that Danvers Carne had been thrown and dragged immediately, which meant that he would reach the chalk-pit almost an hour before the right time. It was not my affair, however, and Brade had disappeared. By that time I cared less about the success of the experiment than to see Mimi home.

"Are you all right?" I asked.

"Yes, just wrenched my shoulder a little. It's nothing." But her attempt to reassure me with a smile miscarried and ended in a twist of the lips that had the opposite effect.

Furness followed Barnet as we made our way to the spinney.

"Time this carefully, Frank," said Carne-Hilton at his elbow. "At three forty we move off."

Most of us involuntarily glanced at our wrist-watches. I looked around for Brade, but he was not there. Three minutes more to wait. I thought of the trenches in Flanders and remembered how a tuft of long grass had blown into my eyes once while I was waiting, and though, a second before, I thought I was calm enough, panic had seized me when I lost the deliberate stepping of the minute hand.

Four forty. Frank, from the forward edge of the spinney, gave the signal and we were off.

The private park of Lord Hillborough skirted the village at this end and we had to cross a corner of it— fretful work for the horses. There was a carefully mown border to a drive, and a shrubbery which Frank avoided. Here we met with the rails Carne-Hilton had mentioned and here Furness appeared, cutting across a field from the Wilderness. Carne-Hilton waved him back. "He jumped that stile into the right-of-way," he shouted to me.

Furness drew up, bewildered. I could see what Carne-Hilton meant. A footpath ran through the park, and to reach us Furness must have left the Wilderness farther along and found himself on the wrong side of this fenced boundary, jumped the stile, and arrived at the stream where it widened out, while the main field would have avoided the stile and leapt the stream under a willow where it ran between deep banks, it seemed odd that he should have strayed just there, since a man riding a young horse belonging to someone else might have thought twice about these two obstacles.

"He's forgotten," said Carne-Hilton. "He was never near us until we crossed the stream. Good God!"

This last exclamation was caused by Pink Livery, who suddenly seemed to have gone quite mad. The timber infuriated him. Whether he was attempting suicide or murder, I don't know, but after jumping two fences insanely at top speed with room to spare, he took a third as if it were a mole-hill, put his chest into it, went headlong, with such a display of steel hoof and belly as I'd never seen before, and lay there sprawling and struggling, half in the fence and half out, with Revel underneath.

It was not so long as it seemed before Revel rolled clear and stumbled to his feet, got Pink Livery by the bridle, hauled him out of the mass of broken rails, and persuaded him to rise. The horse stood there, shivering, while we formed a group round them and Otway came towards us up the lane, from which we were still separated by a cut-and-laid fence and a bank. I dismounted, but Frank was examining Pink Livery's off foreleg. "Shouldn't be surprised if he's done for," was his curt comment, "and a good job too. You can't ride him, Mr. Revel."

Otway opened a gate and joined us, and suddenly

Brade was there, though where he had been or how he got there I didn't know.

"What's to be done?" Furness asked.

"Oh, we'll go on," Brade said calmly. "Otway's part is finished anyway. He rode straight home from here, didn't he, Sir Ralph? Jerry, suppose you take his place and let him lead Pink Livery to the farm. It can't be far in a straight line from here. Billiam's friend, Mr. Vane, will know what to do. Then we'll get the timing, and that's all we want. Mr. Revel can go on with Otway's mount."

"Yes, that'll do." Carne-Hilton considered. "Mimi went back through the Wilderness. It's just after five now, so that's all right. I make it five three."

"Five four," Brade corrected him. "We allow one hour four minutes difference in the time from here. Mr. Furness spoke to Mrs. Carne. What did you say, Mr. Furness?"

"Oh, I asked her why she was going home."

"Is that right, Mrs. Carne?"

"I didn't hear what he said, but I guessed that was it. So I called back, explaining that my mare had cast a shoe."

"Did you hear what he said?" Brade asked Carne-Hilton.

"No."

"You, Otway?"

"No, sir."

Furness looked quickly from one to the other. "I should have thought one of you must have heard," he protested. "You were both as near as Mimi was."

No one replied.

"Five seven," remarked Brade.

I saw Mimi turn away towards the distant wood, and rode on with the others until we reached the lane. There I parted from them, hacking along towards the high road, glad that Mimi had finished with her part of the experiment. I could see Otway trudging across the field towards Cranmere Farm. The horse was hobbling on three legs, his head drooping, and I did not think he would jump another fence. His day seemed to be ended.

We were now distributed like figures moving along the sticks of a fan; Mimi on the extreme right, hacking towards Marpen, Barnet next to her, Otway on an almost parallel line in the middle, I coming next, and Revel, Carne-Hilton, and Furness with Frank, each group out of sight of the others. I did not know where Brade was. For all I knew, he might be following Mimi. Her direct way would take her well to the north of the fallen tree, according to the rough map which Carne-Hilton had made for us. But to avoid jumping the stream and to make use of gates in the fields, she would naturally have ridden due east and met the ride in the wood almost exactly where her husband had fallen. By her own account, that was what she had done.

I remembered that Brade had been missing some what longer than Furness. Of course, it struck me suddenly, he had followed on and instructed Barnet not to leave the Wilderness until after four thirty and to arrive at the chalk-pit after the time when Billiam had left it. So Mimi and Barnet might meet, and this would make it seem probable that Mimi had seen Carne, dead or alive, in that wood. It seemed to me that only one thing could save her, and that was to fasten the guilt on Revel. But how? What had happened to Carne between three thirty and four fifty or thereabouts? Why, if he had been able to move about after his fall, had he not walked home? There was a possible solution which no one seemed to have considered. Suppose he couldn't walk so far. Suppose his ankle was sprained or his leg injured. Suppose he had heard the horn and knew the hunt could not be far away. Might he have tried to get to Cranmere Farm, after waiting awhile, hoping someone might come along to help him? Might he have met Revel in that way? It was worth a thought.

I had nearly forgotten that I was impersonating Otway when I turned down the high road and saw the car waiting at the edge of the Wilderness. Jennings was at the wheel, and Lady Carne-Hilton was standing on the grass waiting for me.

"Where is Otway?" she demanded hysterically.

I explained, but she only seemed half to understand.

"That's the gate to Marden, I suppose." I pointed to the small gate opposite.

"Yes, sir, that's the way Otway went," Jennings answered, "across that field, straight to the stables."

Lady Carne-Hilton was recovering from her surprise as Miss Legend strolled out of the wood toward us.

"I walked home, of course. But not until I'd been looking for Brune for a few minutes."

"And I drove on with Miss Legend, as soon as she came back," Jennings added.

"Well, go ahead, Jennings." Averil Legend climbed into her seat and drew the rug over her. The time was twenty to six, and dusk was falling fast.

I had a sudden impulse to go through the Wilderness to the chalk-pit, to see the end of the drama. For a moment I thought of asking Jennings to take my place — ride my horse in to check Otway's time—while I walked back. Then I remembered that the others had their parts to play too and decided against it.

I opened the gate and rode across the field, through another gate, and round by a path to the stables.

"You're late by seven minutes," Marion Trent said as she came forward. "Rogers has gone round to take Sir Ralph's horse. Mimi brought hers in nearly to time."

"I suppose I must walk down to the Lodge now," I remarked. "That checks up Otway's movements."

It was farther from the stables to the Lodge than from the gate by which I had entered to the stables. Unsaddling my horse and leaving him comfortable, I turned down the drive. "That disposes of Otway," I thought. Just as I reached the Lodge, I wondered why I had not met Lady Carne-Hilton, and then realized that she had probably taken a short cut too.

The woman at the Lodge had been told to time Otway's arrival there, and I had to make my explanations to her too, so it was a quarter past six when I came out and started back towards the house. When I had walked a few steps, I heard a horse galloping behind me. The hoofs scraped the gravel, and Revel drew up, his face showing white in the dusk.

"Take my horse and ride back to the chalk-pit," he shouted, jumping down. "Otway's lying there and I think he's dead.

6.40 p.m., Saturday

As I look back on the half hour that followed, I am reminded of the mad artist in Dunne's Serial Universe. He set out to paint a picture of the world as he saw it and found that he saw himself painting the picture, and then saw himself seeing himself painting, and so was constrained to go on painting an infinite series of artists painting pictures within other identical pictures of artists painting pictures.

I galloped along the grassy edge of the high road, aware of the cars that slid past, their lights streaming far ahead, growing to blinding brilliance, blackened out behind me, aware of my horse and the need of watching the uncertain going, aware of the grotesque horror of my errand, and aware of myself looking on coolly, observing my own reactions to the event.

Plunging into the Wilderness where the darkness thickened, I made for the lighter edge where the sky had not given itself to the night. Out in the open, lantern-lights moving on the edge of the chalk-pit directed me. Someone took my horse as I jumped down.

"The doctor!"

"This way, sir!"

An electric torch was thrust into my hand and I flashed its light into the pit. It caught on a paleness of hunting pink and a brightness of brass buttons.

For a moment I thought I was seeing a ghost. That was not Otway's body. No one had worn hunting pink today.

"It's only a potato-sack, Jerry," murmured a voice at my elbow—Brade's. "Now, watch your step. We don't want another casualty. Come along, Otway isn't dead."

"Did it give you a start, sir?" asked Barnet. "It was Mr. Brade's idea for me to drag that sack, dressed up like that. She didn't like it, didn't Sarah, and I can't say I blame her. I said there'd be a haccident, didn't I, sir? I'm glad it was only Pink Livery—and, of course, Mr. Otway too."

Brade was right. Otway was not dead. He lay just under the edge of the chalk-pit, but his fall had been broken by a cushion of gorse which he must have struck with his shoulder, rolling over it aslant to the bottom. His head was badly cut, the skull fractured above the right ear, and three ribs broken.

By the time I reached him, darkness had settled close upon us.

Furness was there, with Mr. Vane from the farm, and Billiam's father, a stalwart labourer. While I was examining Otway, Carne-Hilton joined us with Revel. They had driven back together from the house, and before we had carried Otway up the far slope and lifted him into the Ford van which Mr. Vane had brought, the local constable arrived. A soft rain had begun to fall. We made the unconscious man as comfortable as we could and drove off, Mr. Vane at the wheel, the policeman beside him, and I inside with Otway, my fingers on his pulse.

I had not had charge of a surgical case since the early part of the war, but I knew that Otway would hold out until I could get him into more experienced hands, and my mind turned from my patient to the problem his injury presented. He had certainly not fallen into that chalk-pit from sheer carelessness. Mr. Vane told me over his shoulder that Pink Livery was at the farm, where Otway had left him. I guessed that, instead of going straight back to Marpen, he had walked to the chalk-pit to see the end of Brade's plan, just as I had thought of doing. What then? Had anyone witnessed the accident? Was it an accident? Revel's story, as I had grasped it while busy over the injured man, was that he had reached the chalk-pit, seen the pink coat, descended just as he had done on the other occasion, and then discovered Otway, whose dark garments had been obscured by the dusk, half sheltered by the tuft of gorse above.

The van jolted over the cart-track and into the road, but Otway lay inert, so deep in coma that his battered body made no protest. It was five miles to the hospital at Stanbury.

If this was not some incredible accident, it looked like an attempt at murder. Who could be responsible? The person who had killed Carne and feared the servant? Revel? What more likely?

My spirits rose in spite of the tragedy. A car at the rear threw its lights into the van and showed Otway's face. The moment passed, leaving me pitiful. Otway was no saint, but he had never pretended to be better than he was. At least, his devotion to his master showed a dogged faithfulness and he had suffered for it. He was, I guessed from his face, so helpless now in its unconsciousness, an arrogant and vain man for whom the sheer joy of living was absent, who had to have expensive stimuli, money to buy his women, his excitements, his showy clothes. But, serving Carne, he had shared these things, and he had probably worshipped in his master a more refined and complete model of himself. So, at least, I read the relationship. Otway was virile, Carne aesthetic; Otway was direct, Carne devious; Otway probably took no trouble to rationalize his passions, Carne managed to hold the stage as a superman in spite of his behaviour; Otway had excuses which he did not realize himself, perhaps; all Carne's excuses were such as only the psychologist could fathom. I was sorry for Otway.

They were waiting for us at the hospital, and I was busy for nearly an hour with the surgeon in charge.

Then I left Otway, about to be carried into the X-ray room, and went downstairs. Jennings had come for me, but before I could step into my car, my sleeve was grasped and I turned to see a girl standing there. Her face had a robust prettiness, refined at the moment by emotion.

"Will he die?" she asked me. "No one will tell me. Will he die?"

"You mean Otway?"

"Yes—Jim. I am Carol Vane. We are engaged to be married."

"I can't tell you, Miss Vane. But I will telephone later when I hear the result of the X-ray. If the injury to the brain is not serious, I think he may recover. You live at Cranmere Farm?"

"Yes. But don't send a message. My father doesn't know I'm going to marry Jim. They have no idea that I'm here now."

"I will ask for you, then."

"Oh, doctor, if someone could explain to my father! Then perhaps the hospital people would let me be with Jim. If Father would tell them we were engaged, they'd let me see him again—if—if—"

"I don't know your father, Miss Vane. If he disapproves of the engagement—"

"He has no reason. It's only Jim's ideas. You see, he doesn't hold with the silly rules people make for other people, like getting married. He promised to marry me because I hated to hurt Mother. But he taught me to understand that it isn't a wedding that matters, but love—"

"And your father objected to these ideas? I see."

"Doctor—did anyone do this to Jim?"

She pulled me aside, away from Jennings, who was listening.

"I don't know."

"I think—if anyone did—it was that Mr. Revel."

"Why, Miss Vane?"

"Because Jim suspected him of murdering Mr. Carne."

"Mr. Revel was Mr. Carne's friend."

"I know. But people were like that about Mr. Carne. They turned against him. And Mr. Revel asked Jim, the day before Mr. Carne died, if he knew that his master rode Cat o' the Hills under Pink Livery's name in that race. He thinks Mr. Revel was suspicious of Mr. Carne — someone had made mischief. I think it may have been my father. When Mr. Barnet told him that Pink Livery was at Marpen, my father was furious. He said he'd tell Sir Ralph a few facts about that business, and I think he told Mr. Revel instead. Mr. Revel owned the horse, you know."

"That was the day before Mr. Carne died?"

"Yes. Mr. Revel came to look at one of our horses, and Father was in the stables with him a long time."

"Thanks, Miss Vane. I'll remember what you say."

I was not likely to forget it. It fitted too well my own line of reasoning, my own wishes. Not that I had any grudge against young Revel. The truth was that I saw the line tightening around Furness and Mimi Carne, and the only hope was in Revel's guilt. The motive, the opportunity: Mimi and Furness in combination had both, judged by the appearances. There was no one else, so far as I could see, open to the same suspicion, unless it was Revel. Once proved, the attempt on Otway's life weakened the already discredited theory that Danvers Carne had met his death by accident.

As I got into my car I was stopped again, this time by a reporter from a local paper, eager to make use of any scraps of information I would give him. I got rid of him quickly, took the wheel from Jennings, and drove away, but the incident prepared me for the change I found at Marpen. Up to now, whatever had been said in the cottage and pubs, the farm kitchens and country-house dinner-tables, the family had escaped persecution by the public. All that was to be changed. We were not the only ones who had realized that there was a difficulty in explaining Otway's fall as an accident. Suicide from grief? Hardly. Such a drop would be too uncertain a method. Reporters from three London papers were pestering Colman at the front door when I drew up in front of it. The old servant welcomed me.

"Sir Ralph is talking to Colonel Shields, sir," he whispered, "and Mr. Ives is there too. I can't get rid of these gentlemen. Here's another." The excited hoot of a siren from the drive punctuated the exclamation.

"Gentlemen," I addressed them as a group, "we cannot make any statement at present. As you know, Mr. Danvers Carne died as the result of an accident last Tuesday. This evening at six, or shortly afterwards, his servant, James Otway, was found seriously injured, lying near the spot where his master was killed. Those are the facts and you know as much as we do about the matter."

"But we should like to hear about the circumstances. We are told that there was an organized attempt to reconstruct the hunt of last Tuesday. Is this true?" The young man drew out his note-book.

"I am unable to reply to that question."

"You and other members of the party had been riding this evening when the accident was discovered?" He glanced at my riding-kit.

"That is true."

"Will you give me the names of the persons?"

"No, certainly not. I am only a guest in this house, and you will understand that I can't answer such questions. I have no doubt Sir Ralph Carne-Hilton will make a statement later."

"We will wait," said the young man cheerfully. I left them in the hall.

The dining-room door was half open, and the table set for nine was occupied, with a ragged effect, by Mimi, Lady Caroline, and Furness. The footman trying to serve them was completely demoralized, as nothing in his training had prepared him for ladies and gentlemen who began their meals at intervals of a quarter of an hour apart, so that soup was being supplied to one while another was pushing away a half- finished savoury. Lady Caroline was making a determined effort to talk to Furness. Mimi was smoking and the ash-tray before her was already full of cigarette ends. She got up when she saw me and then sat down again, pushed out a chair for me, and asked: "How is he?"

I understood why this second catastrophe had shaken her as the first had not. Her husband's death was the climax of a situation already ominous. She had expected disaster and was prepared for it. This was unforeseen.

The young footman put a fruit plate before me, removed it hurriedly, and retired in quest of soup.

"He's in a serious condition. They've promised to telephone later."

"I can't bear it!" she half whispered. "That he should have suffered for his loyalty to Dan. I suppose that was why? *Could* it have been an accident? Could it?"

"We must wait."

"I don't think I can wait. It is intolerable. Why doesn't someone speak—tell the truth? Oh, why?"

Revel entered with Marion Trent. Neither of them had changed from their riding-clothes. Both looked haggard and spent.

"We've been to the hospital." Marion Trent sank into a chair. Revel hovered over her, and the footman, putting down my soup, went back for more, while Furness got up and left the room. Lady Caroline followed him, and Mimi said: "Otway must be saved. He shall not die for Dan. Will you do all you can, Dr.Jerrold?"

"Sorry, sir, there's no more soup. The kitchen lad dropped it. Will you begin with fish, miss?" The servant offered Marion Trent a perfectly cooked sole, which she allowed to cool on her plate. Revel scowled at the boy, who apologized miserably, although Revel, I am sure, did not know he was there.

Colman came to my side. "Sir Ralph would like to see you, sir."

I ate a few mouthfuls of fish, drank a glass of brown sherry, and went to the morning-room, where I found Brade rolling cigarettes, Sir Ralph leaning back impassively in a big chair, Ives solid and large in a little one beside him. Colonel Shields, a rough-hewn and soldierly gentleman, occupied a seat at the big writing-table facing them all.

"Hello, Jerry," said Brade forgivingly.

Sir Ralph nodded.

"We thought we'd like your opinion on the chances that Otway may be able to tell us what happened, Dr. Jerrold," Colonel Shields explained.

"There is a chance. Not a very good one, I'm afraid, but we shall know better in a few hours."

"I'm just going to question Barnet," said the Chief Constable.

"Interesting," murmured Brade. Colman opened the door. "Barnet, sir," he announced, and Barnet came in, smiled at us amiably, repressed the smile as unsuitable, and coughed behind his hat.

"Barnet, would you tell us again just what happened?"

"Yes, sir." Barnet, loquacious as he was when the subject was a horse, was obviously at a loss and waited for a lead.

"You carried out your instructions?" suggested the Colonel encouragingly. "What were they?"

"I had to ride over Mr. Carne's tracks, like, sir; just 'ack down the ride to that tree."

"And then?"

Barnet shifted from one foot to another and glanced at Brade.

"Sir Ralph, 'e told me to ride straight to the chalk-pit and wait, but when I got to the tree Mr. Brade, 'e caught me up and told me different."

Brade nodded. "I wanted to see if Barnet could fall off too, dragging potato-sacks. And he did."

Barnet flushed. "It was Sarah, sir. She didn't like it. And no wonder. That mare, sir—she—"

"What's this about potato-sacks?"

Brade explained gently. "You see, a potato-sack was the best substitute I could think of for a corpse. I had one all ready for Barnet. I told him to wait till five forty, allowing one hour and seven minutes' difference in the time, and drag the sack to the chalk-pit. Just a little fancy of mine, Colonel."

"I see. So you waited in the wood until five forty, Barnet?"

"Yes, sir."

"And then?"

"I did what I was told, sir. But Sarah, she didn't like it. I've never 'ad trouble with that mare before. Not in all the fifteen years I've known 'er. No, sir. Seemed like she knew there was danger, sir. 'Orses 'ave got better wits than 'umans when it comes to danger, as anybody can tell you, and Sarah, that mare, sir, what that mare don't know—well, sir, it ain't to be found, not in print." He finished triumphantly, beaming on us.

"You tried to take her to the edge of the chalk-pit?"

"Yes, sir, but would she? Not Sarah, sir! And that was when she got me off. Neat as a tape she was. Reared and twisted 'erself into forty knots and just wriggled me off like I was a rubber ball instead of a man with two legs to me. So, as I was hoff, I just let that sack slide over the edge of the pit and rode Sarah round the field to quiet 'er like."

"And what did you do then, Barnet?"

"Let 'er take 'er own way 'ome, same as Mr. Brade told me. But before we got to the gate, Mr. Revel rode by and 'e shouted out Otway was 'urt and to go back, so I did."

"Would you have seen Otway if he had been in the chalk-pit then?" asked Brade gently, looking critically at the cigarette he had just rolled.

"Oh, no, sir, not if he 'ad been in the chalk-pit. What with Sarah tugging at the reins and showing 'er 'eels, sir, I never looked down at all—just give that sack a roll and over it went, so that was all right, and there was the 'orses at 'ome to see to and young Rogers thinkin' more of 'is own importance than usual with all the talk—" he looked reproachfully at me. " 'Orses 'ave got to be fed and watered and groomed. There's those as forget that, though it's 'ard to credit." There was considerable severity in Barnet's tone of voice.

Colonel Shields smiled.

"Thanks, Barnet. That's all, I think."

Barnet looked at Sir Ralph.

"Yes, you can go, Barnet. Thanks!"

Barnet touched his forehead and went out.

"There's one thing about that type: they can't lie," said the Colonel.

"No"—Brade's cigarette end flamed and burnt out — "no, they can't." He glanced thoughtfully at me. "Jerry, could I have a word with you?"

I followed him to the room at the top of the house which he had commandeered. It was fitted with a trestle table, on which was piled a miscellany of maps, typed manuscript, a compass, string, photographs, and his set of bricks. He looked down at the display with marked distaste.

"I suppose you want to know what Lord Belfare had to say?"

"Lord Belfare—did he say anything?" Brade was still regarding the table and its contents in dejection.

"Well, you sent us to ask him questions. I suppose you want the answers." I told him about the letter on which Carne's uncle had acted to procure information about his debts. Brade did not appear to listen.

"I wish Otway had not tumbled into that hole!" he murmured miserably. "I wish he hadn't."

"You think he knew something?"

"He was an attractive little man."

"What on earth has that got to do with it?"

"Nothing, darling—or lots, I don't know. That's the trouble with this case. Things don't fit. They won't fit. They can't be made to fit. What did you make of our ride, Jerry? Be open with your Simon!"

"You must admit I haven't had much time to think about it."

"That's another trouble. Time. Clocks defeat me. I wish I were Einstein—or this fellow Dunne. They don't worry about clocks. Is there a fourth dimension, or is it the seventh or eighth dimension we want, and did everything happen in one of them with clocks sliding through diagrams to prove they don't tell time, but only split up one's hallucinations into fractions of inches? Without clocks, and juries who have a childlike faith in them, I could do the trick for you."

"Damn clocks!"

"I was afraid you'd feel that way about it! Now, read that."

He handed me some typed sheets, and I read over Marion Trent's account of the hunt.

"You see, she and her Dan left the hunt to hold a tete-a-tete in the woods below Noke Hill and they did not ride across Lee Farm with the others. It was agreed between them that Marion Trent should hack home and that Carne should join her about four so that they could have tea together and a nice peaceful talk before the others arrived. I asked her why he didn't go with her then and she said it might have caused comment. They did not want their plans discussed until Mrs. Carne had agreed to a divorce. Her whole account holds together—doesn't it? Did you see anything today to make you doubt it?"

"No."

"Now read this. Look at the passages I have marked."

I read:

"Mr. Brade: 'Please describe the hunt in detail after you rejoined it.'

"Mr. Furness: 'The field was moving across a park. There was a water jump, I think, and some timber. My mount fell at one fence, as I told the Coroner.'

"Mr. Brade: 'Can you describe the obstacles in more detail?'

"Mr. Furness: 'I remember the water and my fall.'

"Mr. Brade: 'How many fences?'

"Mr. Furness: 'Oh, several.'"

"You see? Compare that with Carne-Hilton's account, or Mrs. Carne's. Or Furness's own description of the day up to three thirty, and then remember how things went today. Furness could direct everyone until that draw at

Chess Spinney. After that he was lost. He had forgotten that stile. Well, Jerry, you saw that stile. Would you forget it? It was awkward to approach and uncommonly big and stiff, the sort of thing a prudent man looks at twice even if he's mounted on a foolproof conveyance and Trews was young and half-trained. Yet Furness forgot, though he remembers everything that happened after his spill. *Why*, Jerry, why?"

"Didn't you ask him?"

"If he had wanted to tell me anything more he would have told me, wouldn't he? I hate to beg."

"Did he tell you what he and Otway were talking about so earnestly?"

"He said they were discussing the weather. The weather can be a serious subject of conversation you know—the English weather!"

"And he rode after Came to tell him he'd seen Otway?"

"He said so."

"Did you get anything else?"

"Well, there was Mrs. Danvers Carne's story. That confirmed Carne-Hilton's. And she saw Furness take that stile too. You heard what she said about Furness speaking to her just before she left the field. Sir Ralph said he saw him say something to her. She says she thinks he did, but didn't hear what he said, and thought it was only a natural inquiry about her mare which had cast a shoe. Furness says he doesn't remember."

"Have you any theory about Otway's accident, Brade?"

"Bless you, Jerry, what use are theories? Somebody pushed him in like Pussy in the Well. Anyway, somebody knows how he got there."

"Who could know—except Barnet or Revel?"

"Obvious—who? But has it occurred to you that both Barnet and Revel would know that it would be obvious? Also that half an hour elapsed between Barnet's visit to the chalk-pit and Revel's, and that in any case Mr. Vane testifies that he had five minutes' conversation with Otway about Pink Livery, and Otway left the farm about four twenty, so that if he walked straight to the chalk-pit he must have been there nearly fifteen minutes before Barnet rode out of the Wilderness, always supposing Barnet kept to my instructions and is telling the truth? Otway may have been lying there injured and out of sight when Barnet threw in the potato-sack. Or he may not. He may have been concealed inside the edge of the Wilderness, watching and not wishing to be seen. And we may know more tomorrow when Ives has been over the ground—and we may not. May—may, might —might, if—if. Make what you can of that, my brilliant friend!"

"If Otway dies, there'll be another inquest, of course, and it won't be like the other."

"Not in the least like the other. For one thing, Mrs. Danvers Carne will be asked if she saw Otway on her way home. Has it struck you that a hunting-crop is a handy weapon in an emergency, and that Otway has an ugly hole in his head, so you say?"

"Brade, you are a fool."

He flung himself into a chair and took out his tobacco-pouch, rolling cigarettes angrily.

"I'm not the only fool. There are others. Ives, for one, is sure that your Mimi did it—got rid of her husband and tried to get rid of Otway. That Furness murdered Carne and that she disposed of his body. But I agree—I am a fool. Why did you pester me into taking this case at all? I didn't want to. It's the kind of thing Holloway would dote on. Why didn't you get him? Jerry, what's the matter with Furness? He's the only one who shows hesitation or confusion in his story. He's the only one who certainly is lying about something. He's the only one who behaves like a guilty man, and he's the only one, barring Carne-Hilton, who did not kill anybody. He was seen by three people at points during that hunt which give him an alibi you can't get round. Danvers Carne wasn't dead when he left him. He fell at the tree, recovered, walked about a bit, smoked a cigarette, and had a drink out of that flask or I'm a congenital idiot. Furness was back with the hunt by three forty; you saw for yourself today that he couldn't have been later than that to be where he was when he was, and he couldn't have taken less than ten minutes, riding fast, to make it from the Wilderness to the point where Carne-Hilton swears to seeing him. He left the Wilderness at three thirty at the latest, and Danvers Carne was alive then, and he never had time or opportunity to go back after that."

"I suppose Carne-Hilton's story may have been cooked. It all rests on that."

"Not a hope. It's confirmed at every point by one or another witness—among them Mrs. Carne—and as a whole by the M. F. H. and the hunt servants. His story is gospel truth, if that impresses you. I'd a great deal sooner dispute the Gospel as historical fact than his account of that hunt. He might just have killed his cousin and chucked him into the chalk-pit, for he left the field before anyone else did, if it wasn't for his game leg and the fact that Carne didn't sit under that tree and wait an hour to be killed—too cold! Go and look at his saddles, my boy. They are all creased with the pressure of his left leg and hardly rubbed on the right side. He can't use his right leg, and Billiam and I proved nobody could have done the job who hadn't a masterly seat on a horse and a bit of luck to help him. You'd have to lean right down out of your saddle to free the stirrup at just the right spot, and all the weight would come on your right leg. It was a rodeo performance. It's too much to pretend that he would have shammed his disablement for fifteen years in anticipation of this particular emergency."

"Suppose he suddenly recovered the use of that leg?"

"Yes, suppose! But why, then, did Carne wait over an hour for his cousin in that wood? You've got two unlikely, even highly improbable circumstances to face—no, three, for Carne-Hilton knew his way home, and he did not know that Danvers Carne was in that wood. His direct way from Cranmere to Marpen was through the top of the Wilderness, nowhere near the scene of the accident.

A Resurrected Press Mystery

Suppose, first, a miracle on Carne-Hilton's leg; second, some unthinkable reason for Carne's sitting an hour in the cold, waiting to be murdered; third, Carne-Hilton guessing number two! Too involved, Jerry, for a simple soul like me!"

"Have you thought that Carne might have been hurt badly enough by his fall to make it difficult to walk, or remount, unaided?"

"It did occur to me, Jerry, dull as I am! But he was not helpless or there would have been no mud on those boots, no footmarks in the wood. Put yourself in hie place. You've had a spill and you are lame enough not to want to walk back to Marpen. It is three twenty on a foggy afternoon and it is very cold. For some reason you can't remount—either your horse has made off, or you are too badly hurt to manage it. What would you do?"

"Smoke a cigarette, take a pull at my flask, and think it over."

"Just what he did. What then?"

"Listen. Someone might be about."

"Exactly! Then?"

"Well then—I suppose I'd try to remember the nearest place where I could get help or telephone."

"And that would be—?"

"Cranmere Farm or the village."

"How long would all that take?"

"Depends. I might have been dazed and shaky for ten minutes or so—even unconscious. Ten minutes for a drink and a cigarette—another five, perhaps, before I felt like moving. Then a few minutes looking for my horse, if it had wandered—or attempting to remount it if it hadn't."

"That would make it nearly four, then?"

"Well, by then from all accounts the weather was very thick and I'd feel cold and bored. I'd try for the farm, I think."

"Or the village. The distance is about the same, and you'd have a better chance of meeting with help coming along that ride than by crossing the wood and fields to

Cranmere; and it was better going too. And if you had started for the village along the ride, you would have met—help."

Yes. I saw it. I should have met Mimi Carne. Or heard her horse and shouted to attract her attention. My own reasoning had brought it to this, and, not for the first time, I was chilled by the ugly dovetailing of the minute with the event. The case against Revel seemed weak beside the facts implicating Mimi Carne. Point for point: he had a conceivable motive, she had a clear one; before his opportunity could be allowed, the delay between the fall and the crime had to be explained; it was not so with hers. There might be little direct evidence against her, but Colman's testimony about the string glove would tell with a jury, and if the series of accidents which had preceded Carne's death could be made to look like preparation for a crime, she would stand out as the most likely author of the scheme.

I resolved to say nothing about my discoveries in regard to Revel for the present. Brade spoke again.

"What is the matter with Furness, Jerry, and why won't he come out with what he knows?"

"I suppose you mean he may be shielding someone else," I said at length, for I wanted to know if that was his idea.

"That's my bright boy," he commended me, "and it's a lovely thought, but it doesn't cover all the facts. Why did he lose his memory for that critical quarter of an hour? If he'd just killed a man and thrown him down a forty-foot hole, you could understand it, but he hadn't."

"Perhaps he is trying to cast suspicion on himself. None of these people have our reason for knowing that the murder was not committed so early."

"That won't work either, Jerry dear, for he knew his progress had been witnessed and that it would be no use to deny the facts. He tried to remember. No, the man defended himself exactly like a guilty man who didn't want to be caught in a mistake." Suddenly Brade sat up.

His tobacco-pouch rolled onto the floor and so did the cigarette-papers and the half-finished cigarettes. "Darling Jerry, you've hit it! I see you have. Bless you for ever! By all that's gorgeous, the man thinks he did it, and he thinks we know he did."

"But Brade—"

He paid no attention to me. He was ringing a bell violently.

Colman came running up the stairs and appeared, flushed and out of breath, at the door. "Please ask Miss Legend to come here at once," said Brade.

10 p.m., Saturday

Averil Legend reminded me of certain actresses I have seen and admired because they never waste a gesture. It is a formidable exercise in self-control and the result certainly of long practice. She came in and sat down in the chair Brade vacated. The firelight played on her grey cloth frock and her smooth beauty.

"Yes?" she inquired, lifting her eyes to Brade.

"Miss Legend, will you be kind enough to answer a few questions?" asked Brade. "And if you don't object to dear Jerry, I'd much rather have him here than one of Ives's men. They put me off. They seem to think I'm funny or mad, and it spoils the atmosphere."

"Why should I mind Dr. Jerrold?" She smiled at me. "I think he is charming."

"You see, Jerry!" Brade made a gesture of satisfaction. "I said everyone loved you! Now, Miss Legend, Ming porcelain is an expensive hobby and I have to pay for it by finding out things other people don't think of, and I'm not a clever man at all! I've only got a short-sighted intellect. That's what gives me my reputation—I see what's under my nose. And one or two little things make me think we can be of use to each other."

"I'm very glad to hear that," said Averil Legend.

Brade unlocked and opened an attache case which was among the articles on the table. He took out the manuscript which I had seen and put it into her hands. "I've read it," he said, "but no one else has since it came into my possession, and I'm willing to let you have it at a price."

"And the price?"

"That you will tell me how it came to be locked up in Lady Carne-Hilton's cupboard, why she was keeping it, why you drew from your bank a large sum of money — which, by the way, you sold some valuable pearls to obtain—on the day you came to Marpen Hall, and what exactly were the relations between Danvers Carne and his cousin's wife, our hostess."

"So you know about Vivien and Dan too," she said thoughtfully.

"Yes, dear Jerry told me."

I said nothing, but of course I had no idea what he was talking about.

"You put it under my nose, Jerry," said Brade.

He drew out of the attache case a copy of my notes and showed me two marked passages. The first occurred in my conversation with Lady Carne-Hilton in the Greek room. It was: "I cannot endure the commonplace. Have you ever thought how the average person accepts everything ready-made? Tastes, habits, morals?" The second was from Revel's description of his dead friend: "He had a horror of the commonplace. Most people accept everything ready-made, even their morals."

"That was close enough to be odd, especially as Lady Carne-Hilton repeats rather than originates," Brade remarked, "so I took the trouble to find out if there were other signs that these two great souls had been in touch. I was lucky enough to find a link. I traced the architect who designed the Greek room. He was an obscure young man and had shared his fee with Danvers Carne, who got him the job."

Averil Legend made one of her rare gestures of assent.

"I knew that some man pulled the strings, and I soon guessed that it was Dan," she said. "What do you want to know, Mr. Brade?"

"All about it, dear lady, please. It's so interesting!"

"It is very simple. This manuscript was written by my mother and the royal personage referred to was my father, but not my mother's husband, of course. I want to marry the man who is going as Ambassador to the country where my father now rules. If this story should be published, it would be impossible, as my father's wife is, shall we say, old-fashioned in her ideas and could hardly receive me as the lady of the Ambassador to her country if the truth should be public property. My brother, being in difficulties, sold the manuscript to a man who was evidently acting as agent for someone else. Vivien Carne-Hilton wanted money. I knew she had a lover and that he bled her for cash all the time, but I had no idea who he was until she told me that she was in possession of this manuscript, that she needed money and did not dare ask Ralph for more than he already gave her, and wanted me to promise her a large sum to keep it from the public. I was willing to pay what my brother received, to buy it back, but nothing would induce me to marry, or announce my engagement, until the manuscript was destroyed. The conversations went on for almost a year, and I noticed that when Dan was in England, Vivien's answers were prompt, but when he was abroad they were not."

"What made you think of him at first?"

"First of all, because he went out of his way to ruin my brother. They played bridge together and lost. For Dan the losses were serious—for Frank they were final. He had to leave England. I thought Dan must have had some reason. Then something Vivien said confirmed my suspicion. You see, I've known her all my life. She is a distant cousin, and my mother, in a moment of piety, asked her father to be my godfather, so he felt obliged to teach me my catechism. They used to have me stay at the vicarage when I was a child. And later, when Vivien was so discontented, Mother was sorry for her and had her in town for some dances. That was during the war, and that was how she met Ralph. Vivien was always a bore. She always wanted to be noticed. First she tried to be a beauty like Mother. Then she went in for war work and patriotism. Then, after she married Ralph, she became terribly social. You could always hear the last person she had been talking to when she was speaking. So when I heard her say that money was of no importance unless you changed it for beautiful things, I recognized Dan's voice."

"Go on, please, Miss Legend. This is exciting!"

"Vivien wasn't a blackmailer, you understand. Neither was Dan, so far as I know. That was why it puzzled me. But I did know that Dan's debts were becoming serious, and the man I want to marry is a very rich man. I felt perfectly sure that as soon as I was married, the price of these papers would rise to a fabulous sum. I think they would have waited until I was married to tell me where the memoirs were, but my brother knew that I would not marry until I traced them. I was enraged that he should have sold them without my permission, so he got hold of the man who had approached him. Through my brother they found out that I was privately engaged to this gentleman. I got a detective from Chicago on the trail."

Brade was so excited that he was trying to smoke a wad of tobacco and burnt his fingers.

"Go on," he said, "go on!"

"The detective office in Chicago sent a man over here to see me. They had traced the purchaser of the documents to a professional crook, but he swore he had acted for another man. And without doubt the papers were in Vivien Carne-Hilton's hands. There is just one more curious thing. On Tuesday she again refused my offer, but on Wednesday night she accepted it, if I would increase it by one hundred pounds. I made up my mind to get the money, and, as a matter of fact, it reached me on Friday, and, but for the burglary, the papers would have been in my possession now."

"Did she give any reason for changing her mind?"

"No. She seemed to be very much excited and in a great hurry for the money. I have hardly seen her since that night. But I supposed that Dan's death made the difference, and it only seemed strange to me that she could think about the money at such a time."

"She is a strange woman."

"Did you ever know any other kind of woman?" asked

Averil Legend.

"And what, my intelligent friend, do you make of that?" Brade asked when she had gone.

"That Carne was not only a villain but an unsavoury villain," I answered promptly. The disclosure nauseated me. That Mimi Carne's husband could propose to divorce her and marry Marion Trent might prove him unscrupulous, calculating, and a devil, but it did not obscure the unpleasant lustre which his personality shed, even now; that he could make use of Vivien Carne-Hilton in this way extinguished it. He should not have been able to touch her with the far end of a barge-pole.

"It's grotesque. And it doesn't help us. It doesn't, Jerry. That's the one thing in common with all the elements in this business. None of them fits. Yet it's true. Go away, Jerry, I've got a headache. I want to have a good cry. Give me thirty grains of aspirin. I can't be stupider than I am already. Write up your notes. They're useful. They're so useful that I'll never take a case without you again. Go away! I want to play patience. I've got one that never comes out right, but I always go on hoping it may—just like the crime in the chalk-pit. We'll call it that, shall we? When we write our memoirs!"

10.45 p.m., Saturday

When I came out of Brade's room, I found Mimi Carne waiting for me.

"I've been to see Otway," she said quickly. "Dr. Jerrold, will you go once more tonight? I can't tell you how I feel about him. There isn't any doubt, I suppose, that he is suffering now because of his devotion to Dan. Where will it stop? Please! I shall feel better if you go. You will know if everything is being done."

I promised to go. As I passed along the corridor, I heard voices from the direction of Lady Carne-Hilton's bedroom. That hysterical lady was talking to her husband, for I heard him interrupt her once. "He is a martyr—a martyr, I tell you!" she cried shrilly. Even if Otway was a martyr, I did not see why all the servants should hear about it, so I closed my bedroom door with a bang intended to warn them that her shrill voice could be heard in the hall. Carne-Hilton came out of her room and stopped me as I went downstairs.

"My wife is very much upset," he said wearily. "Her nerves are not strong and the burglary and the outrage on Otway have alarmed her. She thinks no one is safe. She wanted to go and see Otway, but I feel that this would be foolish. Could you see her for a moment, Dr. Jerrold?"

With considerable reluctance I entered Lady Carne-Hilton's room. I was genuinely shocked at her appearance.

"I am just going to see Otway," I said. "I will do everything to make sure that he has the best chance for recovery."

"You will—you will—" she seized my arm. "What that man has suffered! And you won't let them listen to anything he may say—he won't be responsible—Dr. Jerrold! You see that? I ought to go to him, but I am so afraid. Is he disfigured and is it horrible to look at him? I can't bear blood! I am too sensitive—"

"There is no need at all for you to go. In fact, it might be bad for him. You must trust me."

So Otway knew of her connexion with Danvers Carne, and she was afraid he would speak of it in delirium. That was my immediate thought. I soothed her, prescribed a narcotic strong enough to keep her quiet for a few hours, and left her.

There was no change in Otway's condition, and the surgeon in charge had decided that an operation would be necessary to remove a part of the broken skull.

"I have got the best man in London coming down to do it," he said. VI understand that a great deal depends on his regaining consciousness? Of course, the operation will delay that—on the other hand, it is the only hope for him, in my opinion."

"Sir Ralph Carne-Hilton wishes everything possible done for the man."

"Naturally. In any case everything would be done. But if he shows any sign of being able to speak, I will have you notified at once."

We were standing by Otway's bed. I looked down at him. The lights in the room were low, but the surgeon had switched on the lamp over the injured man's head. Did I hope that he would speak? If he did, would the name of Mimi Carne be cleared in a breath?

On the way home I remembered my promise to Miss Vane. There were lights at Cranmere Farm to be seen from the high road, and it occurred to me that I should be doing a kindness to stop there.

My knock was answered by the farmer himself.

"Come in, sir." He made way for me to pass him, and I saw Miss Vane bent over the fire in the sitting-room. She turned to see who it was. Her face was red and puffy from crying, but she forgot her appearance and jumped up when she saw me.

"Is he—worse?" she cried.

I told her all I knew.

Mr. Vane brought out a decanter. I accepted a whisky and soda.

"My daughter has told me that she was engaged to Otway," he said. "I'm sorry for her. But I don't trust him. Like master, like man. It's bad to speak ill of the dead, but she's my daughter and the only one I've got."

"You don't understand him, Father. He's above the common herd."

"That may be." Mr. Vane's dark face looked grim to me. I did not think he wished to understand Jim Otway.

"Mr. Vane, did you tell Mr. Revel that in your opinion Mr. Danvers Carne was a party to the fraud when Cat o' the Hills was ridden in Pink Livery's name over a year ago?"

"I said I wouldn't put it past him—nor Otway either. In my opinion, there was a lot of dirty work Otway did for his master that Mr. Carne took care not to know too much about. But he wasn't above benefiting. Otway did quite a bit with horses on the side, and he must have done it with his master's money."

"Did Mr. Revel believe you?"

"I don't know. He shut me up, and he was angry— or let on he was. I don't know which."

Nor, unfortunately, did I.

1.30 a.m., Sunday, February 12th

When I had written up my notes that night, I sat down by my fire and thought over the case. I could not see how Averil Legend's story affected it unless to throw suspicion on Carne-Hilton. If his wife had been in love with his cousin and under his influence, and he had found it out, a new element would have entered into his hatred, and he would have been capable of violent action perhaps. But Brade had summed up the arguments against this theory and I admitted their weight. What, then, was I to think? Who alone had the time to carry out the dragging of the body? Who had motive and opportunity? Who had destroyed the string gloves? There was only one person whose name fitted an answer to all these questions, and that was the name I was determined to protect. Put Lady Carne-Hilton in Mimi's place and I would have pointed to her as guilty.

Then I put aside the evidence and went back to my own field. The person who had murdered Danvers Carne, it seemed to me, must have been one of those who, having been under his influence, had suddenly found him out. Not Mimi, who had known him too long to suffer any shock from further disclosures. Not Furness either, for the same reason, nor Carne-Hilton. Whom did it leave? Vivien Carne-Hilton, Marion Trent, or Revel. Any of these, it seemed to me, might have arrived at the crucial point at that particular time.

What evidence had I accumulated against Revel? I reviewed it dispassionately and found it weak, if looked at with the practical eye of a British jury. Yet, from my own point of view, it seemed more and more possible that he might be guilty. Carne had cheated him and taken away the girl he was beginning to care for; if he had been convinced by Vane's account of the fraud about Pink Livery, the whole extravagant structure of illusion which he had built up around Carne must have fallen at one sweep. He was capable of violence, as was proved by the man he had attacked before he was sent down from Oxford. And he had hunted on numerous occasions with the South Lodesdale hounds in his undergraduate days, so that he must have known the country better than he admitted.

I sat there in that pleasant room and worked out the murder as it might have been done by Revel. Give him time to ride after his victim, accuse him of his treachery, and perhaps be maddened to sudden action by a selection of self-made moralizing which he now recognized for the devil's own religion. Suppose him to have killed Carne— with his hunting-crop—concealed the body, and then ridden back later to cover up his crime, having had time to think out the plan which nearly succeeded. Against this I set his own attitude after the event; but might he not have realized that no one was satisfied with the verdict at the inquest and have taken up his truculent pose to hide his guilt? The boy, swayed for a year or more by this man's persuasive philosophy, might have been left without principles or standards for the moment and be resolved on escape from the consequences of what he had done, ruled by a sense of self-preservation. Why not?

I took up my notes and began to write.

2.30 p.m., Sunday

The next morning I was roused from a heavy sleep by Colman who told me that I was wanted urgently on the telephone. My assistant begged me to come to London, so I dressed, ate a hasty meal, and ordered my car. But before I left I went to see Brade and found him playing patience.

"Everybody's so busy," he complained, looking with annoyance at the cards, which were behaving with their usual obstinacy. "Nobody seems to realize that it's Sunday. And they do neglect that wretched poodle. I took her for a walk, and our friend, the French lady, is very much annoyed about it, as she had just brushed her and she's all over burs. As for Ives, his temper is positively atrocious and he's dropping proverbs all over me too. I can't bear it, Jerry dear. He says: 'Haste makes waste,' and 'The watched pot never boils,' and 'One swallow does not make a summer.' So I decided to play patience till he stops. It annoys him."

"Brade, I'm going up to London, but I'll come back tonight. By then I may want to talk to you about a theory of mine. What is everyone doing?"

"'Everyone' is out walking with Mr. Furness. I saw her start ten minutes ago, and there's an inconspicuous little man with field-glasses dodging behind hedges. I rather think he's watching them. Don't look so fierce, darling. It's not my idea—it's Ives's."

"Where's Revel?"

"Amusing Miss Trent, I believe, somewhere about the house. And our hostess is being temperamental, pacing up and down with green light and Greek pillars for company, and Sir Ralph is in the smoking-room totting up figures, and Miss Legend is being massaged by her maid, and Lady Caroline is dealing with a domestic crisis. The chef has given notice at last, so Colman says."

"They won't arrest Furness at once, will they?"

"Bless you, my lad, they can't. Not unless Otway dies. But he's still unconscious, and I don't think the doctors are too hopeful."

"I'll be back about dinner-time, I expect."

"You will, won't you? Your energy is so bracing and I'm sure my blood-pressure is low. Besides, Lady Carne-Hilton wants you. She said so. You've made a great impression on her, Jerry!"

Thus warned, I made my way cautiously through the house to the door, where my car was waiting, and escaped.

There was so much work for me in London that by dinner-time I was still busy and it was nearly eleven before I came back. I went to my room and sat down to re-read my notes, with the idea of deciding on what I should tell Brade. It must have been about twelve when a light tap on my door startled me. The house was so quiet that the slight sound was like a sudden light in a dark room. I opened the door to let in Richard Furness.

His face was sullen and hard with suppressed emotion.

"I want to talk to you," he said, and walked over to the fire. His dressing-gown flapped round his legs, his strong throat was bare. He held his pipe in his hand, but it had gone out, and now he relit it, unsteadily.

"Jerrold," he said abruptly, "are you a friend of Mimi Carne?"

"Yes."

"You'd do anything to shield her?"

"Yes."

"By anything, I mean anything," he said fiercely.

"I think so."

"Then you won't use what I have to say if it might hurt her—under any circumstances whatever?"

"No, I won't."

"Are you in love with her?"

"I believe I am."

He laughed.

"Well, I've been in love with her for five years, but I never told her so until today." He looked at me sharply. "You may not believe that now, but you will when I've told you the rest. To the best of my knowledge and belief, I killed Dan."

"What do you mean?"

"Exactly what I say, for once! You've heard what I told Brade. It's all true, only I left out a bit. I had my suspicions of Dan's intentions when I went out on Tuesday morning. There was something in the air between him and Marion Trent. Carne-Hilton seemed to know, but I couldn't get it out of him. So I tried Otway, and Otway was more forthcoming. He said Dan meant to divorce Mimi, mainly on his evidence. You see, in getting Dan out of scrapes, Mimi and I had been thrown together in an intimate way. Once, especially, Dan was nearly poisoned. I was with Mimi. We were almost sure a fellow he had ruined playing piquet when the boy was drunk had done it. Mimi was in a state of collapse and I sat with her half one night. Otway was with Dan, and he knew all about it. Mind you, I expect Dan would have allowed her to divorce him, but he meant to threaten her with action if she wouldn't, and she wouldn't have done it to free him in order to make another woman wretched. I know Mimi. Otway was trying to convince me that Mimi must divorce Dan to save herself. He was playing his master's game.

"Well—I leave you to imagine my state of mind. I followed Dan into that wood with every intention of killing him, I think. But before I caught him, I had time to think of Mimi, and I saw I couldn't do it. To drag her through a business like that would be as bad as Dan's plan. So I rode more slowly, and when I caught up with him, I told him I knew, and meant to expose him if I could without hurting his wife. Dan was bland. He traced out the story he had concocted, which Otway would support. It was so devilish in its cleverness—finished as a pastrycook's birthday cake—that I lost control of myself again. He'd made use of the very acts of friendship I'd gone out of my way to do him, and, worse, he'd made use of Mimi's pluck and faithfulness, to fix up a case that would certainly smirch her name if it did no worse. And he'd manoeuvred us into situations through our care for him, with every intention of using them against us.

"We reached that overhanging tree, and I ducked and just missed being thrown. Dan was behind me. At that moment he said: 'It was really a mistake, my dear Dick, to pretend you wanted to reform me when what you really wanted was to corrupt my wife.' Instead of holding the branch for him, I let it swing back in his face. I heard it strike him. I heard Sarah jump and plunge, but I never looked back. I rode away from him as I'd have ridden away from a regiment of demons. If I hadn't done that, I'd have turned round and killed him. It was one thing or the other. I might as well have had the satisfaction of doing it, I suppose. How I got back to the hunt, and what happened after that, I have no idea, until I saw Mimi Carne. Then I caught myself up with a jerk. *I told her to see if Dan was in when she got back—he might have had a spill.* Jerrold, she must have passed under that tree, found his body, and worked out the rest to cover up what I had done. But for that, I might have told the whole story—I'm not sure, for even that would have brought her in, and once a woman's name appears in such a connexion, God help her! She may be as flawless and above criticism as the new moon, but no one will believe it. And, as it was, what could I do but keep silence? Now Brade has taken up this case, and he's after the truth, and nobody knows better than I do that I've made a blotch of it. I never expected he'd question me so closely about the hunt just at the time when he knew I was there, or I'd have taken good care to know my lines. It put me out when I realized that I'd forgotten nearly everything about those few minutes. It must be clear as a pikestaff to him that I was in no state of mind to know what I was doing."

"I suppose it is."

"Exactly! So I thought I had better talk to Mimi while there was time, and I asked her to go for a walk with me today. I told her that I'd never admit to anyone what I said to her as she left the field that day. She asked me what I did say. I tried to tell her that I didn't murder Dan—for of course I didn't, technically speaking, though, heaven knows, I had murder in my heart, and but for her, I think what was more or less of an accident would have been murder. But she wouldn't let me finish. She ran away and shut herself in her room. I've come to you because I can't get at her. I know any move I make to see her may react on her, and at any moment I may be arrested. I want you to take care of her, Jerrold. When I think of what may happen—I'm nearly mad with thinking of it. Promise me you'll stand by her! If there were any way of making Brade believe I had time to go back and finish up the business, I'd tell him the whole thing now and hang for it. But for her to suffer—"

"Why are you so sure she did it?"

"Because when she found Dan she must have guessed more or less what had happened from what I said to her, and who else had time to do it? She didn't know it was practically an accident. She thought I'd killed Dan for her sake, and she meant to save me if she could."

"I don't believe it."

He looked at me in amazement. I don't think he had for a moment considered that his reading of the case might be wrong. I didn't feel free to tell him that he had not killed Carne, but I said: "Furness, you don't know everything about this business. You aren't even sure that the fall you gave Danvers Carne was fatal. Go to bed and go to sleep. Keep quiet for the present, and I'll think over what you've said. You must trust me. I'll save Mimi Carne."

He looked at me for a moment. His face was stupid with weariness and relaxed strain. The relief of telling someone the truth was for the moment enough to ease the tension of his nerves. "I'm pretty nearly done, and that's a fact. I believe I can sleep—I've got some stuff."

"You'd better let me measure it for you," I said, somewhat grimly, but he shook his head.

"I'm not that sort of coward."

I went with him to the door. There was a light in the passage and I saw the figure of Lady Caroline, larger than ever in a substantial dressing-gown, coming towards us. "I want to see you for a moment, Dr. Jerrold," she said. Furness passed her without looking at her, and I heard the door of his room close quietly. Lady Caroline put her hand on my arm. Her big, pleasant face was sick with dismay.

"Mimi has gone!" she said in a whisper. "Someone must find her at once."

12.30 a.m., Monday, February 13th

In the little sitting-room where I had had tea with Lady Caroline and Mimi, the latter's trembling maid was waiting. Her story was soon told. She had been off duty that evening and went to church. When she came back she looked into her mistress's room to see that the housemaid had put things as her lady liked them, but Mrs. Danvers was not there. Later she went in again, feeling anxious about her mistress; nothing had been touched. She supposed Mrs. Danvers to be downstairs and that for some reason she had not changed for dinner. It was much later that Colman remarked that Mrs. Danvers' dinner had gone up to the sitting-room, but that she had eaten nothing. Still anxious, but not dreaming that anything terrible could have happened, she arranged her mistress's room for the night and went to bed. Mrs. Danvers never allowed her to sit up for her, and since the accident she had become used to Mrs. Danvers being irregular in her habits.

It was about a quarter to twelve that Lady Caroline had come to her room and asked if she had seen her mistress since dinner. They had then looked everywhere and had failed to find her. Mrs. Danvers had changed to a dark blue frock, which she had not worn since her husband died, and that seemed strange. So far as either of the women knew, Mimi had not been seen since tea-time, when the housemaid had brought her tea to her bedroom and found her lying face-downward on the bed. The maid spoke to her, but Mimi answered that she had a headache and would be all right soon.

"I am horribly frightened," said Lady Caroline.

There were two things we could do: rouse the house and notify the police, thereby setting every machine going to trace her; but what would be the result of that? If any suspicion slept in any mind against her, it would be wakened to full activity. Why should she have disappeared, unless to avoid questioning? I was the only one who knew the shock she had received that day. If what Furness had told her was news to her, if it was true that she had not heard what he said to her as she was leaving the field on Tuesday, consider her state of mind now! She did not know that her husband had not died as the result of his fall. That Furness could believe that she had disposed of the body must have made her certain that everyone would believe it. I don't think it ever occurred to me to think she might be guilty, and this an attempt to escape justice, but I understood that it would seem so to everyone else. If ever a woman had reason for desperation, she had, and this blow came as a climax to years of strain.

It seemed likely that she had gone out soon after the housemaid had left her. Allowing time to change her clothes, it might have been between half past five and six. She had worn tweeds and walking-shoes and a soft hat, but nothing else was missing. Her maid was sure that she had not taken a dressing-case. I thought of the chalk-pit, and so did Lady Caroline.

"Don't tell anyone until we must," she begged. "Perhaps she has only gone out to walk and some accident has happened."

"I'll get my car and Barnet," I said, thinking of him because I liked him and could reach him without attracting attention. He and Rogers slept in the groom's cottage, and the rooms were all on the ground floor.

"There's the lake in the park," Lady Caroline whispered.

"Don't!" I ejaculated.

"Barnet will know," she directed me.

No one who has never made such a search as I did that night will understand what it was like. I wakened Barnet and told him what had happened. His usual inclination to talk deserted him completely, and he dressed and helped me get my car without speaking. He seemed to know where I meant to go first. We drew up in almost the same spot where we had stopped when going to view the scene of Carne's death.

I had a powerful torch with me and another for Barnet. The chalk-pit lay beneath us—grim with shadows—the lights playing over it bit by bit. While we still looked, the moon shone out. Startled rabbits scurried away before our lights. The chalk-pit was empty and sinister. We went back and cautiously examined the neighbourhood of the house, but the hard gravel drive had nothing to tell us. Outside in the lane that ran past the gate were footprints, but they were not Mimi's.

"There's the footpath through the park, sir. She might 'ave taken that and made the six o'clock bus."

We had already looked in the garage for missing cars, but it was locked and we could see through the glass that the cars were all in their places.

I led the way to the footpath, and here we found what we sought. Light prints of a lady's walking-shoes led steadily towards the high road, but led, too, towards the big lake which stretched along the road just there. The hard macadam of the road showed no prints. We went round the shore of the lake in silence, examining the soft grass almost inch by inch. It was raining now, and our torchlight caught the raindrops as they swept past. There were more footprints beside the lake, among some reeds, but they were confused and difficult to read.

"The poor lady!" said Barnet, and he took off his cap.

"Put it on," I said roughly.

He obeyed me in silence.

I told Barnet he could do no more. We walked back to the house as silently as we had come. Lady Caroline was waiting for me.

"Ought we to telephone to the police station?" she asked, helplessly. Then she resumed her air of control. "No; if Mimi is dead—let's face it—we can't help her. If there has been an accident we shall hear of it. And if she has simply run away, give her time. You may be sure of one thing—in the end she'll be sensible. She might—yes, she might do away with herself under some sudden shock. But if she gives herself time she'll come through. Do you know anything that might have upset her tonight?" She must have seen my answer in my face for she said: "Dr. Jerrold, you do!"

"We have to think of the chance of her wandering about, not herself, and coming to some harm which might be avoided if we roused everyone."

"I can't bear the idea."

Neither could I.

"Think," she continued, "if she has had some bad news, and is in such a condition, of the effect of her being tracked down by the police."

I considered that.

The trouble was that any step we could take meant publicity. The local stations, the bus routes, were all manned by persons talking of the Marpen Hall mystery. The press had been active night and day. I was known to the neighbourhood by now and there was no hope of keeping the matter a secret if I went about asking for Mimi. The house still slept on, undisturbed, apparently, by our goings and comings. Mimi's maid could be trusted.

"Wait till morning," insisted Lady Caroline.

I sat with her a little longer, while she talked to me about Mimi. There was not much I did not already know, but she gave me a picture of her life with Danvers Carne which was indescribably painful. "She was used to hard jobs. Her father was a difficult person, and she stood between him and her mother. She never looked back. At first I think she had some happiness with Dan, for he could be delightful, and he was in love with her. She knew the family depended on her and she was fond of us all. Then Dan was faithful to her, so far as I know, and there seemed little chance of divorce. She had a terrific pride, hated to admit failure, and loved him as long as she could, and then remembered that she had loved him."

Then she said something more: "I used to have doubts

as to whether Dan was a villain or a saint. I have none now—he was a devil!"

It was three o'clock when I went back to my room.

The first thing I noticed was that the notes I had been reading when Furness came in were gone from the table where I had left them, and the next was that Brade was asleep in my armchair, the note-book open on his knee.

I don't know how long I stood looking down at him, but, without opening his eyes, he murmured: "Don't shoot. I knew all about the string glove. Jeemes, the odd-man, told me." Then he looked up at me gravely. "Have you found her?"

"How did you know?"

"I was working in my room, and I heard you go out. Then I made a few quiet observations for myself. Don't worry, Jerry, she'll come back!"

"I'm not so sure of that." I told him as briefly as I could Furness's story. Since he knew of the burning of the glove he had the most damning evidence against Mimi and it was useless to keep the rest from him. Indeed, as I felt then, Mimi was beyond his power to harm. I believed she was dead. "So you were right; Furness does think he killed Carne," I finished.

"And he thinks Mrs. Danvers Carne covered up his tracks. I'm half-witted, but only half-witted, you know. I did work that out eventually. But the trouble was the importance of keeping the facts to ourselves in this case. Otherwise I could have told him some time ago that Mrs. Danvers Carne knew nothing about that murder until she was told by Lady Carne-Hilton on Tuesday evening.

"Brade, I thought you suspected her."

"Well, I can't read your thoughts. And, mind you, my opinion wouldn't satisfy a jury. It's based on two things— the embroidery she was working on and the letter she wrote and sent her maid out to post. I've examined that embroidery. She did the last stitches in her room just before the news was brought to her. Every stitch is perfect, and it is fine and difficult work. Can anyone with any imagination believe that she could have chosen that occupation at that moment and concentrated on it with a steady eye and hand if she had just been through the process of harnessing her husband to a horse's heels and tossing his body down a forty-foot drop, or even if she had witnessed his death? And she wrote a letter in her usual hand, ordering more embroidery silk of a special colour, and sent her maid out to catch the evening post with it. I ask you, my brilliant friend, does it fit?"

"You know I never thought it fitted."

"You must remember it's the little things I see. And little things tell me that she will come back. She changed her clothes. Why? Because she would be more likely to be recognized if she wore mourning. She needn't have bothered about that if she meant to drown herself or jump into the chalk-pit. She had money with her too. Believe me, Jerry, she couldn't stand the atmosphere of this house one moment longer, so she went away. I feel like doing the same thing."

I don't know why I had not thought of all this for myself.

"There's another thing, quite enough to explain her running away. She had a visit at tea-time from that temperamental lady, Lady Carne-Hilton."

"Don't joke about this, Simon."

"It's true. Do you blame her?"

He got up and mixed me a drink from a tray Colman had left for me. "Now, Jerry, be a patient for once and humble yourself to take a prescription from my hand. Here it is, stiff and strong and comforting."

I must say, if the drink was comforting, so was he.

"Tomorrow," said Brade, "at eleven o'clock we're going to have a little consultation, and if you'll go to sleep like a good boy you shall come. I shall never be able to do another case without you, Jerry. Your notes have seen me through the worst places."

"Simon, have you thought about Revel?"

"I have, Jerry, I have. He's coming to the consultation.

And so is Lady Carne-Hilton. I have enormous faith in that woman. You see, Jasper, if we're to free some of these nice people from suspicion we've got to fix the guilt on somebody else. Unless we do, they are all suspect. It's an awkward point about this case. And one thing more, Jerry: there is no hope whatever of Otway's recovering consciousness. Don't forget that!"

"But, Brade—the doctor said—"

"Don't forget it!" he repeated, and went to the door and opened it. There he paused and looked back at me, as much like a wicked sprite as if Barrie himself had created him.

"I always knew you'd find it out," he said. He pointed to my note-book. "You've got it at last. The secret's there."

Gently, but firmly, he closed the door.

6.40 a.m., Monday

I don't know if Brade dosed that glass, but I do know that I sat down and went to sleep, and that when I woke up, Mimi Carne was standing at my side. I must have been half dazed still, for I jumped to my feet and took her in my arms. She stood there leaning against me. All the horrible circumstances surrounding us seemed cleared away. This was what I had been longing for, I believe, ever since she walked into my consulting-room a week ago—the woman made for happiness, and the woman to whom I longed to bring happiness. If that is not love, what is? As she rested against me and I felt her relax in my arms, I think she knew that it was there her birthright would come to her.

In a moment she drew away and looked up at me.

"I meant to run away," she said softly. "I thought about the hills and the sea in Argyll. I couldn't think of anything else. Just getting out of this house and thinking about them all night brought me back to my senses. I knew I had to go through with it. Whoever suffers, I've got to tell the truth—be myself. But that Dick should pay such a penalty for loving me—that he could believe me capable of doing such a ghastly thing—oh, can you understand, can you begin to understand what I felt?"

I made her sit down. It was not seven o'clock, but I could hear the servants stirring in the corridor, and I went out and found a young housemaid and sent her running for some tea and whatever food she could find. I made Mimi take off her wet clothes and brought her a warm dressing-gown, made up the fire myself, and took the tray from the housemaid at my door. Then I sat down beside her.

"My dear," I began, "Furness did not kill your husband. We know that he was living after Furness left him." I let her grasp that before I went on. "Furness told me the whole story. He thought you heard what he said to you as you left the field that day. Brade knows you did not and knows you had nothing to do with the crime."

"But, Jerry—you don't know the rest—" Her eyes were black with horror. "I am thankful—God only knows how thankful—that Dick did not do it. But who did? Let me tell you what happened when I was in my room after I left Dick."

"Drink your tea first," I insisted, and she obeyed me. Then she told me.

"I was frantic with fear and misery. If I kept secret what Dick had told me, I should be as bad as he. If I told, I should be punishing him for his friendship and devotion. I saw no way out. And while I was walking up and down my room in the most awful agony of mind, Vivien Carne-Hilton came in. She shut the door and locked it. Then she flung herself on me. I'd never seen her as she really is before. You know how she dresses for the public, even when the public is only her own maid. Well, she wore her own clothes, but they didn't seem to belong to her. She had not attended to her face, and her skin is ugly and greasy. She looked common and frightened and utterly helpless. When I drew away from her, she stood there twisting her fingers together and began to talk. I couldn't understand what she was saying. It was incoherent and rambling, like a bad dream. I think she was talking about Mr. Brade. She called him that horrible man. She seemed to think he had found out something. Then she was complaining about Ralph. She said she had always been unhappy with him. He was cold and narrow. He could not understand why she was not contented to be ordinary, mediocre, why she needed passionate love, money. 'Some people are meant to stand out,' she said, 'they can't be limited, cramped. *He* was like that!' It took me a little while to understand that she was talking about someone else, and then, quite suddenly, she was repeating stock phrases of Dan's. Oh, you can't imagine how horrible it was—like hearing him mocking me in her shrill voice. He had persuaded her that she was unique, that it was her only duty to express her personality. I know how he could talk. And then, from things she said, I knew he must have been her lover. She spoke of getting money for him. I thought Dan despised her—he used to make fun of her. I could hardly believe my ears. She was like a bad gramophone grinding out a record of his cant. She excused herself just as he did, but without his peculiar charm and persuasiveness. I tried to quiet her, thinking of Ralph, but she went on and on, and then she drew a crumpled paper from her pocket. It held four questions and was signed: 'S.B.'

"'How did you know Mr. Carne had been murdered before anyone else did?' was one. 'Why refuse Miss Legend's offer on the 5th and accept it on the 6th?' another. 'Who was Rufus M'Lean?' the third, and 'Why destroy that string glove?' the fourth. It ended: 'At eleven tomorrow, when you've thought everything well over, will you meet me in the morning-room and answer these questions, please?'

"Jerry, I shrank from her in horror. I did not understand the questions, but I knew they must point to her guilt. She took hold of me and held me, like some animal that sticks." Mimi paused, shuddering. She went on in a forced voice; "Then she cried and wailed and talked all at once about how she adored him, how he loved someone else. 'Sometimes I wanted to sleep with him, sometimes I wanted to kill him, but I always loved him. He meant to marry that girl, but I didn't care. I couldn't let him go.' I can't remember all she said. She was so hysterical that she had the strength of ten women. I couldn't have struggled harder to get away if she had been trying to murder me. Finally she weakened and I pushed her down into a chair and ran for her husband. He came and took her away.

"Then I changed my clothes, got some money, and went out. I thought if I could go home to Scotland I might be able to think. And then when daylight came, the dawn so slow and gentle, yet relentless and awful, spreading everywhere though I tried to stop it with my two hands, I came back to my senses. I remembered that you were here." She looked at me. "I thought you would tell me what to do."

If I had done what I knew was right, I should have gathered her into my arms again and put her to sleep there in front of the fire. But it did occur to me that other people might not see the perfect logic of such a course. Instead, I took her to her room, called Lady Caroline, and went to wake Brade.

As I got to the landing outside his door, a shot rang through the house.

8-10 a.m., Monday

In a second it seemed doors were opened all round and people were scurrying after me as I bolted down the hall. The sound had come from the direction of the room occupied by Revel. I threw myself against the door, but it was locked. In a second I heard his voice and the sound of hysterical crying.

"Who is it?" he demanded. "Wait!" He unlocked the door and I heard Brade say, behind me; "Keep the servants away," and, turning, saw Colman, half-dressed, shooing a group of terrified maids down the stairs. Revel opened the door and, seeing me, let in Brade, Carne-Hilton, and myself. Revel was holding a small revolver in his hand. Vivien Carne-Hilton was lying, half-fainting, in a chair.

"Luckily, she is not shot," said Revel. "I was in bed, drinking my tea, when I saw the door open and she came in. She pointed this at me, and I ducked, and it went off. As she fired, she said something—God knows what. She must be mad!"

Brade touched me on the arm. "I want you, Jerry," he said. Then he turned to Carne-Hilton. "It isn't as bad as you think. Get her to her room, and don't let the servants know she was here. Mr. Revel was cleaning his revolver, of course, and it went off. Don't leave her alone." Brade drew me with him to his room and shut the door. "I'd never have given her the credit for so much real feeling," he said thoughtfully.

I told him Mimi Carne's story. "What possessed you to give that woman those questions and leave her unwatched?" I asked Brade. "You must have been mad."

"It was all your fault. I meant you to go and explain it to her, and you were out looking for lost ladies. And then I felt sorry for you, and thought it would do her no harm to worry for a bit. Now, Jerry, I've a job for you, and I don't say it will be to your liking, but it is in a good cause. In your professional capacity you are to visit Lady Carne-Hilton and you are to prepare her for our little drama at eleven o'clock. I'll explain. She likes to be important. You are to show her she can be the most important lady in the British Isles—for a day or two—and one of the most important for quite six months, at a rough guess. She's afraid of going to jail. You are to assure her that she won't have any such luck, and if she seems too disappointed, cheer her up by assuring her that if she does just what you tell her to do, the distinction will cast a glory over her for ever. She can talk as long as she likes and we shall all hang on her words, and later every man, woman, and child in England, and lots outside it, will be doing the same thing. Heads normally crowned with coronets will be turned her way, and at the most celebrated dinner-tables her name will be on every lip. Later she will refuse the pressing invitations of duchesses, to accept those of greater beings. Help her with her story. Show her how she can pose as the victim of romantic love. At the same time suggest, as I know you can, that the love isn't half as romantic as she thought it was and that there are better things ahead. All this as a trifling reward for telling us *why* she opened those awkward shutters to watch for the news of Danvers Carne's death last Tuesday, *why* she left her pet poodle wandering in those dangerous woods, *why* she burned the glove (Jeemes saw her do that, you know, and Colman was really unjust in blaming him about that fire), *what* she saw in the Wilderness that frightened her and led her to guess that a tragedy had taken place, and why she was willing to take that money from Miss Legend one day when she had refused it the day before. Now, Jasper, fortify yourself with the best breakfast you know how to order, shave that interesting face of yours, dress yourself in your usual quiet and distinguished style, and then if, in addition to all this, you can suggest that, as a stop-gap, an eminent psychologist with a reputation for unsuspectibility isn't a chance to turn down offhand, you'll have won my awestruck admiration, for I know it's asking too much!"

11 a.m., Monday

When I joined the others in the morning-room at eleven o'clock, I felt I had earned the most exalted praise Brade could bestow. At the end of that interview with Vivien Carne-Hilton she was weeping in my arms, and I was in a condition of mind which I will not attempt to describe. I did not care who had murdered Danvers Carne. I did not feel any curiosity about Otway's fate. I wanted to take Mimi Carne to the most remote and inaccessible spot on the map and keep her there for ever.

I found Brade and Carne-Hilton waiting, and Revel came in a moment after I did. Mimi Carne entered later with a short, square little man who seemed to be a stranger to everyone except Brade. Ives was there, of course, and with him was the local inspector and the shorthand-typist I had seen before.

"This is Mr. Bliss of Chicago," explained Brade, as if we ought to know all about it now.

"I guess I better explain," remarked the stranger. "I'm a member of the firm of Bliss & Jonby," Surprised, apparently, at our polite but blank reception of this news, he added, in a mortified tone: "Private detectives."

"Of course," I observed soothingly.

"The fact is, we are interested in this business. It crosses a little affair of ours. Mr. Brade has asked me to explain, and as time is money, I'd better begin. Mrs. Carne has been giving me some useful information. You see, a client of ours missed a manuscript and asked us to trace it. We did so, and found it had been bought by a man well known to the police of New York City, and handed over by him to another character who'd attracted our attention in the past. Mrs. Carne thinks that her late husband was behind the transaction. He was in a position to know the value of the material. I may add that our interest in the matter is ended by the safe return of the missing manuscript to our client, and any little help we can give is welcome and gratis. But the character I refer to was the late Mr. Carne's confidential servant, a man going by the name of Otway. He had reason to leave the United States, as he had acted as informer against a gang of swindlers. I guess it was a good deal of a shock to him to see me. I attended the hunting meet on the day which proved fatal for Mr. Carne, and this man Otway recognized me. I made an appointment with him which he did not keep, and I may add that I took the liberty of hanging around the premises, hoping to get a word with him without attracting too much attention. I am sorry to say I alarmed Mrs. Danvers Carne on one of those occasions."

"The man in the garden!" Brade waved a hand, like a showman.

"Exactly so! I greatly regret the incident."

"It is quite all right," said Mimi with a faint smile.

"The only point on which my information appears to be of use is that Mr. Danvers Carne had befriended this Otway by helping him to get out of the country at a time when this was essential to his safety, and also that, *if* Mr. Carne was the principal in this affair, he may have been as displeased to see me as Otway certainly was."

"Of course it makes it clear why Otway was so devoted to Dan," said Mimi. "He was grateful, I suppose."

"He told us so," Brade added.

"But I don't see that it throws any light on either tragedy," said Revel.

"We are very much obliged to you, Mr. Bliss." Brade turned to the American. "And though I know that Sir Ralph would not wish to hurry you, as you said, time is money, and the car is waiting for the train you said you would like to catch."

"I'll take it as a favour if you'll excuse me, then," said the little man, briskly. "The fact is I've other little matters to look into and I sail on Tuesday." He bowed to everyone, and Sir Ralph rang for Colman to show him out.

"Otway's devotion to Dan always puzzled me," said Carne-Hilton, "but now I understand."

"Gratitude is a touching trait in human nature," mused Brade. I looked at him sharply.

Revel spoke. "Do you seriously imply that Dan was guilty of some sort of underhand work—blackmail, in fact?"

"There are many surprises in store for you, Mr. Revel," Brade replied sweetly. "For instance, why have you so completely forgotten those hunts with the South Lodesdale Hounds when you were an undergraduate? The huntsman remembers you quite well. But you didn't tell the Coroner anything about it."

"Of course I wasn't going to tell him, when he tried to bully me."

"So you knew the country quite well. Better than Mr. Furness, for instance?" Brade turned to Carne-Hilton. "Mr. Revel doesn't know exactly what happened, you see. Will you tell him?"

He told briefly the story Furness had told me.

"I don't believe it," cried Revel. "He is lying!"

"We'll ask him," said Brade sweetly. "Here he is! Mr. Furness, your story of your quarrel with Mr. Danvers Carne is under some suspicion in—er—certain quarters."

"I think it may be right enough—except the theory that an accident ended it," Revel blurted out; "but if it is true—" He wheeled round on Mimi Carne. "Furness says he told you to look for Dan when you left the field. What have you to say to that?"

"What I have said all along. Dick spoke to me as I left the field that day, but I did not hear what he said. As a matter of fact, I had a cold and I am still deaf in one ear. He spoke on that side. I am quite willing to have a doctor examine me and I think you'll find it true. I've had the same trouble before."

Revel turned to Brade. "Can you accept anything so thin as such an excuse?"

"It's no less credible than your explanation of why you rode to the chalk-pit, which you knew perfectly well, at the end of a tiring day."

"I'd never seen that chalk-pit before. It's quite true I'd hunted a few times with the South Lodesdale Hounds, but never in this particular bit. I don't see what you're driving at." The boy's face was flushed and angry. There was fear in the glance he turned from one to another of us.

"The truth," sighed Brade. "And the trouble is so few of you seem able to tell it. Even Jerry has been trying to keep things from me. Mr. Furness, do you think anyone else heard what you said to Mrs. Carne?"

"Anyone might have heard it. I had no idea that Dan was seriously hurt. I thought he might have had a fall, and spoke to Mimi because she could send someone to look him up. I was uneasy. Why, Revel himself wasn't far off. I remember now. He and Carne-Hilton and Otway were all there."

"What are you insinuating?" demanded Revel, taking a step towards Furness. Carne-Hilton stepped between them. Brade spoke.

"Remember, Mr. Revel, you were a disciple of Danvers Carne, and none of his admirers took their morals ready-made. The rest of us, presumably, do, even when we act against them. Ready-made morals have this advantage: The average man knows more or less what they mean. Somehow or other, original morals don't inspire the same confidence. I don't know if any of you are acquainted with the farmer at Cranmere. But he was complaining to me that his daughter won't work because she has an untrammelled soul or something of the sort."

"What has the farmer at Cranmere got to do with it?"

"Oh, it's only a case in point."

Colman opened the door. "Did you want to see Barnet, sir?" he asked.

"Ask Barnet to wait," Brade directed. "Jerry, would you ask Lady Carne-Hilton to step this way? Her nerves are very much upset and I do think a doctor is the best person to go for her."

Revel was shaking with anger now. "I hope someone has taken away her gun," he said; "she's crazy."

"Oh no, Mr. Revel. She has impulsive ways of showing her suspicions, that's all!"

"Do you mean to say she thinks—you all think—" He was livid. "I loved Dan," he stammered.

I went upstairs—there was no help for it. I found that a welcome transformation had taken place in Lady Carne-Hilton's appearance. Her maid was still working on her face when I was told to come in. She rose from her dressing-table, a tragedy queen.

"I am ready," she announced, loud enough for a Drury Lane audience to hear her. I was proud of my work.

I must say everyone played up to her. She was given the stage. She took up her position at the door facing the light. Her husband placed a chair for her, but she paid no attention to him. One flicker of genuine emotion crossed her face as she looked at Revel. She pointed to him with a shaking finger. "He is the guilty man," she said. "I will see him hanged."

"Sir Ralph," said Brade, "are you willing to have me ask your wife certain questions before the persons here? I think, if you will allow me, it may save more publicity later on."

"My wife has exposed herself to any sort of investigation you think necessary," he answered with an effort.

"Then, Lady Carne-Hilton—but I do wish you would sit down—"

Perhaps she felt that need of all bad actresses— something to do with her hands. Anyway, she swept herself into the chair and gripped its arms till her knuckles showed white.

"That's better," sighed Brade with relief. "Now, tell us why you knew of the tragedy before you left the Wilderness on Tuesday."

"I told you that Brune, my poodle, bolted after a rabbit. When I found her she was worrying a string glove. There was a stone inside it, and the glove was soaked in blood."

Mimi started and shrank back in her chair. Revel leaned forward, his eyes scorching hot. Carne-Hilton wheeled round and looked at his wife for the first time.

"Do you know anything about that, Mr. Revel?" asked Brade.

"I?"

"Yes, you."

"I should have told you before if I did," answered Revel.

"Then you don't?"

"No," shouted the boy. "No, no, no!"

Brade looked pained, and turned back to Vivien Carne-Hilton.

"What did you do then?" he asked.

Her eyes shifted. "I hid it in a tree."

"Why?"

"I saw my husband riding through the wood, and from his face I believed that he—I hardly knew what I believed—but I hid the glove."

"You see," explained Brade, "I was always interested in that pair of string gloves. Otway says he placed them in the car. It was usual to supply drinks and spare saddles and anything likely to be needed in this way and he thought Mr. Carne would remember that. But if someone innocent of the crime removed them, why did he not come forward to say so? Where were they? And where is the other glove now?"

Carne-Hilton turned to Brade. "Does the doctor agree that such a weapon might have killed Dan?"

"Yes. He has no doubt that it was exactly the sort of instrument which might have caused the injury to the skull. But when examining the body at the time, the idea of foul play did not enter his head."

"Who was Rufus M'Lean?" asked Brade. He handed

Carne-Hilton a cheque, which Carne-Hilton handed to me. It was made out for five hundred pounds, to Rufus M'Lean.

"That was the name under which Dan and Otway opened a joint bank-account," replied Lady Carne-Hilton.

"And you sometimes paid money into this account?"

"Yes."

"If you had sold the manuscript in your possession which was taken from your cupboard on Saturday night, the money would have been paid to Rufus M'Lean?"

"Yes. We thought we should get much more if we waited till Averil Legend was married. But after Dan's death Otway wanted money at once. He could not bear to stay here and wanted to go away."

"Why did you burn the glove?"

"To shield my husband," she said.

"You got it from the wood where you had hidden it?"

"Yes, the next day."

"And burnt it?"

"Yes, in the furnace."

"You did not know that you were seen by a servant?"

"No. Mimi Carne was in the basement, but I heard her coming out of the store-room and hid. Then Colman came. I waited till he had gone and then went back to my room."

"Thank you, Lady Carne-Hilton. That's all for the moment."

She had answered the questions exactly as Brade had told me to direct her, but now she pointed at Revel. "He is the murderer," she repeated. "I shall see him hanged."

"Thank you, dear lady," Brade said sweetly. "You have taxed your nerves enough. Dr. Jerrold will follow you shortly. He knows just what to do for strained nerves." I bestowed my blackest look on Simon. Not for untold wealth would I see that woman again, and he knew it.

She left the room with a backward glance at me. Brade gave a sigh of relief.

When she had gone, he moved to the hearth and stood

there looking at nothing, while everyone in the room looked at him.

"My friends," he said, like a person in a trance, "I do not yet know certainly who committed this murder, but murder it was. And the murder was premeditated, prepared for skilfully by someone who was at least ready to commit it if the chance came, and other circumstances made it seem the only way out. But chance had a hand in it too, and I cannot tell at this point whether chance may have decided the issue. For there were others with sufficient motive to take advantage of the situation; that is, the person who planned the murder may not have been the one who carried it out. I have believed for some time that, to bring the murderer to the pitch of killing his victim, some sudden and unexpected aggravation of his or her hatred and fear was necessary, or the sudden conviction that the man who posed as a saint was an unscrupulous villain.

"Bear these three points in mind, Ives:

"Premeditation: indicated by the series of accidents.

"Chance: Carne was felled by that overhanging bough.

"Sudden provocation for the crime: in the case of either someone who already hated him and whom he had driven too far, or someone who had believed in him and suddenly found him out.

"Now, premeditation: Only two people can come under suspicion on this point. His wife and his servant.

"Sudden provocation: His wife, because it was only in the last twenty-four hours before his death that she had learned his complete faithlessness. Mr. Revel, because he, too, had been told that Carne meditated the cold-blooded and cruel action of getting rid of his wife and marrying Miss Trent, whom Revel had love, for her money, and because he had reason to know that Carne was a cheat and a liar. Miss Trent, for the first reason. Carne-Hilton, possibly from facts which have come to light, because he believed his wife was Carne's mistress and dupe. Otway, because, after seven years' devotion, his master had turned on him vindictively, *or*, as an alternative theory, because he saw the American detective at the meet that day and thought Carne had betrayed him, as he had perhaps threatened to do before. Furness, because of Carne's foul suspicion of his wife and his scheme to get rid of her.

"Now you know the evidence. Carne was killed, not when he fell and Furness left him, but not long afterwards. But his body was not disposed of until an hour or more had passed. Furness's story is borne out by his presence with the hunt so soon after the accident, and his telling Mrs. Carne to find out if her husband had reached home. He certainly did not drag the body to the chalk-pit.

"Otway has an alibi which satisfied Ives. The attack on him also diverts suspicion.

"Carne-Hilton is crippled and the dragging of the body was an athletic feat. He was nowhere near the place where Carne was killed at the time.

"Miss Trent was at Marpen Hall about the time the crime took place and afterwards.

"Mr. Revel has no satisfactory alibi for either the killing or the disposal of the body and he has misled us about his knowledge of the hunt country.

"Mrs. Carne has no alibi for the masking of the crime as an accident."

"The accident to Otway complicates the case. If we find out who did that, we'll find out the rest," said Ives.

"Very well!" Brade rang the bell. "Ask Barnet to come this way," he directed Colman.

"Barnet," said Brade, when he appeared, "we are getting near the truth in this matter of Mr. Danvers Carne's death. We know your master did not kill him. We think you can tell us something further about Otway's accident."

"Yes, sir," answered Barnet serenely, as if the remark were connected with his routine work in the stables.

"Do you know how it happened?"

"Yes, sir."

"Will you tell us?"

"Certainly sir, as it can't 'arm my master. Sarah kicked 'im."

"How do you know?"

"I was on 'er back at the time, sir."

"Would you tell us just what happened?"

"Yes, sir, I'll be pleased to. You see, when Otway left the 'all that evening, there'd been some rough words. 'E gave us to think 'e suspected someone of 'avin' a 'and in 'is master's death. Well, I did too, knowin' the kind of a gentleman Mr. Danvers was. It seemed natural somebody might lose 'is temper, like, and Colman 'ad told me my master and Mr. Danvers 'ad 'ad words the night before. Something about Mrs. Danvers, Colman thought. 'E 'eard Sir Ralph say to Mr. Danvers: 'You belong to a family as doesn't allow itself to be disgraced.' Them was the words Colman 'eard. Well, I made up my mind to find out if Otway 'ad got some mistaken notion in 'is 'ead about my master. An opportunity did not present itself until Saturday. You see, sir, when I followed orders and dragged that potato-sack out of the wood to the chalk-pit, I found Otway there. I 'ad trouble with Sarah, same as I told that gentleman," he pointed to Ives, "and did a voluntary." He chuckled softly. "Wouldn't 'ave thought the 'orse lived as could do it, but that mare, sir, she's got a will of 'er own—never see the like—though gentle as a lamb when not crossed in 'er wishes, you hunderstand. Well, Otway, 'e give me a leg up, and then we 'ad some words, and 'e went so far as to name my master, showin' 'ow 'e might 'ave murdered Mr. Carne. I'm a peaceable man most times, but I got angry, in a manner of speaking, and Sarah was upset with our voices getting loud and all, and I said: 'If anybody murdered anybody, I'll pick you to 'ang,' and that upset him bad, and he grabbed at Sarah's bridle, and she reared and kicked. The first thing I knew, 'e was down that chalk-pit. I could 'ave got down, but I began to think, and Sarah was still a 'andful, and I thought 'e was better where 'e was than worrying my master. So I rode 'ome and left 'im, knowing Mr. Revel would come along shortly according to plan."

Carne-Hilton gave a great sigh. "Barnet, did you think of the consequences to yourself?"

"Yes, sir. I ain't a married man. And I 'adn't killed Otway. 'E'd attacked me. And if it meant prison, why, I'd do more than that for you, sir."

"Why didn't you tell all this to Ives?" Brade asked.

"Mr. Ives, sir? That gentleman? 'E didn't ask me straight out, same as you 'ave, and I didn't want to tell what Otway 'ad said about my master—not until the murderer was found."

"Brade, how did you guess it was Barnet?" I could not help asking.

"It was Barnet or Revel, obviously, so I thought I'd ask. That's all, Barnet, thank you!" Barnet went out.

"What is to be done?" demanded Carne-Hilton.

"Lady Carne-Hilton concealed the facts to shield her husband," said Brade thoughtfully. "Barnet was attacked and there was an accident. He was guilty of negligence in not going to the assistance of Otway, but this will not be a serious matter, and he has confessed the facts. Now, look at this map." He spread out the map of the hunt, which we had studied before. "Danvers Carne was killed by a weapon made by the string glove with a flint inserted. He must have been killed soon after Mr. Furness left him. Someone found him, brought his horse up, and probably attacked him from behind while he was trying to remount. The body was hidden in the bracken. Later someone caught Sarah, fastened the stirrup to Carne's foot, mounted, and dragged the body to the chalk-pit. He had luck all round, of course, or he could not have done it, and he was an expert horseman and very strong.

"Now, who had the chance to get those gloves out of the car? Revel did. Who knew the country well enough? Revel may have done so and has already tried to conceal the fact that he had ridden before with these hounds.

Who had time to murder Carne and also to dispose of the body? Revel. Who had motive? Carne had taken away the girl Revel loved, and within a few hours of the crime, Revel had been told that Carne meant to divorce his wife and marry Miss Trent from the basest motives. He might not have believed it if he had not found out at the same time that Carne had been party to a swindle about a horse. Revel may have been suddenly enlightened as to Carne's true character and may have been so appalled and shaken by this that he was irresponsible. Well, Ives, what do you say?"

"I say it's enough to issue a warrant on."

The boy had been listening while Brade calmly discussed his guilt. Now he turned a wild face on me. "It's lies—all of it! I never doubted Dan." He was almost crying, and Mimi herself was trembling. "If I've got to doubt him now, it will be worse than anything. I may have been a fool, but he—he—" He broke down completely.

"I felt like that once," said Mimi quickly.

Colman opened the door. "The lad from the village says he must see Mr. Brade at once. Mr. Brade said I was to admit him if he came."

"My Billiam!" cried Brade.

It was Billiam, grinning, in the doorway, and holding out a white string glove. Brade pounced on him.

"Billiam, where—oh where?"

"Lee Farm," said Billiam, "caught on a thorn in the third hedge after you leave the covert."

"In plain sight?"

"Yes, you only 'ad to look to see it."

Brade pounced on the map. Then he went to Revel and grasped his hands, shaking them up and down warmly. There were tears in his eyes.

"This is perfect," he exclaimed, "absolutely perfect! I had to make sure. This settles it. Ladies and gentlemen, Mr. Revel, as he says, is a fool, but he is not a murderer. The man who planted that glove did it to make us think that both gloves had been dropped during the hunt, but he made a mistake. He didn't know that Carne couldn't have dropped it there, because Carne and Miss Trent were elsewhere and never rode over Lee Farm at all. But Revel knew. He was there."

"Who is this boy?" asked Carne-Hilton.

"He is my Billiam and a future sleuth. But he can go now. Billiam, wait for me somewhere. I can't be parted from you! But go now!"

Billiam gave one adoring glance at Mimi and went.

"Then we know no more than we did before," Carne-Hilton exclaimed.

"There's many a slip—" murmured Ives.

"On the contrary, my dear man! Jerry, tell them who did it," he cried.

"I have no idea."

"But you told me yourself. It's in your notes. The only trouble I had was to read your writing."

Brade drew from his pocket the gold coin and handed it to Mimi.

"Is this the coin your husband lost?" he asked.

"Yes." She grew whiter and whiter as she looked at it "Where did you find it?"

"In Lady Carne-Hilton's cupboard," said Brade.

"But why—how—oh, he must have given it to her."

"That is what I thought, but I was a fool," answered Brade. "It was stolen from him, because he trusted to it to bring him luck."

"No—no!" cried Mimi. "No!" She stared at Brade in horror.

The door opened and Lady Carne-Hilton came in.

"I can't stand this," she said. "You are cruel to leave me all alone."

As she spoke, the telephone bell rang. Brade snatched up the receiver. "Yes? What? Dead?" He rang off abruptly. "Otway is dead," he said.

Mimi covered her face with her hands, but Lady Carne-Hilton screamed shrilly. Then she seemed to lose all her strength, and Brade guided her to a chair. He stood beside her and glanced at me reproachfully.

"Do you understand now?" he asked.

I looked at the woman. Her eyes had filmed over with a kind of blindness. Her hands lay dead on her lap, all their nervous activity gone. "Jim," she whispered, "Jim—dead!"

"Lady Carne-Hilton was not shielding her husband," said Brade. "She was shielding the man she loved."

We talked there before her, cruelly, as if she could not hear. I don't think she did.

"Dan?" cried Mimi. "It was Dan she talked about to me. She said she loved him."

"Did she mention him by name?" asked Brade. Mimi tried to remember. "She was so incoherent, I could hardly understand. No—I don't remember her saying his name, but she repeated his words—the very phrases he used."

"How often had Otway heard those phrases? What was to prevent his using his master's philosophy for his own ends, whether he believed it or not? He must have seen it was useful."

"Oh," cried Mimi, "but he never did—to me."

"He wouldn't!"

"And Miss Vane of Cranmere Farm, she has caught hold of the same cant," I exclaimed.

"Exactly. Miss Vane has been a help." Brade looked at me with melancholy reproach. "Oh, Jerry, I'm disappointed in you! Read that!"

I took the sheet he handed me and read my own words. "'I had a sudden impulse to go through the Wilderness to the chalk-pit, to see the end of the drama. For a moment, I thought of asking Jennings to take my place—ride my horse in to check Otway's time. . . . Then I remembered that the others had their parts to play too.'"

If I could have sent my horse in by someone else, Otway could have done so. But Jennings drove Averil Legend home. Vivien Carne-Hilton walked. She could have taken in the horse. Rogers was not there to see who unsaddled him.

"But Otway's alibi!" Ives broke in ponderously. "His horse was in. He couldn't have had her in the stable, unsaddled and blanketed before five if he had done it. He was in for his tea at five himself."

"Because Lady Carne-Hilton took his horse home for him, my good man. She followed his directions. He told her to take the horse in when no one could see her. She sent the car home and led or rode the horse across the field. Otway may have found Sarah, done the job, galloped back to the edge of the Wilderness, which is only five minutes' walk from the Lodge, though much farther from the stables and house, and walked in, leaving Sarah to find her way home. The time gained by Lady Carne-Hilton taking in and unsaddling his horse, added to the time required to get him from the stables back to the Lodge, is the time he used."

"But why risk it?" I cried.

"Let me describe what probably happened. He had already worked Furness up to a murderous pitch by telling him his master's plans. He saw Furness ride after Carne and followed. He came up immediately after the accident and found Carne stunned but not killed. He murdered him and left him hidden, believing that Furness would be accused and convicted of the crime. Then he had misgivings. There were those gloves. And he heard Furness tell Mimi to look for her husband.

"Suppose he had been found at once, while the hoof-marks and foot-marks were clear. How could he be sure that the story was not written plainly in the ground? He had trusted to delay and meant, perhaps, to find the body himself, when the marks of his horse's hoofs and his own boots would be explained. But if Mrs. Carne, made anxious by Furness, went to look for her husband and found him, what then? Or if she sent someone out at once, before Otway could get there? Yet he did not dare to act immediately. Also, Furness's remark to Mimi would make a jury doubt his guilt.

"He rode home thinking hard and saw his chance when he met Lady Carne-Hilton. He knew she would do anything for him, and this was a simple thing. It was dark and misty and Rogers was the only groom in the stables, and he had to wait at the house to take horses coming in, so she could choose a time when he was not about. Perhaps he thought of the chalk-pit and realized that Furness himself would believe that he had been responsible for Carne's death, provided Otway could make it seem that Carne had been dragged after his fall. It was worth risking and he was desperate. Is that reasonable?" He looked down at the drooping creature beside him.

"You have heard what I said. You sent the car home, went into the field, took Otway's horse and led him in, unsaddled him, and came into the house, all in the time which it would have taken to look for your dog and walk home?"

She said: "Yes."

Suddenly she started to her feet. "Oh, Jim killed him. He had a right to kill him. Dan had made a slave of him. Jim had to make money for Dan to spend. Jim had to cheat and steal and blackmail and Dan took the money and pretended not to know how it came. When Jim arranged about that race Dan won on Cat o' the Hills, Dan dared to pretend he did not know he was not riding Pink Livery. A hundred times he threatened to expose Jim for doing the very things he made him do. At first Jim was grateful—then he understood that he had put himself in Dan's power and that Dan was a devil, with the devil's own luck. What was there for Jim to do but to kill him and be free?"

Revel had been watching her with horror. Now he abruptly left the room. Mimi touched Sir Ralph's hand. He was motionless, but Mimi's touch roused him. He looked at his wife with such loathing that Mimi drew away from him. She got up and went to the window and flung it open.

Ives came forward. "I shall have to take her ladyship's statement," he said clumsily.

"Take her away," said Sir Ralph. He was shaking. Ives took her arm and led her out. She went with him blindly.

Sir Ralph got up and followed them.

For the first time he walked without a limp.

That night, in Brade's room, Carne-Hiltdn joined us. He limped in, in his usual way, and sank into a chair beside the fire. Rain was purring against the roof. The room was full of tobacco smoke and the steady brightness of the burning coals. We were all so tired that our minds worked on a plane where the events of the last week seemed remote and unreal. We might have been ghosts with human brains, discussing something that interested but did not concern us.

"Is Ives satisfied?" asked Sir Ralph abruptly.

Brade tried to smile, found it was too much of an effort, and abandoned it.

"Ives is delighted," he said mournfully, "and so am I." His voice trailed away in dejection.

"Then it will rest there?" asked Carne-Hilton.

"Eternally, I hope," Brade answered, shutting his eyes.

"Perhaps you'd like to hear what happened?"

"If you tell us tonight, I shall probably be faintly interested by this time next week," Brade sighed.

Carne-Hilton drew out his pipe and lit it. Then he said: "Well, you see, Sarah heard me riding home through the Wilderness and followed me. When I saw her, I realized that there had been an accident. I caught her and rode back along the trail she had made—you know one of her shoes makes quite a distinctive impression, so that was easy, and it was not yet so dark that I could not see the ground. I found Dan's body concealed in the bracken. He was dead, of course, and of course I thought Furness had killed him. I saw also how nearly it looked like an accident, and how, with help from me, it might pass as one. I thought of Mimi, and everything I had against Dan came over me like a madness. I vowed he shouldn't ruin his wife, bring disgrace on our name in death as he had nearly done in life. The doctors have told me that the use of my leg might come back suddenly after a shock. I don't know how I managed it, but I did. I fastened his foot to Sarah's stirrup, dragged the body to the chalk-pit, and flung it in. I knew that the hounds were on the other side of the hill, but I trusted the mist and the failing light to shield me from any chance rider passing along the top. I rode Sarah back, remounted my hack, and galloped home. Sarah must have followed. For all I know, Otway may have seen me. I realized this morning when I shut that door, and found that my leg was aching, that I had walked out of the room like a sound man. You see—I didn't know that my wife had been living as the mistress and dupe of a servant." He got up and went away.

Brade turned listlessly to me. "Otway needn't have taken all that trouble, you see, and if he hadn't, and if there had been no Billiam, even Lady Carne-Hilton need never have known the truth."

I was feeling considerably humiliated.

"After all," I remarked, "it's not my province to solve crime mysteries, but it is to understand character. I ought to have known from the beginning that, whatever Carne was guilty of, he could never have been that woman's lover."

"Console yourself," Brade murmured. "Next time your wits will be clearer. Let us hope you won't fall in love with the chief suspect."

"There won't be a next time," I vowed fervently.

Brade yawned. "And so to bed!"

Mimi never knew all the truth and I have never felt any inclination to tell her. In fact, we never speak of the murder. The new inquest went through without a hitch. The evidence that Otway had schemed for his master's death was overwhelming. It became evident that he must have followed Furness, when Furness followed Carne into the Wilderness, carried out the murder, concealed the body, and used the opportunity Lady Carne-Hilton gave him later to return and mask the crime as an accident. His feelings when he discovered that his job had been done for him must have been mixed.

Lady Carne-Hilton's genuine grief for Otway was soothed by notoriety, and she is living in Monte Carlo now, attended by a following of foreign titles, some quite genuine, I believe.

Mimi and I are going to Australia for our honeymoon, unless we can think of some place still farther away.

Brade says the story ought to be on record, because it is the only case he knows of in which the crime as a whole was carried out, without voluntary collaboration, by three people and a horse.

Resurrected Press books in A. E. Fielding's
The Chief Inspector Pointer Mystery Series

The Eames-Erskine Case (1924)
The Charteris Mystery (1925)
The Footsteps that Stopped (1926)
The Clifford Affair (1927)
The Cluny Problem (1928)
The Net Around Joan Ingilby (1928)
The Murder at the Nook (1929)
The Mysterious Partner (1929)
The Craig Poisoning Mystery (1930)
The Wedding Chest Mystery (1930)
The Upfold Farm Mystery (1931)
Death of John Tait (1932)
The Westwood Mystery (1932)
The Tall House Mystery (1933)
The Cautley Conundrum (1934)
The Paper-Chase (1934)
The Case of the Missing Diary (1935)
Tragedy at Beechcroft (1935)
The Case of the Two Pearl Necklaces (1935)
Mystery at the Rectory (1936)
Black Cats Are Lucky (1937)
Scarecrow (1937)
Pointer to a Crime (1944)

RESURRECTED PRESS BOOKS IN ELAINE
HAMILTON'S *INSPECTOR REYNOLDS OF
SCOTLAND YARD* SERIES

The Westminster Mystery (1930)
Peril at Midnight   (1934)
Tragedy in the Dark (1935)

The Casino Mystery (1936)
Murder Before Tuesday (1937)

MYSTERIES FROM THE JAMES "BONNIE" DUNDEE
MYSTERY SERIES BY ANNE AUSTIN

The Black Pigeon
The Avenging Parrot
Murder Backstairs
Murder at Bridge
One Drop of Blood
Murdered, But Not Dead

**Like us on Facebook to stay up-to-date on
all of our latest releases:
http://www.facebook.com/ResurrectedPress**

AVAILABLE FROM RESURRECTED PRESS!

BRITISH WOMEN OF MYSTERY
Three Novels Penned by
Women of the Golden Age of Mysteries

Three Full Length Novels in One!

- **Whose Body by Dorothy L. Sayers**
- **The Westminster Mystery by Elaine Hamilton**
- **The Clifford Affair by A. E. Fielding**

Prior to World War I, detective fiction in Britain was largely a male preserve, but in the period between the wars—an era that has been called the Golden Age of British Mysteries—women authors in Britain not only embraced the genre, but came to dominate it. Authors such as Sayers, Allingham, Marsh not to mention the great Agatha Christie topped the best sellers lists, but there were numerous other women writers working to satisfy the public's demand for mystery fiction. Unfortunately, many of these authors are virtually unknown today. This volume brings together the first mystery novel of one of the best known of these writers, Dorothy L. Sayers' Whose Body?, along with novels by two of the lesser known women of the period, Elaine Hamilton's The Westminster Mystery and A. E. Fielding's The Clifford Affair, in the hopes that it will serve as an introduction to the British Women of Mystery.

AVAILABLE FROM RESURRECTED PRESS!

THE EDWARDIAN DETECTIVES
LITERARY SLEUTHS OF THE EDWARDIAN ERA

The exploits of the great Victorian Detectives, Poe's C. Auguste Dupin, Gaboriau's Lecoq, and most famously, Arthur Conan Doyle's Sherlock Holmes, are well known. But what of those fictional detectives that came after, those of the Edwardian Age? The period between the death of Queen Victoria and the First World War had been called the Golden Age of the detective short story, but how familiar is the modern reader with the sleuths of this era? And such an extraordinary group they were, including in their numbers an unassuming English priest, a blind man, a master of disguises, a lecturer in medical jurisprudence, a noble woman working for Scotland Yard, and a savant so brilliant he was known as "The Thinking Machine."

To introduce readers to these detectives, Resurrected Press has assembled a collection of stories featuring these and other remarkable sleuths in The Edwardian Detectives.

- The Case of Laker, Absconded by Arthur Morrison
- The Fenchurch Street Mystery by Baroness Orczy
- The Crime of the French Café by Nick Carter
- The Man with Nailed Shoes by R Austin Freeman
- The Blue Cross by G. K. Chesterton
- The Case of the Pocket Diary Found in the Snow by Augusta Groner
- The Ninescore Mystery by Baroness Orczy
- The Riddle of the Ninth Finger by Thomas W. Hanshew
- The Knight's Cross Signal Problem by Ernest Bramah

- The Problem of Cell 13 by Jacques Futrelle
- The Conundrum of the Golf Links by Percy James Brebner
- The Silkworms of Florence by Clifford Ashdown
- The Gateway of the Monster by William Hope Hodgson
- The Affair at the Semiramis Hotel by A. E. W. Mason
- The Affair of the Avalanche Bicycle & Tyre Co., LTD by Arthur Morrison

RESURRECTED PRESS CLASSIC MYSTERY CATALOGUE

Journeys into Mystery
Travel and Mystery in a More Elegant Time

The Edwardian Detectives
Literary Sleuths of the Edwardian Era

Gems of Mystery
Lost Jewels from a More Elegant Age

E. C. Bentley
Trent's Last Case: The Woman in Black

Ernest Bramah
Max Carrados Resurrected:
The Detective Stories of Max Carrados

Agatha Christie
The Secret Adversary
The Mysterious Affair at Styles

Octavus Roy Cohen
Midnight

Freeman Wills Croft
The Ponson Case
The Pit Prop Syndicate

J. S. Fletcher
The Herapath Property
The Rayner-Slade Amalgamation
The Chestermarke Instinct
The Paradise Mystery
Dead Men's Money

The Middle of Things
Ravensdene Court
Scarhaven Keep
The Orange-Yellow Diamond
The Middle Temple Murder
The Tallyrand Maxim
The Borough Treasurer
In the Mayor's Parlour
The Saftey Pin

R. Austin Freeman
*The Mystery of 31 New Inn from the Dr. Thorndyke
Series*
*John Thorndyke's Cases from the Dr. Thorndyke
Series*
The Red Thumb Mark from The Dr. Thorndyke Series
The Eye of Osiris from The Dr. Thorndyke Series
A Silent Witness from the Dr. John Thorndyke Series
The Cat's Eye from the Dr. John Thorndyke Series
*Helen Vardon's Confession: A Dr. John Thorndyke
Story*
As a Thief in the Night: A Dr. John Thorndyke Story
*Mr. Pottermack's Oversight: A Dr. John Thorndyke
Story*
*Dr. Thorndyke Intervenes: A Dr. John Thorndyke
Story*
The Singing Bone: The Adventures of Dr. Thorndyke
The Stoneware Monkey: A Dr. John Thorndyke Story
*The Great Portrait Mystery, and Other Stories: A
Collection of Dr. John Thorndyke and Other Stories*
The Penrose Mystery: A Dr. John Thorndyke Story
The Uttermost Farthing: A Savant's Vendetta

Arthur Griffiths
The Passenger From Calais
The Rome Express

Louis Tracy
The Strange Case of Mortimer Fenley
The Albert Gate Mystery
The Bartlett Mystery
The Postmaster's Daughter
The House of Peril
The Sandling Case: What Would You Have Done?
Charles Edmonds Walk
The Paternoster Ruby

John R. Watson
The Mystery of the Downs
The Hampstead Mystery

Edgar Wallace
The Daffodil Mystery
The Crimson Circle

Carolyn Wells
Vicky Van
The Man Who Fell Through the Earth
In the Onyx Lobby
Raspberry Jam
The Clue
The Room with the Tassels
The Vanishing of Betty Varian
The Mystery Girl
The White Alley
The Curved Blades
Anybody but Anne
The Bride of a Moment
Faulkner's Folly
The Diamond Pin
The Gold Bag
The Mystery of the Sycamore
The Come Back

Raoul Whitfield
Death in a Bowl

And much more!
Visit ResurrectedPress.com
for our complete catalogue

About Resurrected Press

A division of Intrepid Ink, LLC, Resurrected Press is dedicated to bringing high quality, vintage books back into publication. See our entire catalogue and find out more at www.ResurrectedPress.com.

About Intrepid Ink, LLC

Intrepid Ink, LLC provides full publishing services to authors of fiction and non-fiction books, eBooks and websites. From editing to formatting, from publishing to marketing, Intrepid Ink gets your creative works into the hands of the people who want to read them. Find out more at www.IntrepidInk.com.

www.ingramcontent.com/pod-product-compliance
Lightning Source LLC
Chambersburg PA
CBHW070900250626
47159CB00003B/1138